QUENTIN MCFURY

THE LAST DEFENDER

Patrick T. Gorman

I AIN'T GOT NOBODY by Roger Graham & Spencer Williams
(1915) Public Domain

Cover Artwork by April Johnston
Copyright © 2013 Patrick T. Gorman
All rights reserved.
Published by KMRIA Publishing, 2013
ISBN: 0615891004
ISBN-13: 978-0615891002

For Tricia
The measure of my dreams.

CONTENTS

CHAPTER ONE
WREAKING HAVOK

"Yeah, I'm grateful," muttered Quentin McFury. "Grateful not to be dead. Grateful not to be blown into 93,573 pieces. Not yet anyway."

ShrrrrrrrrrrrRRRRAAKKKKKKKKKK!!!

Explosions rocked the ship, but the battered Havok held together barely . . . just barely. Grabbing the stick, Quentin pulled up on it with all his might, until his muscles shook and stretched so much he worried they might snap. His once thin, finger-sized fingers turned red, squeezed out like plump sausages from his "driving gloves".

"I am *NOT* going to die today," he growled.

KrrrrrrRRZZZZZZZZZzzzshhHTTTT!!!

"Ooookay, I might totally die today . . ."

As flames ripped across the back of the cockpit, he now knew for certain that the Striker attack fighters bearing down on him weren't looking to chat about what the best Clash album was. (And even if they were, Quentin didn't have time to argue it was clearly *Combat Rock*.) Hell, he didn't even have time to put out the fire, even though he knew *not* putting it out would be suicidal with an added dollop of burny.

So, as blasts flew across the bow, the Havok's pilot had a decision to make. A decision other pilots never had to worry about as all *their* ships had clever fire extinguishing capabilities. (Some even had hovering extingui-bots in tiny red helmets behind *"Break in Case of Emergency"* glass just waiting to show their tiny little stuff.)

Quentin had none of that. All he had was the willingness to hold his breath and crack open a window when the time was right. And that time was now.

Although the Havok moved swiftly for a heavily-modified science freighter, it wasn't really designed for space combat. Four times the size of any of the zip-fast Strikers, the bulky Havok trudged through space like a lumbering sheep dog. Whereas the cat-like, single-piloted Strikers were built for speed, the Havok was single-mindedly built to protect whatever was inside it. Thus, making it easy prey for the faster fighters.

The dark screaming Strikers barreled downwards, each one firing point blank on the Havok, the barrage shredding the shields. No ship could take the beating the Havok now took. Each and every one of those Striker pilots smiled the confident grin of cocky jerks everywhere who knew they were about to get an easy victory, an easy score. Such smirks, however, are generally always premature and not recommended, especially as karma, fate, God, gods, etc. despise such smiles and take a giddy glee in turning those smiles into smashed-up, tear-stained frowns.

In the Havok's cockpit, just as it was about to be obliterated into melting metal and hunks of human chunks, that ship's pilot took several deep breaths. On the last inhalation, Quentin held his breath tight and flicked a series of green buttons above his head. Thirteen microseconds later, all the air from the ship was sucked out with a whooshing clap!

Clinging to the controller as his body flew up out of his seat, Quentin flitted about the cabin like a spider about to be slurped into a vacuum. As his body bounced around the cockpit, the ship twisted and spun through space with a crazed flurry of jerks and turns that made the Havok look like it was having a fit.

The Strikers rapidly tried to scramble out of the spasming freighter's way. But every time those Strikers swerved to safety, they were met with a random move that put them right back into the path of danger. No flight experience in the universe could have prepared those pilots to attack a ship while simultaneously defending themselves from their target's kamikaze-like frenzy.

Without warning, the Havok veered upwards and then back down in the blink of an eye. Unfortunately a Striker pilot blinked and the Havok clipped him, sending his fighter into an uncontrollable spiral out of the action. Even though unintentional, that act showed its pursuers that the Havok wasn't rolling over in this fight.

Inside the cockpit, Quentin grinned widely. He

couldn't believe self-preservation could be so much fun, nor so destructive. If there were air to breathe, he'd have been giggling maniacally that his ridiculous "plan" to put out the fire roaring through his ship by taking out the air fueling it actually seemed to be working. But since he could neither breathe nor laugh, he instead desperately tried to figure out how to repressurize the ship while not losing complete control of it.

I don't know where I am or what I'm doing or who the hell I'm fighting, Quentin McFury told himself, *but this feels just about right.*

Realizing he could only flail around so long while holding his breath, he stretched out a hand to shut the hatches and turn the oxy-generator back on. Desperately, his fingers trailed across a host of switches, none of which gave him his precious air. He thrashed like an insect right before dying.

With another mad turn by the Havok, his head smashed against the side of the co-pilot's chair, nearly knocking him out. But what didn't render him unconscious did leave a bulbous red welt as a reminder that no crazy plan goes unpunished.

I'm not gonna cry. Maybe later. But not now.

Outside, the remaining six Strikers bore down on the Havok. They'd had enough of this kid, who they loudly referred to over their comms as "a little twarpo".

"Flash the pan!" Striker Leader 4217 (also known as Bripsy) shouted.

The Strikers sprayed the area with indiscriminate blasts, showing no respect for the hunt or the art of battle. But that wasn't their job. Their job was simple and destructive: wreak as much annihilation as possible with balletic ballistic precision. Years spent honing their piloting skills yielded a level of dogfighting combat that struck terror through all.

Chosen as toddlers, potential Striker pilots distinguished themselves from other children based on how their cunning spatial skills melded delicately with their thirst for blowing things up. (Basically, the assessment involved how well a toddler knocked over other kids' blocks and then how much joy they felt watching their victims cry.) Striker pilots weren't defined just by their appetite for destruction but also by their ace flying skills. It was said that any Striker pilot could fly through the eye of a needle while simultaneously shooting holes in a thousand other needles.

Now though, these ace pilots weren't shooting at needles. They were shooting at a lumbering block of zigzagging metal that annoyed them two steps too far. And they wanted to end this now.

The Havok, on the other hand, did not have such a skilled flier at its helm. To be quite honest, Quentin McFury's flying ability at the best of times would be rated amongst the worst in the universe. But his piloting skills weren't that important as, at that moment, the Havok didn't really have any sort of pilot at all. It just had something with arms and legs trying desperately not to die and praying for a miracle.

With bulging eyes, a giant crimson welt across his forehead, and a spleen about to be vomited out, Quentin could name several moments in his life he preferred over this one. However, it was his deep desire to have more moments – some good, some bad, and some that might include kissing – that gave him the strength to take one last swing to restart the oxy-gen.

So when the ship twirled around with a ferocious gut-wrenching dip, that hopeful pilot let go of the stick and reached his hand out as far as he could . . . so far that the very end of the very tip of the longest fingernail on his longest finger just barely . . . just slightly . . . just ever-so-*gently* tweaked the life-giving switch. And right there . . . right then . . . that fingernail quivered and bent.

In that tiniest of moments, the nail could have bent back and ripped off, leaving Quentin gasping his last breath. It would have been the final, painful insult to the abuse his body took during this little escapade. And if that nail broke, he surely would have nodded at his ex-nail with a smirk that said, "*Fair play. You did the best you could, little fella.*"

But the fingernail did *not* give! The nail held, the switch flipped over, and the oxy-gen roared back to life. And so did Quentin! As air flooded back through his ship and into his lungs, he howled with what little air he had left:

"Yeeeeeeeeeeehhhhhooooooooooohoooooooooo!!!"

Gulping down air, his body ricocheted across the cockpit as the Havok continued to soar wildly out of control. The ship had its air back, but still no one at its controls. Quentin tried to curl up into a ball as he thumped back and forth! Off the ceiling! Against the chair! And then back against the wall!

As the ship took another hard right, his foot got

caught between the arm and seat of the captain's chair, nearly ripping his leg off.

"ArrrrrrRRRRRRRRRrrghhhh!!!"

As the Strikers renewed their assault and tore through chunks of the Havok's remaining shielding, Quentin's body found itself at last hooked into a fixed position as his ship flew out of control. With each swoop and jagged swing of the ship's madness, his leg bent back further, creaking like a tree about to snap and crash to the ground. But even with his leg wrenched painfully in the chair, he now had a thimbleful of hope to get himself out of this mess. And excruciating pain aside, that made him feel almost good.

Grimacing, Quentin pushed against the back wall, spinning the chair around to the console. A tear galloped down his face, but he didn't have time to wipe it. He furiously hit buttons and then pushed the stick straight down, causing his engines to scream in agony. The engines didn't like it. They didn't like it one bit.

Outside the ship, the comms of the six remaining Strikers burst with crackles and wild beeping. A steely female voice followed, shouting in their ears so piercingly loud and with such frosty disdain that if their helmets weren't attached to their heads, the pilots surely would have ripped them off and thrown them into space.

"I want that ship!" the voice yelled.

"That's what we're trying to do!" Striker Leader 4217 (aka Bripsy if you recall) yelled back. Bripsy cringed as soon as he said it. No one spoke back to Baiwyk Stanz, commander of the Striker fleets. No one.

"Sorry, Baiwyk," Bripsy muttered meekly.

The other Strikers said nothing. Despite the ear-splitting engines tearing through space hot on the Havok's exhaust, each of these pilots could only hear the hiss of the comms.

They waited. Waited for a response, any response. Waited for Baiwyk to chew Bripsy out so bad he might wet himself. Waited for Baiwyk to demand Bripsy return to base for punishment. Waited for Baiwyk's hand to rip through the comm and end good ol' Bripsy's day.

Waited for something.

After an interminable silence, Baiwyk spoke.

"Get me that ship."

"Certainly, Baiwyk," said Bripsy. "My fullest apologies. Please don't tell the Mother of this."

"Now!" Baiwyk snarled. "Don't make me come do your job for you!!!"

The comm went silent. The other Strikers didn't say a word. They had pulled back, keeping the Havok in sight but at a distance as it continued to dart back and forth across space. Holding their positions, they awaited instructions from their leader as Bripsy eyeballed the target of his rage angrily.

"Taz the ship," Bripsy barked. "Prepare to hold packages."

Instantly, the Strikers spread out from each other. Their targeting screens glowed with the Havok in their sights. All at once, their engines roared and the six remaining Strikers lined up, ready to unleash a terrible oncoming blanket of destruction. The Havok would soon be toast if not for . . .

With warning clarions echoing loudly and the engines screeching in grievous pain, Quentin wanted to tear his ringing ears off. He'd have felt bad for what he was doing to the ship if he didn't feel so bad for himself. His shields were failing, his weapons – what little pea-shooters they were – were offline, and his engines were millisecs away from shredding and ripping the ship apart from the inside out. All of this would have caused more experienced pilots to cry, eject themselves from their ships, or commit suicide. (In a similar scenario once, one pilot did all three.) Thankfully, Quentin didn't know any better and unleashed a tiny, micro-scopic smile.

Chugging forward, the Havok groaned with purpose. This sizeable green chunk of science-trucking wasn't served well by a pilot who treated the ship like a wrecking ball. Thankfully, the Havok was built to take all kinds of beatings to protect its contents. So even with the shields beginning to fail, the reinforced hull gave its pilot some extra time. It wasn't time he needed the hull for though.

As the Strikers descended on the Havok, ready to finish him off, Quentin McFury watched as their laser blasts bounced off the front shields. Each smack caused a flicker and shook the screaming ship's mad dash, jarring him as he clutched the controls. But as the Strikers bore down to strike their final blow, Quentin hit the brakes and stopped his ship cold, using every bit of the ship's capability for movement against itself. The fore thrusters were aimed against the aft thrusters, the rear engines were focalized directly at their opposite positioning, and all the stabilizers were activated at max capacity as if the Havok was going to land.

The Havok shook violently, the hull almost snapping under the intense pressure. But the Havok took it like a champ and stood still though. The Strikers, however, did not. They shot past, each narrowly missing the sci-freighter. And before they could figure out what happened, Quentin barreled right down on them. It didn't matter that he didn't have any weapons and his shields were down to nil. His ship would be the weapon.

Maxing out the engines, the Havok smashed into each of the unsuspecting Striker ships, crushing them one by one like eggs. (Granted, really explody eggs.) None of the fighters had a chance to get out of the way, so shocked were they by the Havok's stopping still.

SMASH! CRASH! CRUNCH!

Bowling right through each tiny Striker ship, Quentin turned himself from victim into victor. And while ramming through the last of the Strikers (poor ol' Bripsy), Quentin dared to dream that whatever this whole ordeal was was over.

As his ship rattled through the wreckage of his former pursuers, the Havok's pilot shook as though going over a bumpy road. His vessel flew on, but only just. The engines continued their melancholy wail until he hit a series of buttons and they shut down. Drifting on, the whole ship appeared to exhale in relief.

Quentin, himself, sat back in his chair, closed his eyes, and exhaled, too. He wasn't sure he was safe. He wasn't even entirely sure he got every Striker. But it didn't matter. He didn't have anything left anyways. No energy, no tricks, nothing. Thus, he rested his head back and closed his eyes, cherishing the calm darkness.

For the whole minute he was able to savor his little victory, it was brilliant. Then all at once, all the pain that had been taken out on credit came back with interest. His leg suddenly tingled excruciatingly with a thousand little shocks raging through it, followed by his head beginning to throb. All the other bruises, dings, and cuts also decided now was the time to formally re-introduce themselves and did so with a terrible vengeance.

"Arrrrrrrggh!" Quentin groaned, mostly as that's what manly men in pain always said in the comic books he used to read. "Arrrrrrrggh, arrrrrrrggh, and double arrrrrggh!"

In his roughed-up blue jeans and his ragged LCD Soundsystem t-shirt, Quentin limped out of the cockpit and down the passageway toward the med-chamber. A fully stocked med-chamber would have him feeling slightly better (or at least feeling slightly less). Of course, he knew when he got there he wouldn't find a "fully stocked" med-chamber. He might find a couple band-alls and some old school Earth aspirin . . . if he was lucky.

He didn't care though. He survived. Even surrounded by the wreckage that sprawled through the passageway (and probably only gave a taste of the ship-wide disaster he was sure to face), he limped on with a dodgy yet joyful spring in his step. He was alive. *And* it was his birthday. Nothing better than surviving certain death on your birthday.

One year ago, Quentin McFury was the last person

on Earth. And, for all he knew, today he might be the only Earth human in the universe. But that wasn't today's big news. No, the big news was that today:

Quentin McFury turned sixteen-years-old.

Hobbling down the corridor, he snarked, "Wonder if I should go back and take my driver's test?"

CHAPTER TWO
SCHOOL'S OUT FOREVER

*O*ne *year ago . . .*

Quentin McFury woke up angry. So very, very angry. He'd gone to bed angry. Fell asleep angry. Dreamed angry, angry dreams. And woke just as angry as when he went to bed. He never questioned why he was furious all the time. Maybe it had something to do with his name. Maybe it was due to North Platte, Nebraska, the railroadin' cowtown he lived in. Maybe it had something to do with being a boy as boys are built angry. (For most boys, anger was their "sad".) Or maybe the root of his anger revolved around his age.

For today, Quentin turned fifteen-years-old. And the birthday boy felt alone. Awkward. Angry.

Last night, he yelled so much at his mom and dad for "*ruining his life!*" that he wasn't sure if he'd gone too far. Laying back in bed, he realized there was no such thing.

"Stupid parents . . ." he muttered.

All kids at one point or another say it. And they *mean* it. And sometimes they're right. Some parents *are* stupid. Very stupid. Very stupid with cheese, bacon, and a cherry on top. And to be perfectly honest, Quentin's mom and dad weren't the best parents in the world. (That went to Joe and Esther Fudge of Ontario, Canada.) But the McFurys, like most all parents, do what they can, fumble a few bad decisions, and generally don't "ruin" that many lives. Quentin, however, was a teenager. And to him, his parents should be brought up on war crimes.

Slamming the door loudly behind him, Quentin closed his eyes and savored the crushing perfection of that slam. His dad had the gall to ask him why he didn't score any goals like Nick Grabenstein did. After informing his dad that "defenders don't score" and calling him "as dumb as a bag of cat farts" (under his breath), he dropped his spoon loudly in his bowl of cereal, grabbed his bag, and burst out of the door with an idiot-shaming, ear-shaking bang.

Storming away from the house with a satisfactory smile though, his grin turned into a grimace. In the heat of the moment, he forgot one simple, soul-crushing fact: he didn't have a way to get to school on his own. His bike needed a new tire and only now did he remember he had to wait for his driver and oppressor to take him.

With churning resignation, he slunked over and leaned against the crummy old Sentra. He huffed and puffed and pulled out his iPod, cranking the volume up so loud he wondered if his head might actually break. It wasn't smart. It wasn't necessary. It wasn't good for his ears. But as the music washed over him, it made him feel better. (If only *slightly* better.)

As Arcade Fire's "No Cars Go" faded out on his headphones though, the sound of a less angry door shutting popped Quentin's eyes back open. Out of the two-story brown house next door sprinted Steve Zbyszywiski ("Steve Z" to his many friends, of which Quentin was most definitely not.)

A year ahead of him in school, Steve Z outpaced his neighbor by a million miles in popularity and coolness. The two boys couldn't be more different. Whereas Quentin had dark and scruffy hair, Steve Z had a blond crew cut. Whereas Quentin was the left defender on the high school's JV soccer team, Steve Z was the quarterback phenom of the varsity football team. And whereas Quentin was tall and gawky, Steve Z was the good-looking, muscular epitome of the perfect teenage boy.

Jumping into his brand new hulking F-150 truck, Steve Z spotted Quentin staring and chuckled at his odd classmate, "What're you lookin' at, freakjob?"

Quentin hurriedly turned away. But the humiliation already crawled across his face, his cheeks crimson. Not fast enough, the shiny red truck then roared to life and sped off, leaving the embarrassed birthday boy to glare daggers at the four wheels and a bag of macho fading away in the distance.

Nineteen agonizing minutes later, the senior McFury –

proudly wearing a green button-down shirt Quentin thought made his dad look like a bald angry leprechaun – shuffled out of the house and boomed: "Let's roll in the Grey Fox!"

Hurrying into their tombstone grey Sentra, Quentin tossed his bag in and sat down in a huff. On the drive to school, his huff grew more huffy as his dad turned the radio on to HuskerShuck, the radio show that annoyingly blared up-to-the-second information on the state's beloved Cornhuskers football team.

Passing house after house, Quentin eyeballed the well-cut lawns, the pick-up trucks in the driveways, the fact that each house was basically the same. *And the people inside no different from their neighbors*, he sneered, *and no different from anyone else. Hell, there's probably only six or seven real individuals in North Platte. Maybe even the entire state! I'm one. And Jane . . . Jane, too.*

Oh, yes . . . *Jane!* Jane Douglas. A sophomore and not just an "original", but damn near perfect. She dug cool music. She was smart. And she treated Quentin like a human. Jane also just happened to be very, very pretty, which may or may not have played a role in his assessment.

But outside of himself and Jane, Quentin considered everyone else – his parents, his teachers, his classmates, the death-smelling Wal-Mart greeters, the cute Runza clerks – not only not "original" but "mindless, soulless ants, each going about their day with little reason or life."

"*. . . And they'll have to play over their heads just to stay in the game, but I tell you, it'll be one hell of a* *battle! We can win if we just smash it down their throat . . ."* the Husker radio host whooped.

Quentin's dad nodded in agreement as the show went to a commercial and he turned the radio down. This meant he was about to say something for which his son had to listen. Knowing this rigmarole, the younger McFury showed him proper courtesy and removed *one* of his ear buds.

"Since you're fifteen now, Quentin," his father declared, "Your mom and I thought we should get you something, especially now that you have your learner's permit."

The teen's eyes went wide before he could stop them. *A car! They're getting me a freakin' car!!! They might not be the worst parents after all. They might—*

"So, here you go, kid," his dad said warmly.

But instead of magical car keys, Quentin's dad handed him an ugly cell phone. An unimaginably ugly, clunky, old, orange cell phone. At first, the freshly-minted fifteen-year-old wasn't entirely sure it *was* a cell phone. And if it was, if it was made this century. As though being ugly and old wasn't enough, one side of the phone even appeared slightly melted. Plus, it didn't have any screen to watch anything on it and it surely didn't even play music.

The birthday boy glared at the phone as though handed a warm dog turd. Silence gripped the car. Quentin furiously gnawed at the inside of his cheek, apoplectic at his father's audacity.

"Got it free at work and figured you pr'y oughta have one in case your mom or I need to get a hold of you," his dad said. "I want it always on so we know where you are and what you're doing. Not too much to ask in exchange for a free phone, I think."

Pulling up to the school, Quentin stared out at all the other kids going in. He fumed that nobody else's parents sucked as bad as his did. His mom and dad never trusted him! Even though he never got into trouble! He didn't drink! Didn't smoke! Didn't steal! Didn't get into fights! Yet they *never* let up! Always riding him about his grades (even though he got good grades), his soccer playing (even though he was a decent defender), and his lack of a girlfriend (even though he *did* plan to ask Jane out . . . some day)!

It's not that they don't "get" me, he stewed. *It's that they don't "get" anything.*

As they pulled up to the school, Quentin chucked the cell phone into his backpack and opened the door of the still moving car. He stuck a foot out and it scraped along the asphalt as the car slowly rolled on.

Stunned, his dad quickly braked, allowing Quentin to jump out and race towards the school, violently shaking his head in disgust. Passing some cheerleaders working on routines for this week's football game, he heard his dad yell, "You could at least say 'Thanks!'"

Three weeks into the school year and Quentin the freshman was virtually friendless. Before the semester began, he clung to a very tiny hope that once he made it to high school everything would change and magically he'd be kinda cool. People would realize he was a really interesting and funny guy and they'd been wrong not to figure this out before. Not that he wanted to be a jock like his neighbor Steve Z. Jocks weren't even really that much more popular than any other group of kids. They just had a pass from adults who worshipped the sports they played.

No, what Quentin wanted was to find a group of friends who accepted him for him. Unfortunately, he instantly got tagged a "weirdo".

It started on the second day of the semester when Ana Butts called him "creepy", telling him to stop staring at her in homeroom. (He wasn't, but that didn't really matter.) Then, Ana Butts let everyone know – verbally, textingly, Twitteringly, and Facebookingly – Quentin McFury was "totally creepy!"

He probably could have survived that if not for . . . the *second* week of school when Quentin went to SpeedMart to get a huge happy hour pop. Accidentally overfilling his drink, he spilled a little on himself. Nothing too major. Well, not 'til Fred Kisicki pointed at the wet spot on his jeans and giddily exclaimed:

"Look at pee-pants!"

The hordes of surrounding kids immediately roared with laughter as Quentin scurried away. Yet it wasn't until Ana Butts added "creepy" to "pee-pants" to create "Creepy McPee-Pants" that he found himself cast out of decent high school society forever.

And that's not to ignore all the times Steve Z and his brethren snarled insults at him with all kinds of words for "weird" and other worse ones as well. It was part of how young guys vied to be the supreme Alpha puppy. A role Quentin never wanted in the first place, so he never understood why they went after him.

All in all, Quentin resigned himself to the fact that he wasn't anybody's cup of tea and he probably never would be. He tried not to care too much though. He didn't even like tea.

All through first period homeroom, Quentin's right leg vibrated wishing it was somewhere else doing anything else. (Along with the rest of his body, of course.) Staring at the clock, each twitchy tick of the tock carried him tiny skips forward. Interminably bored, he tried to sneak a listen of his iPod, but Mrs. Dockweiller snapped:

"Mr. McFury, no music! I see that device out again and it's mine!"

Other students snickered as he put his head down on his desk, hiding his face from the other prisoners. In his anger, he almost said something nasty to Mrs. Dockweiller about how every outfit she wore was like something from the seventies threw up on something from the sixties, but he didn't. When the bell finally rang, he burst from his chair and out the door.

Only called "Creepy McPee-Pants" once on his way to second period, he considered it a decent start to the day. His vibrating leg at least kept him awake through the monotony of Advanced Algebra, the tediousness of Beginning Spanish, and the atrociously dull ramblings of American History, taught by Mr. Grubbs – someone who clearly hated both America and history, not to mention all the students, too.

Then came lunch. Beautiful, beautiful lunch! The lunch *break* being the beautiful part for Quentin, not the food itself. Passing underneath a giant banner with the words "*Go BULLDOGS!*" written on it, he scuttled to a seat in the far dark corner of the room. There, he cranked his iPod up and drifted away, listening to his music that no one else liked and not caring that no one else liked him.

He knew no one dug the same music as him because no one ever complemented any of the many different t-shirts he wore of different bands and singers. T-shirts were how guys started conversations with each other. A shirt with something on it – a band, a sports team, a comic book character – was a statement to other guys saying, "I like this. Do you like this? If you do, say something and maybe we can be friends."

But no one started a T-shirt chat with Quentin about anything ever. (Although once visiting Lincoln for Cornhusker State Games, a college student running to class spotted Quentin's New Order tee and shouted: "Cool shirt, man!" That moment gave Quentin hope that while high school might not be the right world for him, college might be.)

Thirty-seven minutes later when the bell rang, signaling the end of lunch, the short reprieve of tunes tuning out Quentin's wretched high school world ended, thus leading to the one true horror he had to face every day: Gym.

Arriving in the boys' locker room, Quentin snuck past Steve Z who cracked jokes with his pals in the corner. Reaching his locker as quickly and quietly as possible, Quentin spun the combination to the lock with soundless cat burglar-like skills.

"Eyes on the prize, Stealthy McFury," he whispered to himself. "Only 2,729 more minutes of gym class . . . this year. Man, I can't wait until I don't have to do this stupid bullshirt anymore." ("Shirt" was his favorite cloaked expletive, a kinda-swear he once saw on a t-shirt that said, "*I can't spell for shirt!*" Again, proof that t-shirts have much more of an influence on the world than we like to admit.)

Outside, the class separated into two teams to play wiffleball. Now, even though two big time jocks were made a captain for each team (one obviously being Steve Z), Quentin was not the last guy chosen. He may have been a social pariah, but even jocks know when a guy's athletically useful and when he isn't.

"I'll take McTurdy," snickered Steve Z. It was a joke Steve Z had made at least a hundred times before, yet it still drew laughter from everyone, including the teacher, Coach Thompson.

Grinding his teeth, Quentin trudged over to his new "teammates", hating his life and everyone in it.

A rather boring game, Quentin became happier and happier as it neared closer and closer to the end of the period. Unlike the others, he didn't see the game as a series of scored runs to establish a big "winner", but dollops of action that propelled them forward until the bell rang, thus ending their misery. A foul ball took one minute, a long hit to the far weeds of the outfield past girthy William Gravel took two minutes, and an argued call by the *way-too-into-it* jocks took a whopping three and a half minutes.

"C'mon, c'mon, c'mon," Quentin muttered, literally counting the minutes.

Not many of the students excelled at wiffleball, allowing Quentin to stand contentedly in the outfield, waiting to catch pop flies that never came. So when the girls' gym class emerged and started jogging around the track, the young McFury dreamily wondered if any of them might secretly like him.

This daydream came to an abrupt end though when "Burger" O'Malley's bat smacked one of Steve Z's pitches high up for an easy out. The ball hung in the air as the popped fly flew right towards Quentin. Wafting with the buoyancy of a balloon, the young McFury smiled at the ease it'd take for him to catch the wiffleball, daring even to hope that the passing girls would marvel at his athletic prowess and be impressed with —

"I GOT IT!" was the last thing he heard just before Steve Z smashed into him, causing the ball, Quentin, and Steve Z to crash awkwardly to the ground. It took a moment to realize what had happened, but the flurry of girlish giggles rapidly informed Quentin he'd messed up again.

"I said 'I got it,' you freak!" an enraged Steve Z barked.

"I'm . . . I'm . . . sorry," Quentin stammered. "I . . . didn't . . . I didn't hear . . ."

Incensed, Steve Z got in his face, their eyes inches apart: "You're mine, McFury!"

"I'm 'yours'?" Quentin said, his smart mouth running faster than his smart mind. "What does that even mean? Did you just adopt me? Because I'm gonna need to see some paperwork. And not paperwork filled in with crayons and stickers again."

"You're mine!" Steve Z repeated. "You think you're so smart, don't ya? You won't be so smart when I'm done with you! And don't think I don't know where you live!" He then leaned close and spoke low with a flurry of curse words, each one making Quentin wince.

Coach Thompson jogged up and separated them, shouting: "That's enough, fellas! Everybody to the lockers!"

"You're mine, McFury!" Steve Z growled again while running off, his friends eyeballing Quentin as well.

As everyone scurried back inside, the birthday boy stood alone on the field, desperately trying to figure out exactly why his life sucked so much.

As much as he hated Gym, Quentin loved his English class that followed it. He liked reading the assigned books and dug his teacher Mr. Doyle, a guy who impressively caught The Clash, The Smiths, and even The Replacements in concert when he was Quentin's age. (All bands his ignorant dad had never even heard of.)

But the overriding reason he cherished English came down to something simpler: Jane Douglas. The only class he shared with her, Quentin lapped up her funny comments, her thoughts on a Zadie Smith short story, her gasping laughter with friends – all with silent adoration. His desk right behind her, he longingly gazed at the auburn ponytail that hovered just above her long neck and lamented never being able to string more than three words together for her. On a good day, he could manage a "Hi, Jane." But usually any more would cause his tongue to spasm as though it was a prisoner trying to break out of his cheek jail.

Quentin had a plan though: *Today, I'm going to ask*

Jane to . . . Am I going to ask her <u>out</u>? No. But . . . I could . . . ask her if she's heard the new Pictures of My Pocket album. She told Maia Goodoff she liked them, I think, and so that . . . that could bring us together. A start. And that could lead to . . . a date . . . and then dates . . . plural . . . then hugging . . . then kissing . . . then . . . well, other stuff . . . and then . . . maybe getting married . . . and then . . .

With an afterschool death warrant, Quentin figured he might as well get shot down by the girl of his dreams as well. He was really going to do it! *Really* talk to her. Maybe even change things up and ask her out. Right . . . *now . . .*

"Jane," he said, his voice only slightly louder than a whisper, "I was . . ."

Before she had a chance to turn around though, Mr. Doyle stormed in angrily, (a rarity as Mr. Doyle was the calmest, coolest teacher ever.)

"No talking for the rest of class," Mr. Doyle grumbled. "You can get a jump on your reading for tomorrow, but I don't want to hear any chatter." He threw himself into the raggedy chair at his desk, twitched and muttered: ". . . Head . . . bursting . . ."

Simultaneously disappointed and relieved, Quentin cracked open a book and rested his head on it. Grateful he had an excuse not to take a chance, he glanced up at Jane's long and pretty neck. *I bet it smells nice*, he mused. *Like birthday cake . . . or butterscotch . . . Maybe tomorrow I'll ask her out . . .*

Before he knew it, he drifted asleep, savoring a forbidden mid-period nap. Even as a slight buzz crept in and out of his dreaming, he felt entirely at peace . . .

. . . Until the end of the period bell shattered every-thing and the teen snapped awake. The squeak of his skin off the drool on his desk made him blush. He tried to wipe the drool off his face and act like he hadn't just been asleep. He hoped Jane wasn't staring at him and laughing. Thankfully, no one even noticed.

The classroom was empty. Totally empty. Not Jane Douglas's neck in front of him. Not Mr. Doyle at his desk. No one. Books lay splayed open on desks, backpacks hid under chairs, and Mr. Doyle's steaming coffee sat on his desk. After checking his face again for drool, Quentin grabbed his bag and stood up woozily.

"What . . . I miss a fire drill?" he wondered.

Walking into the hallway, Quentin shivered, taken aback by a complete and utter stomach-churning silence. A quiet too quiet to be anything but foreboding. He glanced at his watch. 2:42pm. Everyone should have been loudly heading to their last class.

"Helloooooooo?!!" he shouted. It was a question, this hello. A question that eerily received no answer. *Maybe there was a tornado warning and everyone's in the gym together and they left me behind. Because no one likes me. No one. Maybe Jane hates me more than everyone and told them all to 'leave the weirdo there'.*

He descended the stairs and noted a lonely cigarette burning down to its filter. Passing the gym, scattered basketballs covered the floor; the only face there the painted Bulldog mascot on the wall, starting back at him mid-growl. That killed the tornado warning hypothesis.

"This is beginning to feel like a dream . . . a real shirty dream . . ." he mumbled.

His pace picked up as he wandered the deserted hallways. With each personless hall, with each step echoing with the volume of timpani drums, Quentin began to freak out. Breaking into a full-fledged sprint, he ran down what he always viewed as the longest hallway in the universe.

As he burst out the doors into the outside world, he hoped to hear sirens. Or cars racing off. Or the class-skipping skaters zipping along the sidewalk.

Instead, all he heard were birds. The sky was full of them. And not just a flock of any one kind. There was every kind, flying about the sky with no sense of order, just confusion. Occasionally, they'd knock into each other, bounce off, and then resume their insane zigzagging through the air.

"This is messed up . . ."

Birds soared straight up, climbing high into the sky, and then plummeted straight down, pulling up only inches from hitting the ground. In the madness circling above, a robin drilled a pigeon straight on. Both shook it off – as much as a bird can shake anything off in mid-air – and went right back to flying and squawking as though nothing had occurred. A few gray and brown feathers wafted gently down in front of the frightened teen.

"Ooookkkkkaaaaayyy . . . Guess I'll just go . . . home. Yeah . . . home . . ."

Beginning the long walk to his house, Quentin McFury hoped for the first time in recent history that his parents would be there. That they'd be there with a ready explanation and a hug.

With each step, the birds' creepy squawking thankfully faded into the distance. As he staggered home in a strange daze, dark clouds grew in the western sky. Clouds with purpose. Clouds that knew what they were doing. And as those dour shadows on the horizon approached, the teen's walk advanced into a hurried skip before turning into a full-fledged gallop. He passed a car stopped on the front lawn of a house, its engine still running yet no one inside.

I don't know what Armageddon's s'posed to look like, but this has gotta be pretty damn close. Wished I paid more attention in those CCD classes mom and dad made me go to. Should I see horsemen? Should there be –

Suddenly there was a flash of light and – CRRRRRRRRAAACKKKKKKK!!! Quentin sprinted as fast as his horse-like legs could go, now certain it was totally an apocalypse. Still two blocks from home, the rain came battering down in torrents. By the time he reached the front door, he was drenched as he'd never been drenched before.

"MOM?!! DAD?!!" he yelled as he burst into the house.

Throwing down his bag, he raced upstairs and then downstairs to find no parents anywhere. He rushed to the living room and turned on the TV. Surely there had to be some news of something. But there was nothing. Reruns on some networks, movies on others. The news channels only carried live shots of empty chairs where newscasters should be. The sports stations showed static images of empty soccer stadiums, baseball fields, and basketball courts. On one channel, a couple of pom-poms rested forlorn on a football field.

Quentin scrambled to the downstairs computer. He checked site after site. No news about people disappearing or anything weird. Just one thing that stood out: every site's last update was no later than 2:23pm.

"2:23? What the hell happened at 2:23?!! What the hell happened?!!"

Quentin began to think (and hope) maybe this actually was all a dream. A very bizarre, very unnerving, very real dream. This couldn't actually be happening – whatever *this* was. Shortly he'd wake up back in his miserable yet relatively normal existence.

As lightning and thunder flashed and cracked in the ever-descending darkness, Quentin bolted up to his room and leapt into his bed. He buried his head under his pillows, blocking out the storm, the oncoming night, the everything. Completely covered up in blankets and pillows, he built himself a cocoon with the hope that when he awoke, everything would be fine. In his bed cocoon, he kept repeating to himself:

"Everything will be fine. Everything will be fine. Everything . . . will . . . be . . . fine . . ."

Downstairs in his bag, unheard over the raging storm's din and the comfy pillows' muffling, Quentin's new cell phone rang a jaunty ringtone song. And then stopped. A moment later, it chirped and flashed:

"One missed call."

CHAPTER THREE
STOWING AWAYS AWAY

Staggering towards the med-chamber, Quentin's eyes tracked along the snaking crimson energi-tubing that weaved along the ceiling like a bulging blood vessel. With head throbbing and body aching, he hobbled forward, unaware he'd passed the med-chamber until a clicking down the corridor snapped him out of his daze. He whipped his head around but didn't see a thing. Just maybe a shadow that he chalked up to the ship moving. Probably a screw shaken loose after the rough-and-tumble with the Strikers.

"C'mon, Qwenty, my boy," he said. "Just your head messin' with ya."

The battle with the Strikers had turned the tiny med-chamber room inside out with everything in it scattered to the floor. So much so that when Quentin opened the door, meddos and syr-puffos spilled out like a medical piñata.

"Brilliant," he snarked.

In the best of the times, he'd have had great difficulty making out what meddos to take when they were all in their respective well-labeled sections. With the floor coated with multi-colored pills, tabs, and other medicine, the task was damn near impossible. Looking down, he couldn't tell if he'd be taking a pain-limiter or a pain-enhancer from the pill pile littering the ground. (Now, most reasonable people would question why you'd even have a pain-*enhancer*? Quentin asked himself that same question after he accidentally took one and had a raging pain in his left pinky toe for two hours.)

As he fumbled through the pills, he spotted an all-purpose pill at the back. But when he reached for it, his foot slid on a syr-puffo, dropping Quentin's already rumpled and bruised frame to the floor with an agonizing crunch. Wafts of crushed pill powder poofed tiny little clouds into the air.

Extremely annoyed (and with a brand new bruise on his butt), Quentin McFury did what anyone else would do. He threw a full-on kicking and screaming tantrum.

"Stupid pills . . . stupid spaceship . . . Stupid LIFE! STUCK WITH A CRAPPY HUNK OF JUNK ONLY GOOD FOR CRASHING! ALL ALONE FOR-FRAKKIN'-EVER!!! THIS ALL SUCKS, SUCKS, SUCKS!!!"

His words echoed and ricocheted throughout the ship, bouncing along the corridors and even down to the engines and out into space itself. (As it turns out, in space people *can* hear you scream. Parts of space any way.)

Legs splayed, the angry, angry teen roared and stomped on the ground like a two-year-old being forced to go to bed. However, instead of giving him the satisfaction of blowing off steam, the steel-grated floor just hurt his feet. But before he could add "*hurty feet*" to his long list of aches, pains, and bruises, the engines suddenly staggered to life and the ship stumbled forward in fits and starts, heaving like the ship had been food poisoned.

"What the hell?!!" he exclaimed.

Ships don't start themselves up and go. They just don't. Which is precisely why right then Quentin frantically bolted for the cockpit.

The Havok wasn't enjoying being a spaceship right then. The engines grinded so earsplittingly loud it sounded like ten-thousand tin cans being cut up by a thousand chainsaws. Of course, the ruckus kicked up by the engines was only a symptom of the harried state of the Havok. The oxy-gen wasn't back up to snuff, the stabilizers were pretty unstable, and one of the wings even flapped like a wounded bird.

With ears shattering and a stomach on the way to Regurgiville, Quentin burst into the cockpit and leapt at the console, quickly shutting down the engines and everything else except for the oxy-gen. The Havok again went silent.

As they drifted on peacefully, he sighed and wondered what just happened: *Okay, only two possibilities. First one, the just bad one: the ship's in far worse shape than I thought. Which ain't good as the ship's in pretty horribly crappy shape to begin* with. *Now, the second one (the <u>really</u> bad one) is that I'm not alone. The shadow I saw, the clanking "screw" . . . I . . . am . . . not . . . alone.*

Quentin always wanted someone to talk to, but he wasn't sure if what he'd find onboard here would be the talking kind. And even if it was, sometimes talking wasn't the greatest. Especially if the life-form said something rude like "Now, you die!" and then shot him. (Sometimes he went to the least happy possibility first.)

So, Quentin McFury – being the bold interstellar explorer and adventurer he was – instantly jumped up and courageously slammed the cockpit doors shut. Then he hit the red panic lock buttons, which shuttered the doors with a series of satisfying clangs.

"What now, what now, Quentin, buddy boy?" he asked himself, pacing quite a small pace in space. "If it's a creature, an alien, a . . . monster . . . what do I do? I could blow the airlocks . . . *again* . . ."

Scanning the readings on the console, he realized the oxy-gen hadn't replenished itself since the battle and blowing the airlocks on his limping ship might be the last straw, ripping the thing apart like an exploding gumball.

"Of course, who knows if the thing breathes air anyways," he muttered. "I can just wait it out and maybe the creature . . . the monster . . . the alien . . . the giant-jelly-filled-donut-squirrel will just spontaneously die . . . or jump off . . . or turn into a giant furry Wild Thing and hug me and make everything feel better."

The ship's inertia kept it moving – barely – as its pilot did nothing. The Havok wobbled towards a small, grayish planet, dotted with reddish clouds that festered like pimples. From this distance, Quentin couldn't fully see the industrialized squalor that covered the planet Jebel. From this far out, he could only see a sickly red cloud burst and dissipate over the big ball of grey like a disgusting sneeze.

Also in view, just outside the planet's orbit, a Fly-Ring had ships jumping into and out of the area like a magician making bunnies disappear and reappear. Quentin watched transfixed, kinda wanting to clap each time a new ship popped into existence out of nowhere.

The Havok drifted silently on. The continued silence – almost an hour now – began to convince Quentin that maybe his adrenalin-fueled mind had just been playing tricks on him. Exhausted, battered, and bruised, he conveniently turned a blind eye to the possibility of a bloodthirsty monster onboard. And as the stars danced outside his ship in a crimson tint from the system's auburn sun, the boy's eyes grew heavy.

"Nothing, it was nothing," he said. "Just my head playing tricks . . . tricks . . . Maybe it was a ghost . . ." He laughed to himself. "A space ghost . . ."

Soon after, he fell asleep in his large pilot's chair, curled up like a broken cat.

CLANG-CLANG-RRRRRGRANG!!!

Brutal clanging brought his rest to a premature end though. His eyes, tiny and blurry from coming out of his much-needed sleep, tried to focus. Creaking as he stood up, Quentin peered out the cockpit, trying to spot whatever was banging on his ship. Getting up on his tippy-toes to peer further outside, the echoes ricocheted down the hallway in a way that could only mean one thing: the noise wasn't coming from outside the Havok . . . it was coming from *inside* it! From the sound of the echoing clangs, the impromptu concert must be coming from the engine room, which made his bold plan to "just wait it out" no longer an option.

"Tearing *my* ship up?!!" he spat out. "That's not cool! Not while I'm on it! I don't care who you are! Damn it if I'm gonna let whatever you are kill me this way! If anyone's gonna kill me, it's gonna be me!"

Amped for action, Quentin swept the cockpit door open and grabbed the fraktor hanging above the entryway, wrapping his fingers around it as he stomped down the hallway. He had only used the weapon once. Shaped like a rounder version of brass knuckles, he startled himself the one time he picked the fraktor up and a pulsating blue blast shot out into the cargo bay. He was even more shocked when the blast sent three heavy crates hurtling at him. Crates he just narrowly avoided being crushed by.

With such a wobbly introduction, he'd hoped to have some proper fraktor-time on the first planet he'd land on. Maybe even get to do some target practice.

CLANG-CLANG-RRRRRGRANG!!!

But it seemed target practice had come to him as he journeyed into the Havok's belly to take on whatever was destroying his ship. Quentin didn't care how big of a monster would be waiting for him. He'd had a really bad few hours in the midst of a really bad couple weeks in the middle of a really, really bad year, so he had some aggro to work out.

"I'm the captain and no one messes with my ship!" he said, psyching himself up.

The corridors' greenish walls seemed to pulse as he barreled towards the engines, hoping he wasn't too late. He'd imagined all those skeleton pilots in inert ships that lost power, engines, etc., and he refused to be one of those. He was young and didn't know what he was going to be, but he knew he'd rather leave a bloody mess behind than a moldy skeleton.

CLANG-CLANG-RRRRRGRANG!!!

Quentin slowed as he neared the engine room. He tried to peak inside, but a tiered status console obscured his view. What little he could see moved unimaginably fast. He caught glimpses of someone knocking a pipe against the engine-silos, which gave off tiny yellow sparks. The figure's motion raced across the room with purple trails . . . or maybe green. It all went too fast for Quentin's eyes to catch a good look. That, combined with witnessing the hell being ferociously beaten out of his engines, was almost enough to make him turn back, all his prior courage seeping out of him.

The only thing that kept him there was the scent. The scent of something . . . he couldn't place. Maybe because he'd never smelled anything like it. But something drifted out from the engine room that smelled . . . nice. Not food nice. Just . . . nice nice. Thus, Quentin's curiosity to step into the room could be reduced to one thing: his nose. And so, led by that nose, he jumped in with his fraktor up, ready for action.

"Stop or I end you now!" he screeched, much more high-pitched than he wanted.

The figure stopped and stared at him. Holding up a long pipe as though the shouting boy carried no threat, the figure eyed him up and down. To her, Quentin looked small, almost pet-like.

What Quentin stared back at was this: a tall, lithe human female with slightly violet skin and tornado-swept emerald green pixie hair. Easily over half a foot taller than him, she was maybe a couple years older, too. Along with all that, she was without a doubt the most beautiful person Quentin had ever seen and this made him feel giddy (even as she glared at him with her ferocious yet haunting blue eyes.)

With a voice that spoke with an accent somewhere between Irish and snake, the lovely alien woman commanded in jagged English: "You fly crap. Now, help get engines give us the go before you ship-ships blow you to hell tries again."

He didn't quite understand her, but even if he did, he'd probably still do what he was doing now, which was nothing. Thus, the Earth boy just gazed at her dizzily, marveling at how pretty she was and smiling like a fool.

CHAPTER FOUR
GHOST TOWN

*A*pproximately *343.3 days ago . . .*

In the first days of the aloneness, Quentin ran through town banging on doors, hollering through the police station, grabbing free drinks at the Mall's food court, and smashing the front windows of the giant box store that destroyed most of the town's other businesses. Everywhere he went, he bellowed at the top of his lungs, hoping somebody would appear.

"WHERE IS EVERYBODY?!!"

"COME OUT, COME OUT, WHEREVER YOU ARE!!!"

"IF THIS IS ONE BIG JOKE, I'M GOING TO KICK ALL OF YOU IN THE BALLS!!!"

Day after day, he kept crying out for attention. (Sometimes he even just shouted, "Attention!") But no matter how loud he yelled, no matter how much destruction he caused, no one came.

After a full week alone, the initial waves of paralyzing fear, worry, and unease yielded to an acceptable numbness that then led to pure thumb-twiddling boredom, especially as Quentin had been behaving as though everyone might show back up at any moment.

"Well, forget this!" he grumbled. "If no one's here, I'm gonna do whatever the hell I want. And . . . and . . . to start . . . This is no longer North Platte but . . . North . . . Quentin! 'North Quentin'? Yeah, North Quentin! Welcome to North Quentin, everybody!"

For his first act in North Quentin, the town's sole resident crept through an open window in Jane Douglas's house and felt a shiver run down his spine. He knew this wasn't the classiest thing he'd ever done. But these were extraordinary circumstances. And since the girl of his dreams might not ever be coming back, he figured . . . why not?

"Wow, her house even smells like her," he whispered.

Walking through the dining room into the hallway, he raised his eyebrows, astonished that her family had embarrassingly awful family pictures on their walls – just like his house! One photo even had Jane, her sister, and her parents all dressed as reindeer for a Christmas card years ago.

"Now, that . . . *that* is horrendous. And look at her braces! Holy shirt, she is human!"

Not knowing exactly why, he tiptoed through the house, bemused by the smallest things. Things such as the gaudy furniture in the living room. Things like the kitchen being a huge mess with cereal bowls left dirty on the table. And how her parents' room overflowed with junk in boxes and piles of clothes on the floor. He didn't know why he imagined her life so different than his but he couldn't be more pleased to find out she wasn't some princess in a pristine castle. She was normal. Like him.

Upstairs, Quentin approached Jane's bedroom with a solemn reverence. At the pink door with orange flowers painted on it, he stopped for a second and thought twice about going in. Both times, he came back with a tentative "Yes".

Listening for a moment to be sure that no one was about to catch him, he entered unaware that by doing so his chaste adoration of Jane would turn into something very different.

"Hello, Jane," he said, surrounded by pictures of her.

Images wallpapered the room, like a little museum to her young life. One photo showed her at age nine, dressed up as a cute little rancher and petting a lamb at a 4-H fair. In another snapshot, Jane and her younger sister pulled each other's hair in front of a Miss Piggy cake for Jane's 11th birthday. Around her mirror were more recent pictures: Jane playing on the volleyball team, Jane decorating for a dance with other student council officers, Jane singing at a church retreat, and Jane goofing around with her friends.

Of course, not all of the photos warmed Quentin's heart. The most painful was the one of her at Homecoming with Steve Z last year. She smiled enigmatically in the picture, inscrutable, like something was slightly off. Quentin couldn't add up why though. All he could do was seethe with anger at Steve Z's luck, finding only small consolation in the fact she broke up with the jerk jock not too long after that.

Seeing her iPod, Quentin started it up. Instantly, Joy Division's "Love Will Tear Us Apart" filled the room. In class, in the halls, in the school, with everyone else, Jane wasn't *this*. Jane was mostly pop crap and reality TV. But there were a few times in references she made in class and other times talking to others where he picked up on the fact that she liked real music, good music. Once, he even overheard her talking about the Yeah Yeah Yeahs when he sat a couple rows behind her at a movie. That moment set his heart on fire and now as the strains of Joy Division filled the room, his adoration kindled further.

"Oh, sweet Jane . . . We *are* meant for each other. It's so perfect."

Swooning, Quentin playfully grasped his heart and fell back into her bed. Pillows went everywhere and exuded the lovely scent of Jane. He then promised himself that if she returned, he wouldn't wuss out and not talk to her again.

"Oh, Jane! Come back, Jane! If you come back, I'll ask you about music and we can talk about the Cure and Very Dangerous Asps and Belle & Sebastian and The Velvet Underground and LCD Soundsystem and The Sick Sycophants and Lykke Li and The National and . . . and . . . and everything," he merrily imagined. "And then we'll talk about movies and books and how stupid school is and how we're so much better than everyone else. Maybe we can go to a concert in Denver or Omaha – maybe even . . ." But his enthusiasm trailed off as he noticed the sycamores gently swaying outside. "Yeah, me and my non-existent girlfriend can go see a non-existent band in a town filled with no people."

Plopping down at Jane's desk, he dejectedly turned on her computer. It started up with a background of a cat getting eaten by a dinosaur. He smiled.

Scanning through her messages, he hoped to find that perhaps she, too, had nurtured an unspoken crush on him. She didn't. And he was crushed to find out that this wasn't so. That's not to say he went unmentioned. He was. He just didn't fare too well. In one message to Erin Stobler, she said: "*Qwentin (sp) totally stalker-gazed me in Eng today. Creepy, creepy, creepy!*"

"How could she say I'm 'creepy'?" Quentin asked himself while continuing to search through her messages.

An email titled "*Guys I'd Never Date*" sent to Amy Parker didn't do him any favors either, describing him as "*smelling weird and wearing that stupid Clash snake shirt again.*" And finally, in email messages and a private diary entry, Quentin found out Jane would never-ever-*ever* be his gal. He also discovered that her public persona and her private one were two very, very different things.

"*They can't know!*" she wrote. "*I just don't know why they should CARE. It's nothing to do with them! But if they knew, if they found out or GOD FORBID caught us kissing . . . I don't know what. Would they kick me out? Lock me in a closet? (HA-HA!) What? Maybe after I graduate, Rhonny and I can . . .*"

Jane was gay. Gay and so very, very secretly dating Rhonda Perez. Rhonda was second chair violin in Orchestra, loved anime, and was an even smaller blip in the school than Quentin. Perusing further, his unfettered, unrequited love for Jane turned into something else: a profound respect with a touch of pity. Pity that Jane couldn't be the truest Jane she could be in this world. But not too much pity as she did have something very, very real with Rhonda. Unlike the completely fake relationship he'd just generated where he and Jane became friends, dated, and then broke-up over her newfound sexuality in less than five minutes.

Quentin nodded a *"good for her"* nod. Good for Jane. Wherever she was.

The rest of the day, he spent breaking and entering into other people's houses finding out everyone had secrets, everyone had layers, everyone wasn't all that different from each other. Even Steve Z had a whole secret closet overflowing with Legos including a mini-Lego North Platte with the water tower, Buffalo Bill's Ranch, and the high school all in Lego form.

"Guess it's all about survival," he muttered. "Nobody can be who they are."

When he returned to his own home, Quentin bounded up the steps, ready to zonk out for the night. But reaching the top step . . .

Chirp . . .

Turning back, he slowly descended the stairs. The metallic chirp could have been anything, even if it wasn't a sound he'd ever heard before. Standing still in the kitchen, he waited to hear the tinny chirp again. He hoped it wasn't a creepy cricket or a —

Chirp . . .

His head swiveled and spotted . . . his backpack. Left on the floor from the first day of his aloneness, he hadn't touched it since. He whipped off a shoe and held it, ready to smash the chirping intruder into a thousand bloody pieces. But as he shook his backpack, all that fell out was that ugly orange phone.

He breathed a sigh of relief and —

CHIRP!!!

"Holy shirt!!!" he yelled, jumping back in fear. It was so much louder outside of the bag. He chuckled and picked it up. "Just that crappy phone, you goof."

Looking at the ancient monochromatic screen though, something was off. It listed one missed call. *No biggie*, he figured, *probably just Dad calling to yell at me for not saying 'Thanks'. The jerk.*

He gasped when he noted the time when the message was left: over two hours after everyone disappeared! He rapidly hit the voicemail button. Frustratingly, it left him with even more questions.

A man's voice spoke through intense static, almost like a robot, some of it garbled: ". . . Not alone . . . Find the . . . rurrrrntt . . . Denver . . . the Mother doesn't . . . harvvrr . . . one chance for Eartherrrscraaaaannrr . . . safe. Humans scooped and transported frommmm planet . . . You must . . . grrnn-zrttt . . . Denver and then begin—"

The message then ended abruptly.

The lonely teen listened to it seventeen more times. Words stuck to the inside of him with a new hope. "*Not alone.*" "*Safe.*" "*Denver.*" His mind raced with questions: *Who was this guy? Whose mom is he talking about? And how'd he get my number?* In the end though, the questions meant less than the one big answer.

Quentin now had a mission. He wasn't alone. He was going to find his people. He was going to Denver.

Since Quentin didn't know how to drive (and he didn't want to walk the 262 miles to Denver), he figured he should give himself some lessons first. And for those lessons, only one vehicle was good enough for him: Steve Z's red truck.

Steve Z loved his truck more than a girlfriend. Once, he threatened to beat up Mr. Grubbs because the teacher's bubble butt brushed against it as he waddled past. And being the heralded savior of the school's football program, not only did Steve Z not get suspended, but also Mr. Grubbs found himself reprimanded by the vice-principal.

"Hello, Big Red," Quentin said, buckling himself into the truck. "Let's just try and be friends and see where this takes us."

Now, an F-150 truck isn't an automobile for subtle movement. It's a big, brash piece of machinery meant to get things done. Big things. And big things it did. For it was a big truck.

Things like smashing through a stop sign in the first ten minutes of Quentin driving it. Things like crashing through the fence of the school's football field and tearing up the grass in giant chunks, not to mention bursting back out through a giant Bulldog banner. And things like driving though the indoor mall and crushing everything in its path, including: the pretentious portraits of high school seniors, the Poppy's Popcorn kiosk, and, finally, through the cell phone store amongst much beeping and electrical chirping.

"Woo-hooo-hooo-hooooooooo!!!" the teen yawped.

Back outside the Mall though, Quentin only narrowly missed decapitating himself when his foot forgot which peddle was the accelerator and which was the brake. Thankfully, he remembered which was which just as he smashed into the loading trailer outside the JC Penney's. Slamming the brakes wasn't enough to prevent Steve Z's precious F-150 from total destruction as the trailer ripped through the truck's cab, stopping only inches from Quentin's hyper-ventilating head, nearly ending his driving lessons good and proper.

"Ooooo . . . kkkaayyyy . . . That was . . . yeeeeesh . . ."

Thus learning his final driving lesson (brake and accelerator are *very* different), Quentin decided to go car shopping.

Down at the Renny Garnett Dealership, Quentin found exactly what he was looking for – a black turbo Malatia XXZ. The XXZ was a souped-up, rip-roaring, *I've-got-way-too-much-money-and-really-want-you-to-know-it* high-speed car, the kind driven by obnoxious teen superstar singers that made Quentin's ears vomit. He considered a safer car, a more fuel-efficient vehicle, a less audacious mode of transport. But in the end, he figured: *If they all come back tomorrow, they ain't gonna arrest me any more for stealing a turdy car.*

Rummaging through the dealerships keys, he found

the XXZ's and snatched a sporty set of fingerless driving gloves, racing out of town like a bat out of hell.

"I'm gonna find somebody even if I'm the last guy on Earth."

He knew that didn't make much sense but he liked being proactive. He'd had enough of his little ghost town anyway. He wanted to find someone, anyone. His mystery caller certainly qualified and piqued his interest. Loaded up with a hearty assortment of chips, Dr. Pepper, and hope, Quentin drove off into the sunset.

West, he was going. To the land middle Nebraskans considered a recreational beacon of happiness, opportunity, and fun. To a place he now hoped would have all the answers he so desperately craved.

He was going to Denver.

CHAPTER FIVE
MEET TRINTA

Her name was Trinta. The lissome, slightly violet-skinned alien female's name was Trinta. And Quentin was instantly smitten with her. (He was actually three steps past smitten, but for now smitten will do.) Spending almost a year alone in space would make the first person any guy saw attractive, but she *was* empirically lovely. Which is why he didn't really mind when she slapped him.

"Ww-why'd you—" he stammered.

"Need to stop the gawk and do what the say," she said, her English jagged and ragged like a fork caught in a garbage disposal. "Strikers be missed soon. And missed mightily. If don't up and move, we as under supernova waiting to melt."

"So your sun is really hot?" he asked, trying to figure out what she was saying and also make small talk.

She said nothing. Yet he continued:

"So you're, uh . . . a little purply? Purplish? Purple. Is that . . . normal?"

Trinta shook her head and rolled her shoulders, one swift move so dismissive Quentin felt like an eight-year-old who just pooped his pants. His insecurity wasn't helped by the fact that Trinta was several inches taller than him. (Not to say Quentin wasn't tall himself. He was. For a human. He just hadn't grown into it yet. He was all gangly and jangly, something only amplified through months of flying around the galaxy eating the intergalactic version of Ramen noodles. Which, actually, was just Ramen noodles.) So Trinta's towering stature plus her glaring did nothing for the boy's self-esteem.

"I'm Quentin . . . and you're . . . uh . . ." he asked.

She didn't care about his self-worth and she sure as hell wasn't instantly "smitten" with this strange boy. She didn't really regard him at all. She was only concerned with her own self-preservation and wasn't about to give that up because she found herself stuck with this lump. Hence, she jumped right into doing what she did best. And that was fighting to live. (Although often she was just best at fighting.)

Trinta scanned the room, immediately focusing on the backup oxy-gen tubing hanging on the wall. Leaping up onto the engine core's fusillade, she punched the metal ceiling. As the titaniaplating shifted, a very thin one-foot sheet fell to the ground, nearly slicing off Quentin's left big toe in the process.

"Hey!" he shouted, holding up his fraktor semi-threateningly.

In a split second, Trinta kicked the fraktor out of his

hand with one foot and then smashed it against the wall with the other.

"I wasn't gonna . . ." he protested.

But before he could finish, Trinta grabbed a polarity rod from the ceiling and crushed it in her hand. Green rivulets spilled out slowly. From the syrupy sludge, glowing red bearings separated from the green flowing glob to fall onto the grates below. As the liquid globbed down from the ceiling, Quentin fixated on the wisps of smoke drifting up from the grates.

"Hey, you're ruining my ship!" he said.

"*Your* ship?" she chortled with a husky laugh as she destroyed more and more polarity rods. Soon the whole room rained green with the little flashing bits of red.

"Reminds me of Christmas," said Quentin, oddly delighted.

Trinta hopped off the fusillade and grabbed the tubing behind him. Using her razor-sharp nails, she ripped the tubing into long strips.

"Are you just tryin' to destroy the Havok?" he said. "Because I think that might not be so good for us . . . you know . . . living."

Ignoring the pointless words coming out of the boy's mouth, Trinta concentrated on creating a strange web of tubing. As the polarity streams spurted through one tube into another, the colors would merge and flash and continue on, pumping onwards through the ship. She gave herself a little half-smile as she slid to the ground.

The words "What are you—" spattered out of Quentin's mouth trying to form a question before a trail of purple sped out the door. Frustrated, he ran off after her, feeling like an annoying little brother chasing after a big sister who didn't want to play with him.

Bursting into the cockpit, Quentin bellowed: "Hey, that's *my* chair!"

Unfazed, Trinta didn't move from the pilot's seat, forcing him to fold his arms and give her a very stern eyeballing. His "eyeballing" might have caused her to chuckle (had she noticed it). But she was too busy flipping switches and hitting buttons on the console like a battle-tested, whip-smart pilot. (She even hit the forbidden buttons – the ones in the far section of the console that Quentin tried only once because each time he did, he nearly died.) Trinta clearly had flown a lot and after her flurry of action, the ship groaned and sputtered back up.

"No shut us off another time now!" she commanded.

"We're moving," Quentin said, taking a reluctant seat in the co-pilot's chair.

"You not clever thing."

This quieted Quentin and he simmered as the ship clugged along towards the grey ball known as Jebel, the nearest anything they could land on. Every few moments, the Havok would stagger forward, stop, then hiccup itself slightly nearer to the industrial storage planet. It wasn't smooth, but it was progress.

Quentin went to ask her a question, but held back. He didn't want his new passenger to ridicule him again. Or slap him. *She did slap me, didn't she?* he remembered. *I was slapped.*

Trinta eyed the blurry grey sphere in front of them. The stars surrounding the snot-colored planet made it look like tinsel on a cowpat. For her, despite its rampant ugliness, the planet was an opportunity. If only they could land on it.

"So what'd you do to the engine?" Quentin finally asked.

Before answering, she stretched out in the chair, resting her very long legs on the console, and stared at him for what felt like a hard hour. She then said dismissively:

"I made Triterrtan Spiral. Take engine's jostrum rods to channel through oxy-gen. Make series of microbursts, trick engines into make ship energetic relay spasms." She then raised an eyebrow, wondering why she even wasted breath trying to explain this to someone so – she couldn't even be polite – *stupid*.

"So sorta like a Tesla coil," Quentin suggested. He wasn't the best student ever, but he remembered a little from science class. She gave him a quizzical eyebrow. "Using a couple different things to ignite each other to generate some energy to . . . well, you know . . ."

Trinta nodded, moderately impressed. She gave a half-smile/half-smirk that fueled Quentin with immense pride. Had he known that Trinta often reserved that specific *smilirk* for her childhood pets when they didn't eat their own poo, it wouldn't have made him any less proud.

"So where we goin'?" he chirped.

Trinta shrugged towards the phlegmatic planet in front of them.

"Yeah, 'course," he said, trying to coolly cover his inability to grasp the obvious.

As they gazed out into space, Quentin tried to take

in as much as he could of the woman now commandeering the Havok from his peripheral vision. She was tall, maybe 6'7", maybe taller. She seemed a year or two older than him. (Even though her being an alien and all purply, he didn't really know how old she was. She could have been 100 years older for all he knew.) Her skin wasn't purple like a crayon, but a very light violet where darker shades undulated slightly across the surface where her veins were. Her hair was a dark tight green pixie cut that stopped before her neck, a long, lovely neck that reminded him briefly of Jane. Her legs extended onwards onto the console like samurai swords, lithe, lethal, and striking. And her clothes . . . her clothes were tight and . . . clingy. The dark black pants with an empty fraktor holster, the black boots with the crisscrossing red laces, the grey shirt with the strange maroon markings. Quentin even dug her navy buttoned jacket and —

"Like what see?" Trinta sneered.

Blushing scarlet, Quentin immediately snapped his eyes back to the planet Jebel.

"Yeah . . . wh-what a grey planet," he stammered. "Is it really cloudy or . . . something?"

Dropping her legs off the console and resting her elbows on her knees, she decided to ignore his gawking. "Not clouds. Grey on grey. Smoky stinson from the secondary cores with grethane bursts charging out of the chem-silos. Then yond boxage towers. Never-ending."

Not a lot of what she said made sense to him, but he nodded knowingly anyway. He wasn't entirely sure he'd been alone so long that he forgot how talking worked.

A giant grethane carrier ship rumbled underneath them and across the cockpit's windows, shaking the Havok as it passed. Two smaller nudger ships pushed the immense carrier towards the FlyRing thirteen parsecs in front of them. The three ships trudged towards the FlyRing before disappearing through it, shot elsewhere into the galaxy with a blinding burst.

Trinta flicked a series of yellow switches on the far left panel, causing one of the cockpit windows to glass over and a 3-D holo-grid to appear. In the center of the grid was the Havok. Occasional blipping holo-reps of ships would shoot up from the planet only to disappear through the Fly-Ring as other blipped ships would pop up out of the Fly-Ring and speed down towards Jebel.

"Wow," he said. "It looks like rush hour out there."

Trinta grimaced as the grid showed the Havok drifting offline from the planet, heading slightly askew of Jebel. Knowing their ship had no capability for any real course correction, she kicked the console angrily.

Picking up on her subtle frustration, Quentin asked: "Are we gonna miss the planet?"

Irritated that the boy spoke (even if it was a good question *and* the truth), Trinta grabbed the stick and pointlessly tried to turn the ship back towards Jebel, but the stick didn't do squat. Not even diddly-squat. She brushed past Quentin and hit the green spin wheel on the far side of the console. Still nothing.

"Damn," she spat.

"Guess my smashy-smashy messed that up. Sorry about —"

Suddenly, the grid lit up with three red flashes about fifteen cubes away.

"Griddle damn," she growled.

"Strikers!"

Trinta angrily folded her arms and sat back in her chair. Her upper lip curled as she shook her head angrily, "Longest of the shots anywhy's."

"What was?"

"Prob not enough gas-go to breach atmo, so no cares if no on line with the Jebel."

"So, what? We just wait for them to . . . what? Blow us out of the stars? Is that it?"

She nodded sullenly, barely acknowledging him.

Quentin didn't find her conceding defeat that charming. He didn't like being ignored either. It reminded him of high school. Regardless, not wanting his time with this lovely new pouty person cut short, he came up with the semblance of a plan.

"Maybe there's another option," he said, cocking his head.

"Yer. Could also run out of air," said Trinta with a sarcastic grin, raising her cheeks so high Quentin was surprised she could even see. He didn't stick around long enough to gauge her vision though – he had things to do.

In the cargo bay, Quentin grabbed a series of enormous mag-nets from behind a heap of crushed metal. It never really was a tidy cargo hold. Most of the time, the hold looked most like a portable junkyard, especially with the two shopping carts in one corner. Once, Quentin even played Hide-and-Seek in there with himself. (It was more fun than he thought it would be, but not enough fun to do more than once without feeling totally pathetic.)

Grabbing seven of his finest (i.e. "working") mag-nets, he checked the charges on each. The mag-nets were long metal nets with circular magnetic pucks attached at the ends. Satisfied he had enough, he tossed them by the airlock doors.

But just as he did, the ship shifted slightly with a roar from another passing ship's entry wash. Such movement in a secured and neat cargo bay would usually not cause the faintest whiff of distress. However, in this technological pigsty, an eight-foot ball of metallized cable dislodged and rolled towards the teen with an intent to squish. An intent that went unheard over the fading roar of the passing vessel and the Havok's own sputtering hiccups.

Turning just in time to see a blur and swallow a burrito of fear, Quentin crashed to the ground in what felt like multiple pieces.

"Grrrrrghgh . . ."

Thinking whatever threw him into this new bout of internal anguish had to really, really hate him and be really, really big, he caught a whiff of something sweet with a touch of mint. His face itched as though tickled with lightly charged strands of hair.

Opening his eyes, glimpses of the cargo bay's ceiling appeared through green strands. Feeling the cool breath on his right ear, he realized Trinta was on top of him: *She must have tackled me just before I was crushed. She likes me.*

"Why smiling?" she asked, eyebrow raised. "Tackle into simpledom?"

"Nope," he said. "Just . . . just glad to . . . uh, to . . .

be alive."

Trinta leapt off the boy and reluctantly extended a hand to help him up. He took her hand, but didn't bounce up with nearly her grace or speed. In fact, he cried out a little as he stood, his body never feeling so abused in its fairly short life.

"What was that?" she asked.

"What?"

"Squeachy throat noise," she said, eyeing him down. "It insult, were not?"

Quentin shrugged, figuring no answer sometimes was the smart choice. (Especially when the truth was just that he was a whimpering wuss.)

"Now, where was I?" he said while surveying the scene. He squinted at the huge ball of metallized cable now embedded in the starboard wall. Nodding, he realized how the scraps of a plan that really had nothing to it became slightly more plausible.

"That looks secure," he said semi-sarcastically, giving the cable ball a firm tug.

Hundreds of yards of cabling littered the hold, snaking around everything and back again. Scooping up the piles of mag-nets he accumulated earlier, he clamped each of their hold-points to the end of the cable. He wasn't sure if the dozen or so mag-nets would be enough to grab anything, let alone secure itself if it did, but it was all he had.

"Strikers in range in five minutes," a gruff voice said, booming through the ship.

"Who the hell is that now?!" Quentin shouted. "Who else is on my freakin' ship?! You tell me and you tell me now!!!"

Rolling her eyes, she said: "It's the ship."

"The Havok can talk?!!"

"Yer. Never dia-logs up?"

"Uh . . . no . . . Guess not . . ." he said, taking it all in before questions came spewing out. "Does he have feelings? Does he tell jokes? How old is he? Does he hate me?"

Trinta stared at him incredulously.

Quentin kept talking: "Because of – you know – my whole racing the ship around and getting it really beat up and . . . the stuff . . . Hell, I wouldn't blame him. I'd hate me, too, for that." He paused, concerned. "Has he been watching me, like, *all* the time?"

Trinta was amazed the boy even knew how to put on pants.

"Or . . . or he's probably like an OnStar or Siri or something, right?" Quentin said. "And he's probably not even a 'he' but just a ship. Just a good old ship. That talks and stuff. And I'm an idiot, right?" Finally, he did the smart thing and shut up.

"Strikers in targeting proximity in three minutes," the Havok declared.

"Well, enough of the chit-chat," Quentin said. "Hold on to something. Papa's goin' fishing."

He grabbed the mag-nets, gave a quick pull to their tethered ball of cable, and threw the mag-nets towards the cargo doors. Hooking his arm around a protruding energi-tubing duct, he glanced over to see Trinta's limbs similarly wrapped around pipes and handles on the other side. She didn't know what he was up to, but she knew how to take speedy direction.

With a rakish wink to his lovely passenger, Quentin

hit the bright orange button next to the cargo doors. A musical alarm sounding like constipated wind chimes screeched for a few seconds and then the cargo doors snapped open with a ferocious whoosh.

The mag-nets immediately flew out of the ship exactly as he planned. But so did crates, tools, and even a shopping cart, all of which turned into flying deadly jetsam that spun towards Trinta and Quentin with a thousand murderous possibilities. As a battery pack shot towards the door and ricocheted off his ear in the process, Quentin screamed silently with what little oxygen remained.

With the draining strength he had left, Quentin smacked the orange button again with all his might. The cargo doors shut just as quickly as they opened and he slipped to the floor exhausted. Before he could breathe a sigh of relief though, he bounded over to the control panel. Trinta's eyes lit up as she got a glimpse of what he was thinking.

"Hope we catch us a big 'un!" he shouted.

Reaching the cockpit, they could see the Strikers bearing right towards them. Jumping into his seat, Quentin hit a green switch and the entire cockpit turned into translucent viewscreens. The translucents made the entire cockpit see-through to assess threats with real eyes. It also made for some nice sightseeing, too. (Even though the first time Quentin hit that button, he clutched the console for ten minutes thinking he was going to fall.) Down below the ship, they could see the mag-nets charged with their radiant emerald hue, waiting for something to latch on to.

"Strikers' weapons systems engaged and targeting," the Havok said.

"Well, that doesn't sound awesome," Quentin said.

As the Strikers tore through space towards the Havok, Quentin's fingers dug into the armrests, waiting for death or salvation. Trinta, however, lounged relaxed, like a cool cat on a sun-baked sofa as their ship kept chugging forward, limping towards annihilation.

Luckily, just as the Strikers were about to fire on the Havok, a large transpo arrival bubble appeared and shot the Havok towards Jebel a couple hundred meters closer. Watching a FlyRing for a couple days when he had nothing better to do, Quentin noticed that the arrival bubbles would forcibly shove anything in the nearby arrival area out of the immediate vicinity to prevent any interstellar crashes.

Shooting the Havok forward though didn't put them out of danger. It only gave them a couple more seconds safety. But that wasn't all to Quentin's plan. His plan really got going fifteen seconds later when a tripled-tiered transport wedge arrived out of the FlyRing from hyperspace. The looming big-as-a-building wedge didn't even wait to recalculate its position, continuing seamlessly toward Jebel without delay.

"There we go," Quentin said. "That's gotta be a ninety-seven footer."

Inside the immense transportation wedge starship, a very late pilot cared less about safety than getting yelled at and put on a twenty-seven time shift penal delay. So as the wedge barreled toward Jebel, it did so directly between the Havok and its pursuing Strikers. And when the mag-nets flashed alive and clung to the metal hull of the wedge, the Havok instantly hitched a ride behind the wedge and whipped towards Jebel with such force that the huge tangled cable ball snapped from the wall it had been implanted in and smashed into the cargo bay doors. Thankfully, the doors held and, in a matter of seconds, the Havok cracked through the planet's atmosphere, trailing behind the gigantic wedge like a piece of toilet paper on a shoe.

Before the Strikers realized what had occurred, they'd futilely flown around the surrounding area for thirty frustrating minutes. When the colossal wedge popped out of the FlyRing and roared down to the planet, it was as though the Havok disappeared, so quickly did the Havok latch on and zoom down with it. The Strikers scanned for their target's jump signature but found nothing. They then searched the area for debris in case it might have exploded. By the time they figured out the Havok must have parasited onto a passing ship, it was too late to save any of their careers.

As the Havok broke through Jebel's atmosphere, it did so while wreaking even further damage to the ship. The Havok may not have used any of its own energy to slingshot down, but their free trip still came at a cost.

Nevertheless, Quentin beamed proudly, "Impressive, huh?"

Trinta gave him a begrudging nod of approval only moments before the cargo doors ripped off the ship, the mag-nets and tangled cable ball shooting off with the wedge. It was too much pressure for those sturdy doors to be pulled for so long with such force. They were lucky they lasted as long as they did.

The Havok now plunged breathlessly towards the monstrous traffic snarls of cargo ships and small transporters. If they were fortunate enough to avoid colliding into another ship, just beyond the traffic waited millions of the grey industrial towers of storage containers that made up most of Jebel. On one hand, this was a good thing. Any chance for the Strikers to get a location on them was reduced considerably as they dived down into the planet's traffic of ships like a needle thrown into a stack of a trillion other needles.

In that respect, they were safe.

For now.

For those few seconds anyway.

Well, as safe as they could be while hurtling towards an unfamiliar planet to their certain death. (Well, maybe not *certain* death. There are more chapters here that Quentin and Trinta should most likely be a part of. Hopefully.)

CHAPTER SIX
DOGGONE IT

*A*pproximately *343.2 days ago* . . .

As the roaring car tore down Interstate-80, Earth's alone and lonely boy Quentin McFury cackled and roared as the Black Keys' "Lonely Boy" blared full blast in the musky dusk. (Even if he had mixed feelings about this song that somehow even his mom knew.) At times like this, he was okay with the world maybe just being him.

Racing towards the setting sun, I-80 became a much more dangerous beast though. In the best of times, the interstate was known for being a boring, flat highway with nothing to fear except falling asleep at the wheel due to the monotonous . . . monotonous . . . monotonous . . . monotono . . . zzzzzz . . . monotonous landscape.

Quentin, however, wasn't bored on *this* trip. That's

what the driver's seat will do, especially when you're clocking 115mph. Especially as the highway wasn't an entirely empty racetrack. The embankments alongside the roads and the median were full of cars. And several miles outside of North Platte, it wasn't just the embankments. Suddenly, handfuls of abandoned cars littered the highway, just like in North Platte where cars were strewn everywhere as though people disappeared right in the middle of driving.

"Wooo-hoooo-hoooo-hoooooo!" Quentin shouted, leaning into a curve.

As the last chip of the sun fell from the sky and darkness took the better part of the dusk, Quentin flipped on the lights as he continued his mad dash to Denver. Barreling down that stretch of highway, his lights danced across shadows up ahead and he slowed. Briefly he thought it might be more stranded cars. But getting closer, he realized the flickering shadows were moving . . . living . . .

"What's that?" he asked. "Maybe it's . . ."

For a moment, he believed it might be other people and his heart skipped a hopeful beat. But as he neared, he realized it wasn't people ahead. From the lumbering, muddling, hulking shadows, he knew it had to be:

"COWS!!!"

The XXZ swerved, just narrowly missing a massive heifer. Bringing his speed immediately down to a crawl, Quentin laid on the horn and weaved in and out of the confused cattle meandering across the highway.

Quentin had forgotten about the feedlot along the highway near Ogallala. On trips to his grandmother's he always held his nose while passing it because of its horrific smell. Somehow the cattle must have gotten out and now the cattle mooed and bellowed, moseying across the pavement like a cow street party.

"Hey, Flossie, great to see you!" Quentin said to a brown cow. "Is that a new ear tag? And Reggie, when are you going to make her an honest woman? Get her a ring already. Enough with getting the milk for free."

Quentin loved talking like a pretend grown-up. Made him feel deliciously ironic. He gave a little honk as he maneuvered between more of the husky beasts.

"How 'bout that 'no humans' business, Bertha?" he asked a big Angus trotting alongside. "I know. Isn't it crazy? I thought maybe it was zombies at first, but . . . Oh, really? A 'smart bomb'? Interesting. Maybe I was too stupid for it to get me." He laughed too hard at that one and thought Bertha mooed a chortling giggle, too. "Me? I'm goin' to Denver. Got a bit of a mission. Top secret, you know."

Bertha mooed again.

"Yeah, I'm just drivin' by myself. Yeah, yeaaahhh . . . sure, you're cute. Wait a minute! Are you hitting on me, Bertha? You're a lovely heifer, but I don't know. My heart's been hurt before."

Quentin awkwardly chewed the inside of his lip, unsure what to say next. He didn't want to break the cow's heart, but he also didn't want to lead her on. He reckoned the best thing to do was to just drive away. And so he did.

"Whelp, byeeeeeee!!!"

Weaving in and out of the rest of the herd, Quentin soon found himself back on a cowless, carless open stretch of asphalt. Flooring it, the XXZ tore through the night with a mighty roar . . . for all of two minutes. Then the mighty roar turned into a horrifying screech.

All because Quentin didn't see the little calf down the road. He hit the brakes as hard as he could but momentum kept the car hurtling forward. The frantic newbie driver yanked the wheel rapidly, desperately trying not to hit the calf, but the XXZ's tires couldn't take it. And just as the smell of burning rubber hit his nose, a tire blew!

"Shirt! Shirt! Shirt! Shirt! SHIRT!!!"

Suddenly, the XXZ flipped, twisting and rolling over and over again, spinning into a ditch. As the car tumbled nine times around, air bag after air bag deployed – making Quentin briefly imagine he was in the world's scariest pillow fight. Eventually, the vehicle came to a stop, landing right side up again.

All was quiet, except for the mooing of the ever-so-narrowly missed calf that continued its wobbly trek down the middle of the road.

"Ugn . . . not . . . cool . . ."

Inside the smashed car, the planet's lone human felt nothing. Nothing *wrong*, that is! Despite the crushed up mess the XXZ was, Quentin checked himself over, pleased to find nothing too amiss. To go through that crash and not be in a minor coma (or major death) was a real testament to the XXZ's engineering safety and/or his good luck.

"Alright, let's check your damage, XXZ. Probably not as bad as I think it is . . ."

He tried the door, but it wouldn't budge. He spun in his seat and used both feet to drill the door open with a giant kick. Unexpectedly, the door shot off the car and clanged to the ground, its echoes carrying into the night.

Stepping out of the car gingerly – still amazed he was in one piece even though the car wasn't – Quentin peered down the road to the lost calf. It mooed a forlorn lament. A lament that the only person on Earth knew all too well. It meant: *"Where is everybody?"* Quentin cautiously approached the small brown calf, the bruised lights from the XXZ providing their only illumination in the darkness.

"Hey there, little guy," he said.

He petted the calf's neck gently. The calf nuzzled into the boy's warm hands. Putting his arms around the animal, they shared a hug both seemed to need.

"You don't smell as bad as I thought you would," Quentin said softly. "C'mon, let's get you back to your people."

Leaning into the calf, the teen used his weight to shift the animal around to face back towards the rest of his kind Quentin had passed some time ago. At first the calf resisted, but with enough pressure the boy nudged him around.

"They're right down there, pal. Just go down about one klick. I think it's a klick. I'm not sure what a 'klick' is really."

The calf just stood and stared at him.

"Trust me. Just go that way and you'll be back with the rest of 'em."

The calf gave him a sarcastic moo which Quentin took as *"Yeah, right."*

Quentin then did something he didn't know was in him. Something he'd only seen in movies and TV. He swatted the calf on the butt. Hard. Not only did he swat the calf on the butt, but he even yelled a cowboy-like, "Yah!" To his great surprise, the startled calf loafed off towards his lost tribe, a hearty hurry in its gait.

"Get a-long, little doggie," Quentin said. "Or should that be little cow-ie." He then groaned at his own bad joke. (This is what happens when the only conversations you can have are with yourself.)

Alone again on the empty highway, Quentin shrugged, grabbed his backpack from the XXZ wreckage, and peered up into the sky. It seemed like there were never more stars out shining and glimmering than tonight.

"Guess I could make a wish on all these stars," he sighed. "What with no one else doing it, I'd have some good odds for it to come true." He wished everyone would be back and his life would be the same again, no matter how miserable it was. But deep down, he knew stars didn't work that way, no matter what cricket sung you differently. "Frakkin' Disney."

Eager to keep his journey to Denver going, Quentin spotted a pick-up truck in a ditch on the other side of the road. Crossing the grassy median filled with garbage, a lost book, and some mice, he found the truck unlocked and happily got in. Inside, the cab smelled musty, smoky, and gross, like an old grandpa. As was the case with all the abandoned vehicles, the keys waited patiently in the ignition. Unfortunately, when he turned the key over, the truck did nothing. The fuel gauge on the dash mockingly winked red on the big ol' E.

"Yeah, guess you can't jump from one car to the

next," he said. "That'd be too freakin' easy!"

He got out of the truck and did the only thing he could do: move his feet, generally one after the other, down the road. He crossed the grassy divide again and began his trek towards the town of Ogallala a few miles away. He figured he'd surely come across another abandoned car (with gas) before he got there, but if he didn't there'd be a gas station to fuel up whatever he wanted.

Strolling through the darkness, he did what he always did when stressed and sang himself a song, this one a tune he dug from last year by some British band called the Echo Waffles:

"The hallways go quiet . . .
My insides tumble and riot . . .
I've seen the last of your kind . . .
And now I'm slowly losing my mind . . .
My home's no longer my home . . .
And maybe it's never been . . ."

The lights of Ogallala drawing closer, he picked up his pace. He'd been doing a lot of driving lately and not much of anything that could be considered physically active. His legs now moved with a little bit of a bounce, happy not to be at rest.

"This ain't too bad," he said. "Got the night air blowing through my hair. The crickets chirping in the fields. The stars shining down. The sound of distant barking and shadowy growling things racing towards me." He stopped and squinted at the low-to-the-ground silhouettes charging towards him. "Wait a minute . . ."

From fifty yards out, a pack of wild dogs descended on him, howling with a primitive hunger. Within a blink, Quentin turned and ran in the opposite direction as fast he could. (A roving pack of rabid canines will do that to you.)

"C'mon, Qwenty-boy . . . Gotta go, boy, gotta go!!!"

His feet beat the pavement in a rapid burst of speed, desperately not wanting to be ravaged and bitten by dogs. His only plan was to make it back to that old truck. The barking grew louder and louder as the dogs got nearer and nearer. There must have been at least a dozen. A dozen dogs feral with hunger, inattention, and shared pack rage. As the carnivorous canines gained on him, Quentin thought he felt drops of spittle from their angry growls.

Arriving where he believed he left that grandpa truck, he searched around frantically. *Surely* he was right where he left it. But he'd forgotten – the truck was on the other side of the highway!

"Oh, come on, McTurdy!" he yelled.

Without a moment's thought, he raced down into the grassy median. When his foot lost hold on an empty pop cup, he nearly went face down into the weeds – a sure easy feast for these fuming beasts. But he put out his hands and kept from falling, barely continuing his mad run to safety.

The dogs literally nipped at his heels as he climbed up the embankment towards the truck. Thankfully, he'd left the vehicle's door open and dived in just as a ravenous pit-bull leapt at him, sinking his teeth into Quentin's shoe and narrowly missing the foot and all five of his toes. With his other foot, he gave the dog a hard kick to the face, knocking it to the ground with a whimper. The young McFury then slammed the door shut, just as another canine crashed into the door as it dove for its prey a moment too late. The thud of the dog-on-door action allowed the teen to breathe a very tiny sigh of relief.

"Man, what I wouldn't give for some Scooby snacks," he said, shaking.

The dogs surrounded the truck, barking at the top of their lungs. A Rottweiler and a Doberman jumped into the flatbed, growling and clawing at the back window. A German shepherd climbed onto the hood, gnashing its teeth with rabid saliva dripping down its maw onto the hood.

"Why'd I have to leave North Quentin? I had my own town. And some Fritos. I was doing okay. Stupid voicemail!!! Stupid mystery dude!!!"

Quentin quivered, trying desperately not to wet his pants. He laid into the horn hoping that it'd drive them all off, but the horn only made them madder. The Rottweiler in the back clawed at the back window and ground its head against it. Quentin hoped the windows would protect him but with these dogs he wasn't sure the metal body of the truck could keep them out. When the back window began to crack though, he resigned himself to becoming dog meat.

And just when it seemed like the cracking glass wouldn't last any longer, there was a tiny yap in the distance. Down the road in the moonlit night, Quentin spotted a little grey schnauzer yipping. The dogs all stopped their ferocious snarls and turned. Breathing heavily, they gaped at the yippy schnauzer for a long moment. Then they all ran off, leaving the boy behind like he never had their attention to begin with.

Inside the truck, Quentin shook uncontrollably with fear, chewing nervously on the sleeve of his jacket like a child wanting his mommy. His eyes fixed on where the dogs ran offfor what seemed like hours. He worried about the calf he almost hit and thought if those dogs hurt that little cow, he'd be furious. But mostly he considered how lucky he was. How very, very lucky. Eventually, while on the lookout for the return of those ferocious beasts, his eyes grew heavy and he fell asleep.

The next morning, he awoke with the sun shining right in his eyes and, thus, a squinty Quentin scanned the road. The road appeared clear. No dogs. No dogs at all. He slowly rolled down the window.

"Don't hear anything," he said, cautiously optimistic.

He got out of the truck and stepped down tentatively, leaving the door wide open. He wasn't taking any chances. Peering down the highway and to the nearby fields, he surveyed everything with a piercing glare. If anything moved (a mouse, a bee, a wind-up monkey with a miniature cymbal), he was gonna jump right back in that truck and live there forever. He'd starve to death in that truck if he had to. He wasn't going to get eaten by dogs though. No way. No how. And as he searched the land around him for anything that might want to bite him, his eyes rested on something he couldn't believe.

"Of course . . ."

A little, four door Mini Cooper sat in the ditch, almost lost in the brush. No more than twenty feet away. He never saw it last night. It was too dark and the weeds too high. Surely, *it* wouldn't have had a gas problem. Surely, *it* would have worked just fine last night and he never would have been put in any dog danger if only he had spotted it then. And when he got in the Mini, he found out that he figured right. A little under a full tank of gas and starting up right away, a very hungry Quentin drove off towards Denver with clear eyes and a newfound focus, shaking his head at the way things work.

"Stupid dogs . . ."

The rest of his trip to Denver was pretty uneventful. Denver, however, was not. Denver even had a spaceship.

CHAPTER SEVEN
BOXED IN FOXTROT

"Are we comin' in hot?" worried Quentin. "I think we're comin' in hot."

As the Havok ferociously plummeted towards Jebel, Quentin and Trinta gripped their chairs with tightly clenched fingers, pushing with their feet against the console to keep from being violently thrown around the cockpit.

The ship – now basically a very large, hurtling boulder – fell helplessly. There was no power for the engines and no control of the ship even if the engines did work. The translucents flickered on and off, so one moment they'd see directly outside to the world below and then switch back to proper consoling and panels. Everything went haywire like an amusement park funhouse ride. All at a thousand miles an hour.

"Well, nice meeting you . . . ." he shouted. "Hey! I never even caught your name!"

Dismissing the boy's blathering, Trinta wondered what kind of sound they'd make crashing into the millions of massive storage containers below them. She wondered if they'd hear any of it before they died. She thought she would. She was an optimist that way.

A hub for the accumulation of grethane produced at the planet's core, Jebel served a dual purpose. It started principally as an immense farm for grethane, a unique fuel that can easily shift from a gas to a solid or to a liquid. But as Grumbolt Industries mined more and more grethane, they needed to store the teeming amounts they were dealing with. So they began to build large warehouse-like storage containers to match the demand.

As they constructed more and more, Grumbolt Industries became very adept at creating storage units of any size on the fly. Quite ingeniously, they mechanized a complex system of nano-construbots to instantly measure whatever item it was – anywhere from 13,000 barrels of grethane to a thimble full of ketchup – and in a matter of seconds those microscopic bots would generate a sealed metal container to exactly fit it. Of course, you could also just send them the measurements, but almost no one did this. It was too damn cool to see the nano-construbots make a giant something out of nothing. Never had storage been so much fun.

After hundreds of years, the planet Jebel now proliferated with almost nothing but container add-ons. From the ground up, covering almost every inch of the planet, the containers reached up into the sky in a colorless Tetris of erratically shaped dark grey boxes. And the planet kept expanding both upwards and onwards, with some projections stating that the containers would reach past the atmosphere in the next few decades.

Outside of the grethane regularly shipped off the planet, Jebel's storage was generally a one-way ride. Very rarely did a customer retrieve anything put in storage. Every person thought they'd be back some time. Maybe when things were less crazy. Maybe when they had a little more space. Maybe when they weren't dying.

But virtually no one came back. Those that did were often disappointed. If the storage keeper could locate the item (something that happened only thirty-three percent of the time), the nano-construbots would generally be unable to retrieve the item due to it being packed deep amongst the jenga-like towers. Sometimes the bots could rejigger a large block of boxes in such a way they could slip the container out, often while jamming in another newly fitted container in its place. But when that was impossible, the customer was sent away with some food vouchers or coupons for minor mental upgrades. That usually did the trick and the customer usually left feeling relatively pleased.

Of course, last year there were over two million storage additions and only three attempted storage retrievals, (with only one person recovering what they stored. And that thimble of ketchup was so mangled he ended up receiving vouchers any way.)

All of this didn't change the fact that the Havok was

hurtling towards a gargantuan skyscraper of container boxes so fast the guy from Earth worried his hair was being ripped out. Overwhelmed by imminent death, hysterical giggles spilled out of him. He wanted very much not to giggle, but the harder he tried not to, the more he did. Trinta glared at him with a cutting disdain.

He giggled: "Sorry . . . hee-hee . . . I can't . . . hee-hee-hee . . . I can't believe I'm . . . hee-hee-HEE . . . I'm gonna die . . . hee-hee-heeeeee-hooo-hee-HEE!!!"

Trinta watched as the ships below dropped colossal chairs, elaborate statues, and even a very frightened seventy-foot Wilsilf whalephant. Each briskly disappeared, amazingly swept up into nano-construbot storage constructions. Extraordinary boxes spontaneously formed around the chairs, the statues, and even the whalephant in the blink of an eye.

Watching those items dropped for instant storage gave Trinta an idea. She spun around in her chair and started punching data into the comm console. Numbers flashed across the tiny screen as she feverishly typed.

"We don't have any power," Quentin said, getting his nervous giggles under control. "Do you know of some miracle code to plug in or something? Or maybe a parachute button? That'd be real handy right about now."

Only moments away from impact, Trinta entered the final numbers into the console. The screen flashed: "*17 Containers* . . ." and then listed a series of measurements, finishing with an amount that went seven digits out. Squinting at the number, she shrugged and typed in a security code. The console dinged with the message: "*Approved!*"

"So did you just . . . order us a pizza before we, like, die and stuff?" Quentin joked through clenched teeth.

She considered explaining her plan to him, but then figured there was no point. Not now. Not where his head was. Why even try? He wouldn't understand what she said anyway. This had to be more of a show than a tell.

The Havok spiraled as it hit its last hundred yards, spinning like a flushed bug down a toilet. With only seconds until they turned into embers and bone, amazing spontaneous generation started directly below them. Suddenly, a vertical set of containers built one on top of the other sprouted up towards the Havok.

At first, Quentin thought maybe it'd shave a few seconds off their imminent demise. But when the ship crashed into the first box, he was pleasantly surprised when they didn't die. Then that first box slammed into the second one, the second into the third and so on and so on, their momentum slowly slowing. It didn't slow enough to stop Quentin and Trinta from ricocheting around the cockpit and off each other, but still they both dared to hold on to a thimbleful of hope. (Which is much better than holding a thimbleful of ketchup.)

By the time the sixteenth box collapsed into the final seventeenth, the Havok came to rest with the impact of an extremely gentle car crash. When it all stopped and the outside of the last box sealed itself over the other sixteen boxes, all was quiet and dark.

The boxed-up smash-down crash was spectacular fun

until Trinta and Quentin's bodies slammed about the cockpit. Quentin went unconscious about box six and Trinta at box thirteen. Although the last one down, Trinta was the first one up.

"Ernn-grnnnnn," she groaned, stumbling to her feet.

The barely lit interior of the Havok didn't give her much to see. The console flashed thirty-one red lights and fourteen orange ones – all insisting that the ship wasn't quite up to snuff right now. Peering outside, she couldn't see anything but a rich blanket of darkness, as being inside a box of a box of a box of . . . etc. doesn't lend itself to any sort of natural (or unnatural) light.

Using the slight tinge of trailing green trim lighting along the ceiling of the ship's corridors, she fruitlessly scanned the room for Quentin. But he wasn't in the cockpit. He wasn't up and at 'em either. For when she limped out of the cockpit, she nearly stepped right on his unconscious face.

She considered letting him sleep. He certainly could use it. And she wasn't sure how much of a help he'd be awake, but right now, she felt he served slightly more use conscious than not. *If nothing else, he could be a bargaining chip or even a shield if they got in a spot of trouble*, she thought. *Plus, there's the remotest possibility he might know something. Verrrrrryyyy remote.* Thus, she leaned over the prone boy. *He wasn't entirely repulsive when his mouth wasn't constantly moving*, she shrugged. He wasn't anything she'd go for, but she could see him appealing to someone somewhere. Maybe with a species that had limited vision or unusual tastes in attractiveness.

Gently, she ran her fingers through his hair. A few

strands fell, sliced off by her razor-sharp nails. Half-smiling, she realized he needed her a hell of a lot more than she did him. Maybe that's why she decided to wake him and keep him by her side.

"Wakey, boy," she said, placing the nail of her left ring finger under his nose.

Bolting up as though his butt were on fire, Quentin jumped around the corridor, shaking his head violently and holding his nose to keep out any more of that smell.

"What the—" he shouted. "What was . . . That is . . . eugghhh . . . what was . . ."

His eyes darted around the ill-lit corridor, finally noticing Trinta watching with a wry grin. He wasn't sure, but it seemed her short pixie hair had grown much longer, now shoulder-length. *Maybe just the lights*, he assumed. *Or lack thereof . . . Or my head . . .*

"Ughhh . . . what . . . happened?" he asked, trying to ignore the gut-churning scent from her finger that still made his left eye twitch.

"Stored us," she said. "Make block of boxes. Fall of pillows."

"'Fall of pillows'?"

She mimed the Havok flying as her right hand and then sent it falling into her left hand, which covered it up. She then flipped the left hand repeatedly as the right hand of the Havok fell with less and less force.

"Oh," Quentin said, "it sorta cushioned our blow."

"Yer. What said."

"So we're in a bunch of boxes now? Like one of those Russian nesting dolls."

She shook her head, confused.

"Of course. Why would you get me talking about a Russian wooden doll thingy? You don't even know what Russia is. Hell, there is no Russia any more. Not really."

Trinta folded her arms and stared blankly at the babbling fool.

"I'll stop talking now," he said.

As she walked off down the corridor, Quentin followed in silence. He didn't stop thinking though. And all he kept thinking was he wished that god-awful smell would leave his head.

Seriously.

In the cargo hold, Trinta rummaged through the mostly mangled tools in the little red toolbox she found cratered under an enormous slate of glaciated marble. Thankfully, not all of the tools were destroyed. Fortunately, the photon torch survived. With an exuberant whistle, she tossed it up in the air with one hand and caught it with the other as she headed towards the gaping space where the cargo bay doors used to be.

"I think I know what you're up to," Quentin said.

Trinta patted his head like a dog and hopped down to the container's hard floor. As she hit the ground, the underlights of the ship bathed the box with orange illumination. Strolling up to a container wall, she placed her hand on it and felt the coldness.

Skipping up behind her, Quentin watched as she aimed the photon torch and a dashed square of light appeared on the wall. Trinta turned the knob on the torch and the dashed grid grew to a 5-foot by 5-foot square. Hitting the red button on the torch instantly caused the grid marks to glow fiery red then to blue ice as the smoke from the heat turned into wisps of frozen vapor. The gridded area crackled, then stopped.

"Guess that didn't work," Quentin clucked.

Just then, the square-cut section of wall creaked and fell back towards them, both of them just barely leaping out of the way.

"Only sixteen go now," she said.

"Only sixteen *more to* go now," he said, correcting her English.

Trinta seethed at him with such hate that he zipped his lip up good and tight. He shouldn't have corrected her. He wasn't even sure why he tried. He should have been grateful she knew any English at all.

"Sorry," he murmured.

Trinta kept slicing through wall after wall, each falling down with a huge clang. Reaching the end and kicking out the last sliced slab of metal, they waited a moment to hear it clang . . . but it never did. They poked their heads out and saw they were miles from the planet's surface. They couldn't see an end to anything from where they were. From every view, the storage boxes went off into infinity. Already dozens of large containers sat on top of their boxes as the "skyscrapers" continued onwards and upwards.

After minutes of silence, Quentin said: "So . . ." He really hoped they weren't going to jump. He really, *really* hoped they weren't going to jump. "We aren't going to jump, are we? Are we? Please say we're not going to jump."

Trinta sauntered back into the cargo bay as he kept gazing at the unending rows of storage containers outside. Every few seconds, small tremors signaled more boxes being built right on top of them. He tried to wrap his head around it, but just couldn't fathom how a whole planet could be this way.

Moments later, Trinta re-emerged from the ship holding what looked like a little kid's four-wheeler that was chopped in two. Half her size, it had two fat wheels connected by a chunky cylindrical bit of piping and wires. Above the front wheel were two handles sticking straight up. It was a frict-bike.

"I don't remember seeing that on the ship," he said.

"Mine," Trinta spat back out at him.

"Yeah, and I still don't know how *you* got on my ship either."

Trinta set the frict-bike down and wrapped her legs underneath its center casing. Her long, lithe body leaned forward and she grabbed the handles. Cocking her head back, she motioned for Quentin to . . . to . . .

"You want me to get on your back?" he asked.

"Yer. Now. No more the talking."

Quentin was torn. He'd been wanting to get closer to Trinta ever since he saw her. But he worried she was going to make him do something extremely dangerous. Especially considering what she wrapped herself around seemed pretty darn death-friendly. However, he also didn't want to stick around the box waiting for her to *maybe* come back. In the end, the idea of putting his arms around a cool, attractive woman – even if it was an unromantic situation – beat out all worries of jumping onto something that seemed so unsafe it bordered on automatically fatal. Awkwardly, he stepped up and put his arms and legs around her.

"You sure I'm not too heavy?" he asked.

"Only hold on," she commanded, flicking a switch on the right handle. The frict-bike hummed to life.

"Where are we going?"

"Shopping."

And with that, the frict-bike shot out of the hole in the box. Surprisingly, it didn't do what Quentin thought it would do at all. Futilely, he tried not to scream.

CHAPTER EIGHT
MILE HIGH CITY

*A*pproximately *341.7 days ago . . .*

It took Quentin three cars to get to Denver. The first, the XXZ that met its tragic cow-avoiding fate. The second, the Mini Cooper that performed as a welcome replacement until it ran out of gas outside of Fort Morgan, (a smelly town his dad always snidely referred to as "Fart Morgan"). And finally, a huge black SUV he grabbed just before the Mini ran completely empty. Driving such a gas-guzzler made him feel slightly guilty. For a second. Then he remembered, *I'm the only real polluter around, so the Earth can deal.*

This was made even more apparent by the highway littered with empty cars. On the drive from North Platte, he passed handfuls of cars and trucks and semis left for dead on the silent roads. But as he neared the Mile High City, it was a whole 'nother world. The interstate overflowed with crashed vehicles.

Weaving in and out of these abandoned automobiles, Quentin cringed as he passed the burnt out carcass of a Volvo pinned against the rail walls by an eighteen-wheeler. Nudging his massive SUV between a crashed Jeep and a station wagon jamming his path, the SUV's front bumper cracked with a gruesome crunch.

"It's okay!" he shouted out the window. "I've got great coverage!"

Spying the exit for downtown, Quentin swerved off the interstate as the dusk bathed the town in a beautiful sunset solely for him. He didn't care though. He wasn't into sunsets at the moment. He only wanted to find the guy who left the message on his phone. He didn't know how. He didn't fully know why. But he knew this guy would have the key to what happened. The mystery guy had to. But that could wait until tomorrow.

The journey here had taken enough out of him and tonight all he wanted was a luxury Denver experience. And he was going to get it.

The Grand Royale was the biggest, most exquisite hotel Quentin McFury had ever seen. And walking through the front doors, he instantly knew what opalescence was. He may not have known it by that word though, for this is how he put it with a really poor British accent:

"Well, I do say, this does look to be indubitably brilliant! Scones for all you charming lads and lassies!"

Quentin jumped on a baggage cart and skateboarded it up the ramp. Pushing with his mighty right leg, the unwieldy cart zipped towards the elevator. Gritting his teeth unsure if the cart would make it between the open doors, the cart did . . . just barely. However, having no brakes, it had nowhere to stop and smashed into the mirrored elevator wall, shattering into a million glittery, shardy stars.

"Crapity crap crap CRAP!!!"

Quentin rapidly rolled into a ball before the splintered glass did any real damage to him and his precious face. His quick thinking, however, didn't protect him from banging into the cart's metallic crossbars and receiving a giant lump on his head.

"Urgn . . . head hurt," Quentin grunted. "Not smart, man . . . not smart at all. Urgn . . ."

Shaking off the blow, he scooted off the luggage cart and stood up, scanning the elevator's buttons. With authority, he hit the button marked "Presidential Suite".

"Guess I'm basically the President now, so why the hell not? I deserve it."

But the elevator wouldn't budge. He tapped the button again. And again. Nothing.

"Maybe the panel's busted."

He pushed the number 17 button to test his "busted panel theory" and shrugged as the elevator doors shut, crackling over the broken glass. Instantly, the elevator swept up through the hotel. When it reached the seventeenth floor, the doors opened with a ding and the tinkling of falling shards of glass that sounded like jingly wind chimes. Of course, this wasn't the floor he really wanted.

"It's the Presidential Suite or nothing!" he shouted.

But as he went to push the "Lobby" button, he stopped. Down the hall, he heard . . . music? And . . . clinking glasses?

"Someone havin' a party?" wondered Quentin.

He was so curious his right eyebrow raised high enough that it threatened to secede and become part of his hair. He giddily hoped if by the luckiest of luck that he hadn't maybe stumbled upon his mystery voicemail dude, the guy with the answers. *It makes sense,* he thought. *Just like me, the guy'd want to stay somewhere nice.*

Quentin stepped out into the hallway cautiously. As he passed a cleaning cart, he zeroed in on the room where the noise was coming from. Room 1709. Outside the door, he heard music – poppy songs he couldn't identify but instantly hated. There also rang out the sound of the distinct clink of glass against glass. His heart raced at the thought of finding another person. Hell, this sounded amazingly like other *people*. Almost like there was a real shindig goin' down.

"Uh . . . hello?!" he said. "Anybody there?!"

The racket of glasses colliding gently continued over the music.

"My name's Quentin!" he shouted. "Are you alone, too?!"

Nobody answered.

"Can I come in? I haven't seen anyone or spoken to anyone in . . . forever. I think I might have gotten a message from you! Do you know what happened?!"

He pounded on the door, but the racket kept on going. His pounding then turned into kicks. And then that turned into a full-fledged attack on the door as he stepped back and charged the door with all his force.

"Arrrrrrrrrrrrrrgghghghhh!!!"

Bouncing off the door to the floor, the furious McFury got up with an angry snort. Remembering the cleaning cart, he rushed over and grabbed the keycard hanging off the side. With a glint in his eye, he slipped the keycard in the room's lock and opened the door wide. Instantly his shoes got soaked as a healthy stream of water flooded out.

"What the–?!!" he yelled, unsuccessfully trying to jump out of the way.

As the tiny river dissipated down the hall, Quentin peeked in the room, desperately hoping to find another soul. But inside, there was nothing. Just an overflowing bath whose faucets spat out water at full blast. The whole room had to have been submerged a couple feet from the stains on the wallpaper. Near the bed, an iPod played on a stereo. And there in the corner, two glasses floated in a puddle, clinking against each other with fading volume as their little eddy of water drained out of the room. Depressed and disappointed, the lonely boy left the room with soggy sneakers and an even soggier disposition.

"Chasing stupid ghosts . . ." he muttered, trudging back down the hall – *squish, squish, squish, squish, squish, squish*. Trudging into the elevator, he bitterly scowled at the cleaning cart left in the hallway as the doors slowly closed.

That night, Quentin got his luxury-filled experience in the Presidential Suite by using that cleaning cart's magical keycard. He didn't sleep in the luxurious

Presidential bed the size of his old bedroom though. No, he did *not*. Not after noticing that the unmade bed had a pair of women's shoes on the floor next to it. Not after noticing that the pillow still held the head indentation of a person as though they'd only got up a minute ago.

"Yeah, that's not creepy," he muttered.

Instead, he plopped down on the plush leather couch in the living room and stared out at an oncoming thunderstorm punishing the peaks of the Rockies. As flashes of lightning skittered across the sky, Quentin steeled himself for his search of the mystery man tomorrow. His trip here had already taken a lot from him and he needed to rest. And as the sky cracked apart with flashing electrical discharges, slumber overcame him. His sleep was peaceful that night, his last night's sleep on Earth.

"Weeeeeeeeeeeee-HOOOOOOOOOOOOOOO!!!" Quentin McFury shouted gleefully.

After four hours of searching fruitlessly through a foreign town for somebody he wasn't sure even existed left him feeling frustrated beyond belief. Driving past a giant amusement park though, he altered his mission on the fly. It wasn't his fault he got a faulty mush-mouthed message mentioning Denver but not *where* in Denver this guy was. It was like being asked to find a lost contact lens in the middle of a swimming pool. And after all he'd been through, an amusement park trumped any annoying mission.

Parking the SUV next to the entrance, Quentin bounded over the turnstiles with glee before stopping and taking in the whole place like a kid in a candy store. However, he wasn't in a candy store. He was in a fan-freakin'-tastic amusement park that actually had a its own candy store to boot! So with all that, he screamed at the top of his lungs:

"Woo-hoo!!! It's McFury time!"

He started his park adventure off slow: first, riding a fine brown steed on the old-timey carousel, then playing some old school videogames in the arcade (including one called *Gauntlet* that he dug and one called *Dig-Dug* that he didn't dig), and finally, whacking plenty of moles with a mallet at the carnival games area.

But then something bigger summoned him with a seductive slithering in his ear. The Black Mamba – "*the Deadliest Rollercoaster in the Country*" - beckoned. (It wasn't *literally* the deadliest. That title went to one in Arkansas made of wood, dirt, and carnie hope that OSHA hadn't investigated since 1972 and was technically "the deadliest rollercoaster in the country".) The Black Mamba only opened last year and it wracked Quentin with jealousy whenever other kids talked about how great it was. He knew the ride was impressive when guys at school spoke of it with a reverence that fully acknowledged their fear – an emotion no teen boy ever admits to out loud.

When Quentin arrived at the towering rollercoaster and stood in its gargantuan shadow, he could almost taste its ferocity as it loomed over him like an evil giant.

"Yeah, you ain't so bad!" he taunted.

The Black Mamba had no response.

"That's what I thought!"

However, the snarling teen found himself disappointed once he stepped into the front car and buckled himself in. Waiting for the ride to go, the rollercoaster didn't do anything. Nothing at all. Of course, it wouldn't.

"Well, shiiiiirt . . ."

Quentin hopped out and ran to the control board to figure out how to start it up. It wasn't that difficult. There was a big green button and a big red button. So, without giving it too much thought, he hit the green button, ran like a fool, and dove into the front car as it slowly pulled out of the loading area.

"This is going to be awesome," he chirped as he snapped the seatbelt over his lap.

The Black Mamba began simply. It was a common tactic in the rollercoaster world to rise deceptively unhurried to the top of the first peak. But as it kept going up and up and up and, yes, up and up some more, Quentin grew concerned that the ride might be too much for him.

Man, I hope I don't mess my pants, he fretted. (His worry wasn't without precedent as he'd heard that actually happened to Joe Josephson, a junior forever known thereafter as "Poopy Joe".)

After what felt like twenty minutes of ascending a mile high above the Mile High City, the ride clicked its final clacks of upwards momentum. Then, as he felt not just butterflies in his stomach but also horses, tigers, and a couple thrashing sharks, the Black Mamba bit Quentin and bit him hard, plummeting down with the hellish din of what sounded like a thousand screams.

"AaaaaaAAAAAAAHHHH-OOOOOOoooooohhhhh-eeiiiIIIII-AAAAAAAAAaaaaahhh!!!"

The Black Mamba dipped and zipped around, slinging its lone passenger from one side of the car to the other before going upside down and doing a loop-de-loop that made Quentin screech for his life, his face tingling from the joy of such breathtaking speed. As the rollercoaster roared through its last few exciting dives and whip-arounds, the boy couldn't keep his face from grinning ear-to-ear.

"This is brilliant!" he giggle-shouted.

And when the Black Mamba raced down to the boarding area and continued on without stopping, Quentin couldn't have been happier.

"Again, again, again!!!" he cried out.

However, on the third and fourth go-rounds, Quentin began to feel sick from the unrelentingly intense, constant movement. And on the eighth and ninth times past, he realized he'd put himself in quite the pickle.

"How . . . do I . . . make it . . . stop?" he whined.

As he rocketed past the coaster's boarding area again, he searched for anything he could throw at the control panel. Horrible at baseball, he still hoped he could get a lucky shot on that big red button and bring this all to an end. Checking his pockets, he found the only throwable object around: the keys to the SUV. Surely, if the keys hit the stop button, he'd be home free. But as he chucked the keys, the speed of the rollercoaster – coupled with the fact that Quentin couldn't hit the broad side of a barn he was standing in – caused the keys to hit a pillar and snap right back at him, nearly taking his head off.

"Why didn't I just keep searching for the mystery dude? Why?!!"

After three more nausea-inducing revolutions, Quentin finally figured out a plan. It wasn't the best plan, but it was the only thing he could think of. Given a chance to think things through on a motionless bit of ground, he might have come up with something a little better, something a little less . . . perilous. But in these circumstances, you make cake with what you got.

"Alright, Quentin, it's monkey-time . . ."

After the Black Mamba raced through the docking area once more and crawled its slow trek towards the apex of its death-defying plunge, Quentin unbuckled his seatbelt and quickly yet carefully climbed into the car behind him. Even if the rollercoaster was stopped, clambering from one car to the next would be challenging. Doing so while it ascended at a seventy-degree angle was downright impossible with a scoop of suicide thrown in.

Scrambling over the set of bars, he tumbled into the next car with a thud, smacking his head on the hard seating. It left him dazed for a moment, but he got back up and rapidly scaled over into the next car, this time falling with slightly more grace as the rollercoaster continued its slow rise into the sky.

"Bang on! Just two more, McFury!" he yawped, pumping himself up.

With only two cars left to traverse, he ignored the whole different bowl of danger waiting for him once he got in the final car. He instead focused on climbing and rolling two more times. The second-to-last one brought him safely down with only a bruised shin (and with the abuse his shins had been through over years of soccer, that was nothing).

The last car, however, wasn't gonna be easy. Yes, there was the overwhelming pressure of it being the last car. But also there was the gut-churning issue of the rollercoaster nearing its apex two hundred plus feet above the ground. And Quentin had less than a minute to not only jump into that last car but also get out of it and onto the tracks at its slowest crawl in a way that didn't send him plummeting off the top. Racing down the rollercoaster was thrilling enough *inside* it. Plunging straight down *outside* of it might be more thrilling, but much more squishy.

"Alright, McFury, let's make cake . . ." he sighed.

Briskly, he crawled over the bars, stumbled, and fell head first into the last car, landing awkwardly on his wrist in the process. Groaning in pain, he considered buckling himself in and riding the Black Mamba until he felt better about jumping out onto the tracks . . . or until his wrist and the rest of his throbbing body didn't hurt . . . or until his mommy came back.

But the adrenalin racing through his body made him hunker down and go, knowing that if he didn't go then, he might not ever. Ignoring his pain, he scaled over the back and clung off the back for the last few yards of ascent, his feet mere inches from the steel tracks slowly passing underneath. Nearing the top, Quentin steeled himself, ready to let go and clutch the tracks with all his life. He closed his eyes and released his grip . . . but something held him to the coaster!

"What the damn?!" he shouted.

He opened his eyes to find his watch caught on a connector hook on the back. He pulled furiously on the watch, trying to escape from being dragged down, torn to shreds, and jettisoned off the rollercoaster like a bloody rag doll. With the last six tracks to the top passing one after the other underneath him, he reached over with his free hand – still swinging back and forth like a piñata in the wind – and undid the watch's strap. Falling to the tracks, Quentin hugged the rails tightly just as the Black Mamba bellowed down on its deadly circuit and rattled on into the distance, the rails faintly quivering.

"Oh, thank . . ." Quentin breathed a sigh of relief . . . until he realized his off-the-cuff plan forgot one key thing – the Black Mamba coming back!

Without relent, the coaster zipped around its course and headed back towards its prey as Quentin slowly and carefully shuffled down the track. Two hundred and sixty feet to climb down at a steep seventy-five degree angle. And in less than three minutes. Give or take. On a bad wrist.

With no other choice, he sucked it up and took it one lick of track at a time, singing himself a sequel to a sequel of a Bowie song by the Very Dangerous Asps to keep calm:

"*There's no one at ground control* – Ow! Stupid finger!

Ev-v-v-veryone's gone out to play . . .
Spinning off the edges of that blue ball . . .
He's not even sure he's in this galaxy . . .
Just a few . . . <u>dozen</u> more feet, McFury . . ."

Midway down, his shoe slipped and he hung for a

moment with what little strength he had in his hands. Concentrating, he forced his foot back into the groove of the track and continued his slow-speed descent. Down below, the Black Mamba rattled towards the docking area. His time was running out. Sweating mightily, he kept climbing down, singing:

"He's no longer a Major . . .

He's no longer Tom . . .

Countdowns count up and down . . .

But he's the asteroid clown . . ."

The Black Mamba now slithering to the top, Quentin started jumping down a few tracks at a time.

"One, two, three, four, five . . ."

He jammed his thumb backwards and almost fell, but shook it off and kept going.

"We're not fit to be alive . . ."

The clack, clack, clack of the rollercoaster rising grew louder and louder.

"Five . . ."

Another fifty feet to get down or he'd be rollercoaster roadkill.

"Four . . ."

Visions of the Black Mamba dicing him into grotesque little Quentin chunks rumbled through his head.

"Three . . ."

He scrambled further down with his hodge-podge descent.

"Two . . ."

The slowly clacking Black Mamba told Quentin he had to speed up or die.

"One . . . liftoff . . . you superstar sun!"

As the Black Mamba reached its peak, Quentin curled himself into a ball and rolled down the final twenty feet along the tracks, smacking his head, elbow, both left and right knees, and spleen (or at least it seemed like that's where his spleen should be) against the hard metal rails. He rolled to a stop in the flat valley of the rollercoaster's track just as the Black Mamba held for one second at the top and then . . . hurtled towards him with an unholy rage! The fall knocked some sense out of Quentin, leaving him momentarily dazed there in the valley of the tracks. But the roar of the deafening Black Mamba barreling towards him woke him up right quick.

"Liftoff! Liftoff! LIFTOFFFFFFFFFF!!!"

Though the Black Mamba was three seconds from crushing him, he was still a good fifteen feet from the ground. So he did the math fast and leapt off, the rollercoaster only narrowly missing its prey. Screaming past, the Black Mamba echoed onwards with the disappointed whine of a beast that didn't get to devour its quarry.

Surrounded by lost baseball caps and strewn garbage in the unkempt brush, the bruised teen gazed up into the sky and watched the Black Mamba cycle around and past . . . around and past . . . around and past . . . thanking all of his lucky stars.

The young Earth boy then wondered if he'd died there and then whether the entire human race would have been wiped out. Wiped out by a stupid rollercoaster.

CHAPTER NINE
NOT A DATE

"It's so quiet!" yelled Quentin.

He meant the frict-bike. In fact, it was the only thing that was quiet. The reverberating winds whipped through the tight boulevards of the skyscraping storage block towers around them, making it feel as though they had little tornadoes in their ears. Every time a ship passed by – even if it was a mile above – the roar would Doppler down, leaving the Earth kid's head ringing for minutes afterward.

However, the frict-bike ran virtually silent, its engine generating energy by friction itself, which also was what kept it clinging to the sides of the "buildings" they were riding across like a spider on a motorcycle. (*It should be called a spidercycle instead!* Quentin thought.) Speeding along perpendicular to the ground, he didn't understand the mechanics of any of this. Looking to his left and seeing the ground far below and looking to his right and seeing the grey sky from which he recently fell inspired him not to question how exactly the frict-bike worked. He worried if he questioned it too much, it would end the magic and cause them to fall to their deaths. Filled with such worries, he clung tighter to Trinta.

"Hold *on* me," she snarled. "Not *through* me."

"Sorry," he said, not lessening his grip at all.

The frict-bike raced along the storage walls, every once in a while hitting a jarring bump where a new container started. With the gusts of air rushing through these endless avenues, Trinta's hair repeatedly smacked her passenger's face – something he didn't entirely mind. It did though make him wonder, *Hey, her hair used to be really short, didn't it? How's it hitting me in the face? How'd it grow so fast?*

After driving for almost an hour, Quentin began to question if she even knew where they were going: *I'm not going to ask and be a back-of-the-bike driver. I'm just along for the ride.* A ride that without warning shifted from its perpendicular route to a diagonal one heading downwards, towards a shining cerulean light in the darkness. Squinting hard to make out their destination, Quentin was surprised to see something so oddly familiar. A tree. An immense orange oak tree.

"Is that a park?!" he bellowed. "Are we going to a park?!"

A patch of grass with a few glowing neon flowers encircled the tree. Drawing nearer, they approached the cornered-in park at its only point of entry . . . from above. This unusual way to get in existed because the tiny park was surrounded by storefronts on all four sides. For a park of no more than thirty square feet, Quentin was surprised to find these little "stores" boxing it in, especially with each store considerably different from the next.

Drawing up on their destination, Trinta slowed the frict-bike. Gently rolling them along the wall and then onto the little sidewalk bordering the park, they came to a full stop.

Sighing impatiently, Trinta waited for Quentin to get off the bike. He, however, gawped at the shops, marveling at how strange they looked walling off that dainty park with one tree. Trinta then cleared her throat in the most melodious way he'd ever heard yet still got the point she *really* wanted him to dismount the bike and let go of her.

"That was fun," he said, stepping off.

Trinta walked up to a black box in the corner between two shops. She held up her palm then pointed twice. The black box sent out a two-foot long tray. Putting the frict-bike on it, the tray zoomed it high up into the air where a cube opened and swallowed the frict-bike up whole, zipping the door shut behind it. She then sauntered towards a storefront with a garish awning and vibrant colors floating holographically over it.

"What's this?" scoffed Quentin. "The Kwik-E-Mart? Can I get a Slushee?"

Trinta hit a button and a holo-figure appeared out of the front "window". Emerging from the waist up and looking like the unloved child of a clown and a frog, the green holo-figure with long brown ears and a cute panda nose patted their heads with an elongated arm.

"Hallo, folkties, I'm Gerny," said Gerny, the shopkeeper. "What can'r do? Buy/sell?"

Trinta turned to the Earth kid and motioned for him to come closer. But Quentin stood right where he was, shaking his head like a scared dog.

"Move here!" she said.

"Why?"

"Move here *now*!" she snapped, losing her patience.

"Are you going to sell me?"

"What?"

"Sell me? Are you going to sell me?"

"How much you think worth?"

Quentin shrugged.

"Not much. That how much," Trinta said. "Now, move here now."

Sheepishly, he clomped over as Gerny surveyed them both with a forced smile.

"Buy/sell, please," Gerny said.

Trinta nodded to the shopkeeper as her eyes darted around the infinite listing of items that scrolled down the front window. Her eyes stopped on one offering.

"Languo Upgr-8," Gerny said. "'Course." He clucked his head at Quentin as though her choice explained everything. A small silver tab with a tongue emblem on it rolled down the shopkeeper's holo-arm and Trinta grabbed it. She eyeballed Gerny for a moment before he bowed to her and said, "Thank payment. Good nightly."

Gerny disappeared as the listing of items on the front "window" dimmed but continued to scroll on endlessly.

"What'd ya get?" Quentin chirped. She held up the thin grey strip in front of his face. "Hey, I think I licked something like that once. Does my breath smell that bad? I thought it might –"

Without any warning, she slapped the little silver wedge onto his forehead.

"Hey!!!" he cried out. He tried to pry it off but it was too late. The silver wedge fused to his forehead with a burning sizzle. Quentin winced, even though it didn't hurt. It just felt tingly and . . . *weird*. Like something was marching through his head. His eyebrows went up as the wedge melted into his skin, leaving only a faint outline behind. "What'd you do?" He pinched his forehead frantically. "What'd you do to my head?!"

Suddenly, words spilled out of Quentin's mouth: "Why . . . my brain . . . juxtaposition . . . turtles . . . enchiladas . . . love . . . nutmeg . . . punk . . . fairytale . . . elbow . . . husking . . . poop . . . turbulent . . . butter-scotch . . ."

With more words rolling unwittingly off his tongue, fizzy sounds danced inside his head like someone poured root beer on his brain. Then his toes started to tingle. And his heart went techno. These were pretty common side effects for anyone partaking of cerebro-enhancers. Quentin didn't know that though. But when Trinta finally spoke, he realized that whatever just happened was a good thing.

"Hello, Quentin," she said. "My name's Trinta. Pleased to meet you."

Her words were crisp and precise. She sounded nothing like she had before. Not at all like someone who formerly used words like blunt tools. Now, she sounded . . . normal. (Or normal enough considering the circumstances.)

"Sorry I didn't get your okay for that, kid," she said. Quentin flinched, not liking being called "kid" by someone probably only a couple years older than him. "But I couldn't talk to you with what you had. The upgrade you had going was like talking to a Stitko monkog."

"A 'monkog'?" he asked. "Is that like a monkey-dog?"

"Yeah, guess so. Look, already we're having a relatively coherent conversation. A conversation more suited for children still in diapers, but it's something. At least you don't sound like a total moron anymore."

Hurt, he snarked: "Guess it's slightly better than your normal talking of, '*You, no go-go in the ship ship! Fire BAD!!!*'"

She smiled at him, liking that he might not always take her guff.

"So, what'd you do?" Quentin queried. "Did you fiddle with my brain? Am I on drugs? Did you put me on drugs?! Am I high?"

"No. Gave you a languo-upgrade. Seems you had the barebones package before. You were only a step above baby-talk. Now I won't have to kill you because you can't understand me. I don't like being misunderstood. I also don't like to repeat myself."

"You don't like to what?"

"I don't like to . . ." Trinta stopped, getting his little joke and smirking.

Quentin slyly grinned.

"So what now?" he asked. "More shopping?"

"No. We eat."

She walked over to the storefront with the fluttering

bird wing awnings. Earlier, all Quentin saw on the storefront was a bunch of squiggly lines that didn't seem to make sense. Now, it read: *Gourmandizing Gourmets of the Galaxy (and Beyond).*

"Wait, it didn't say that before," he said.

"Yeah, it did. You just couldn't read it. Your upgrade allows you to understand more in spoken and written language. So anytime you want to thank me for your new head, be my guest. You're now an almost fully functional person. Almost."

"Thanks," he said with a wince.

Trinta ambled up to the door, which opened automatically by sliding swiftly out of the way. Quentin paused before going in.

"You amazed by the moving doors?" she asked sarcastically.

"Yeah," responded Quentin even more sarcastically. "Mesmerized. Moving doors. We don't have those where I come from. Except *everywhere.* Like the store . . . the library . . . the gas station . . . the . . ."

Shaking her head, Trinta strolled into the restaurant. Quentin followed her inside and then stopped, truly and unsarcastically totally amazed. The restaurant definitely smacked Quentin's gob, leaving him far more speechless than he thought he could ever be. Which was odd. Because now gifted with all languages, he suddenly had no words to explain what he saw.

The *Gourmandizing Gourmets of the Galaxy (and Beyond)* – or *3G&B*'s as they were known – were a chain of restaurants spread throughout the universe, the true numbers of which were never really known. Some thought there might be over twenty-three million of the eateries. Others posed there were really only seven. Regardless of how many there were, each one felt uniquely infinite unto itself.

Entering a *3G&B*, the first-time visitor would immediately be taken aback by the thousand-plus people floating around a giant cavern, all hovering at tables with each dining party in their own little floating realm. This was the restaurants' main draw as every customer had their own perfect eating experience as they spun through the spacious cavern. And no two sets of customers were ever the same. So while a pair of growling Tentions might each dive with their gaping, roaring teeth into the fresh carcass of a still-heaving griddle-beast, another "table" might consist of the Mantii snacking with their long-spoons from a small bowl of purp-grass clippings.

After all, *"To each their own to eat"* was the *3G&B* motto.

The only place Quentin could remotely compare this to was Casa Bonita in Denver. He'd only been there once with his parents but it had blown his tiny nine-year-old mind. The restaurant had divers leaping into pools, singing mariachis, and other entertaining strangeness, all happening while you ate, which made it extra-cool. Plus, the food was awesome! They had damn fine chimichangas, tacos, and sopapillas . . . oh, the sopapillas! But this restaurant was so far beyond Casa Bonita that it definitely earned the "beyond" in the *3G&B* name.

"This is . . ." he started to say. "What is . . . I don't . . . This is all so . . ."

"What *are* you?" Trinta sneered.

"What?"

"Are you a Killiarn? A Specksenian? An Abdilliam Crawil?"

He stared at her dumbstruck.

"What . . . are . . . you?" she repeated.

"Me? Me . . . I'm a . . . a guy . . . a human guy . . ." he stammered, not sure what she meant. She squinted at him as he continued. "I'm, uh . . . an American. From Nebraska. North Platte . . ." Nothing registered on her face. "I'm a Bulldog, a North Platte Bulldog," he flailed jokingly. "Go Bulldogs!"

"So you're all called Bulldogs?"

"Uh . . . sure. Why not?"

"Alright, Bulldog, act like you've been in a restaurant before and shut your mouth. Look a little less like this is your first time off-world. Give nothing away. Just be cool. I don't want anyone marking us for their meal."

"Somebody might eat us?!"

Trinta pulled him by the collar and stormed up to a five-foot tall green egg. This was the Host. Three eyes popped out of the top and glowered at them. Instantly, Quentin and Trinta were swept up into the air.

"What's going—" Quentin exclaimed before a seat scooped under his butt and a table popped into existence in front of him. And on top of that table was a beautiful Casa Bonita chimichanga with a whole plateful of sopapillas right next to it. Then, a giant glass of Dr. Pepper appeared with a long and windy straw stretching up to his lips, beckoning him to pure happiness.

This all occurred as they were lifted into the air and swirled around the room in an anti-grav bubble. Sipping on his soda, Quentin gazed across the room at the assorted eaters, all consuming strange foods in so many bizarre and different ways. He gasped as a chunky bear-like creature shoved fruit into its armpits.

"Eat up," Trinta said. "We don't want to stay long, Bulldog."

"Why? You got a date or something?"

She shot him a crusty glare and he rapidly took a bite of his chimichanga. It was hot. It was cheesy. It was perfect.

"Mmmmm," he said. "Hrmmm, hrrmmmm, hmmmm. And on top of that: mmmmmm-mmmmmmm-mmmmmm-mmmmm . . ."

"You okay?"

"Yeah. Just haven't tasted anything that good in . . . forever."

As Quentin sat in a brightly colored chair, Trinta sat with legs crossed on what looked like an oversized silver golf tee. Next to her, a metal vase rested containing a large fork and knife. On the table in front of Trinta, a yellow crystal bowl materialized with what appeared to be a gigantic salad of lettuce, tomatoes, and shaved carrots. At the top of the salad, dollops of blue rice glimmered. Trinta grabbed the seven-pronged fork from the vase and stared at her meal intently.

"Goin' for the salad, huh?" Quentin said. "Yeah, I'm doin' the McFury diet. Nothing but cheese and meat. I know it might clog me up but – "

At the bottom of her bowl, something moved.

Quentin was about to warn her when unexpectedly a grub-snake slithered out of the leaves to the top. The grub-snake – resembling a cute hot dog with eyes – poked its head up out of the salad. Not missing a beat, Trinta stabbed her fork through its head, flicking the head off down below where it missed everyone it passed before hitting the ground with a sick slop. She then grabbed the knife from the metal vase next to her feet, tossed the ex-snake into the air, and sliced it into a dozen pieces that fell gently on her salad. (Both disgusted *and* impressed, Quentin made a point right there never to fight Trinta with utensils.) She took a big bite of the meaty salad and gnashed her meal with relish.

"This place is fantastic," Quentin said.

"It's alright. The food's tasty. All the other stuff . . ." she gestured to the other floating eaters, ". . . isn't necessary. If I wanted all this, I could go to a zoo."

"I . . . I . . . think it's kinda cool."

"'Course you would, Bulldog."

Ignoring her disdain, he continued downing his chimichanga. Cheese dripped from his mouth in a long strand back to the plate. He tried to lick it into his mouth with little success. Eventually, he just grabbed the cheese, wrapped it around his finger, and stuffed it all in.

As the invisible sphere they ate in continued to circumnavigate the room, there wasn't just a plethora of species eating (and usually eating other species). There were also a number of stages where people sang, told jokes, and one where a spindly Prelarian with twelve hooven legs danced a merry jig. Quentin bopped his head to the music and the Prelarian noticed, winking at him with five of her eight eyes.

Trinta used *her* eyes to roll them at his astonishment at the whole spectacle. She didn't know what to expect from the Bulldog, but the fact that he actually *liked* this place made her blood curdle.

"Why are you here?" she questioned, narrowing her eyes.

"Because *you* brought me here," he answered defensively. "It's not my fault. *You* chose the place and you shouldn't rag on me for digging a place you chose. That's not cool."

"No," she said, starting again. "Why are you out traveling? You seem more like a planet-lubbing kid. Not someone for celestial voyages."

"'Planet-lubbing kid'?" he scoffed. "I'm not a kid. I am a . . ." Quentin just barely stopped himself from shouting "I am a man!" (Even he knew nothing makes you seem more like a child than screaming that you aren't one.)

"Alright, you're not a 'kid'," she sighed.

"No, I'm not. Hell, I'm the only one of me around from what I can tell. It's not like I asked – "

"Where are your peoples?" interrupted Trinta.

"Dunno. Gone."

"Gone? Your family, your tribe, they're gone? What? Dead? Kidnapped? Turned into meat?"

"Dunno. I'm the only one. My whole planet. It's just me."

"You're the only Bulldog?"

He wavered on whether to correct her assumption that all Earth humans were Bulldogs. He decided not to explain as he liked the thought that everyone from his planet were now named after his school's mascot. (Even though he didn't give a rat's carcass about his school until it didn't exist anymore.)

"Yup," he said. "I'm the only . . . Bulldog. A year ago, I'm in class counting the minutes until I get my butt kicked by a giant jerkface jockbag and then one tiny nap later I'm suddenly completely and totally alone. Almost made me swear off naps altogether."

"So nobody of your kind exists?" Trinta surveyed him inscrutably.

"Not that I know of."

"None were off-world?"

"Nope. We weren't really an off-world people. Until me really."

"You Bulldogs weren't even interstellar?"

"Nope. We had a thing that went to our moon. That's about it. Oh . . . and we shot things at Mars. But nobody was on those ships. Don't know if that counts."

She couldn't believe what he was saying. *I knew he was green,* she thought, *but not that green.*

"Then how'd you get out here?" she asked.

"I stole the ship of . . ." he trailed off. This dinner began to feel like an interrogation to him. At the same time, it also kinda felt like a date. He was too young to know there wasn't much of a difference, so he continued. "I stole a ship. That's all. But enough about me. Tell me something about you."

"No."

An awkward silence gripped their "table" as they traversed and bobbled about the dinner cavern. A hulking red Crittenden cloaked in a cape of flowing shadows crunched on a bowl of bones. The crunching helped fill the uncomfortable quiet.

"But I just told you a lot about me," Quentin whined. "I mean . . . a *lot*!"

"And . . ."

"And now, you should tell me something about you. Anything. Just to be cool."

"'Just to be cool'? Kid, being cool's about the *less* others know, not the *more*. Something you and your mouth might be wise to learn."

The lone Earth human felt like a dork. He felt embarrassed. He felt like he did back in high school, the dorkiest dork of all the dorks. And unbeknownst to him, he still had a gooey strand of cheese hanging from his chin.

"So how'd you get *your* ship, kid?" Trinta leaned in. "Tell me everything."

CHAPTER TEN
NOT E.T.

*A*pp*roximately 340.2 days ago . . .*

As the day dusked turning afternoon into night, Earth's lone human lumbered through the park, hurt, hungry, and tired. (Not to mention still a little wobbly after surviving the Black Mamba.) After stopping at a snack stand called the Corndogger and nearly frying off his fingers, Quentin eventually whipped himself up six corndogs and gobbled 'em down so fast he nearly ate the sticks.

With the last strands of light falling from the fading sun, shadows came out in force, playing and stretching the length of the boy's shadow to make him look like a spindly ten-foot giant. Feeling guilty for putting the fate of Earth on hold so he could be a kid for one more day, all Quentin wanted was to return to the hotel and sleep. Tomorrow he'd search again for the mystery man. This time without diversion . . . without relent . . . without. . .

"Oh, firetruckin' bullshirt . . ."

Reaching his trusty SUV at the front gates, he too late remembered one key problem: he didn't have the keys. They were back around the Black Mamba wherever they landed after he tossed them in his futile attempt to stop the coaster. And even though he had no desire to go near that ride again, he didn't really have a choice. None of the parked cars in the lot would have had keys in them. Properly parked cars almost never had keys, only the ones apparently abandoned while driving did.

Trudging back, a series of lights suddenly flashed from the far edge of the park near the river. They blinked a strange red and orange come-hither. Familiar with most of the rides, nothing on his trusty map gave him any indication of what it might be. It couldn't be that stupid Hamburger bumper car ride for little kids he passed earlier. Nor was it the Shipwreck Falls. Nor the Halfpipe. And since the map didn't divulge what those mysterious lights were, the temptation overwhelmed him.

"I'll just see what that ride is . . . *then* go look for the keys – which I probably won't find anyways . . . and then . . . *then* head back to the hotel. I promise." He wasn't sure to whom he was promising. He just kept moving towards the blinking luminescence as though under a spell.

Walking on in the last moments of twilight, there weren't any lights on except in the shops. It was a jarring look for the park. One expected it to be either completely lit up or not at all. The scattered illumination gave the whole place a ghostly tinge. The red and orange glow show at the far edge beckoned the teen onwards, even though he knew he should know better.

"If it's just that stupid kiddie Hamburger ride, I'm gonna . . ."

Striding past the spinning carousel, he thought he could make out shadows dancing in the distance. He chalked that up to the fact that with so little light and the constant movement of rides, there would be, of course, a lot of moving shadows. It still unnerved him though. Passing a gift shop with dozens of stuffed animals watching him didn't help either. Regardless, he accepted his mind was probably just trying to scare the corndogs out of him.

"*I ain't got nobodyyyyyy,*" he warbled softly, trying to keep his wits about him. It was some song from the eighties his dad loved. The only song his non-music loving, non-music digging dad ever seemed to have a positive opinion on. "*No-body, cares for me, no-body cares for me . . . Iiiiiiiii'm so sad and lonely, so crazy-sad-lonely . . . Won't some sweet baby mama—*"

But then Quentin stopped with mouth agape before what looked like the coolest ride ever: an awesome spaceship ride! The size of a small house and looking like the bizarre chunky offspring of the space shuttle and an enraged pitbull, a beat-up sign next to the craft read: "*HAVOK*".

"Cool name . . ." Quentin nodded.

The ramp leading up into the ride was lit with a soft, inviting blue light. An invitation the teen accepted instantly, jogging up the ramp and inside.

Going down the long corridor through the "ship", he marveled at the details the park's creators put in so people waiting in line would feel slightly less bored. *A little over the top,* he snarked, *but it does feel sorta "real".* Even the writing on the corridor walls and buttons were in some sort of "alien" language.

Once he made it up to the cockpit though, he had some questions. Questions like: "How does this work? How will I get *this* ride to stop? And why are there are only *two* seats?" Answering the last question first, he posited: "Maybe this is just for the Ritchie Riches!"

Assuming it to be a super-special ride only for wealthy jerks, he wondered if he was now in a whole section of the park off-limits to regular folk like himself. *Hell, maybe there's all kinds of stuff that I can't see in the dark,* he drooled. *Maybe a "real" pirate adventure ship or a "real" underwater submarine battle. If it has all that, I'll live here forever. Forget the mystery dude.*

"Let's see what you can do, Havok," he growled in a steely captain voice.

Sitting in the pilot's seat, he hit some buttons. But nothing happened. He hit a couple more and the interior lights flashed twice but nothing else.

"For as sucktastic as this is, I could've stayed in the car and flipped the high beams on and off."

Clomping out of the cockpit and skulking down the ramp, he cursed himself for not being back at the hotel sleeping. He stopped mid-curse though when he spotted two shadows moving down by the Corndogger. And they weren't fake mind-tricking shadows, but real proper *MOVING-LIVING-THING!* shadows, advancing right towards him.

One must have been some sort of giant. Not a hulking figure, but nine feet tall and thin, moving like a preying mantis. The other figure looked like an ambling four-foot potato with three-to-five extremely muscular "arms". Quentin wondered if his eyes were playing tricks on him, but as the two got closer and closer, he knew that wasn't the case.

The two figures spoke to each other irritably in a strange language.

"Grrer-trik streent mallubitars nek trennos," the tall mantis figure said.

"Nern, dorn edund-edlund," the potato-like figure responded with disdain.

After what he now saw and heard, Quentin reclassified the "fake spaceship ride" as a "really real spaceship". The level of detail put into its "fake" alien touches certainly proved that. (Not to mention the really real aliens currently in front of him!)

"Maybe they know what happened to everybody," he whispered to himself. "Or maybe these dudes are just some E.T.'s lookin' for a buddy."

Good or bad, they sure as hell weren't costumed characters in big fluffy outfits. These things moved with a purpose and gait Quentin had never seen before. The tall one strolled like a slow-motion tornado, rotating as his legs swiveled forward. The other one rolled like an oversized living beanbag, albeit an angry beanbag that could crush things.

Maybe they're a planet response team designed to help people like me, Quentin thought. *People whose entire planet just disappeared . . . Or they might <u>eat</u>*

me. (And he had no desire to be eaten by anybody if he could help it. He was just funny that way.)

"Okay, aliens, let's see what you're all about," he said, doing what boys always do, and threw a rock at them. Well, not really *at* them. *By* them. (And as we saw earlier, even if he wanted to throw a rock *at* them, he'd miss by a mile and probably nail himself in the butt.) And thus the poorly thrown rock bashed into a sunglasses cart causing a loud, cascading sunglasses avalanche.

Instantly, the taller alien shot a brilliant blue beam from his hand, destroying the cart into a million shards of glass and plastic. The stubbier alien laughed a full body heave that shook him from top to bottom.

Frozen with fear, Quentin chose not to move from his position behind the bushes. And although his general body didn't move, that didn't keep his mind from racing and his eyes from almost popping out of his head. *Shoot-first aliens aren't the friendly kind,* he added up. *No big E.T. hug here! These dudes are definitely hostile!*

Arguing animatedly with each other, the aliens stopped as a rat ran through the nearby brush and away. Away *only* a few yards before the mantis figure zapped it into several pieces formally known as rat.

Quentin considered running, although here on the far edge of the park's boundaries, his options were pretty limited. He could try to sneak past the aliens without drawing their attention. The rat, however, showed that didn't seem likely. Another option was to double back towards the spaceship and jump in the river, diving in with the hope they wouldn't be able to get him. Of course, odds were they'd zap him in the water just as easy as on land, so he landed on a third option: the spaceship.

The spaceship option had a lot going for it. For one thing, it'd be impervious to whatever they were blowing things up with (or so he hoped). Also, he'd been driving cars for a while now and driving a spaceship would be a pretty freakin' impressive upgrade. Plus, if he could get that going, he might be able find out what happened with –

ZzzzrrrrrrrrrraaaaaaaakkKKKKK!!!

Suddenly, the Corndogger behind him blew up with an explosion of fried corndogs and splintering wood, forcing Quentin to run for his young life! Another blast shot over his head and hit a tree, the leaves bursting into a hail of orange flames that fell to the ground like a fiery rain. Covering his head, the young McFury sprinted as fast as he could for the ship. He *wasn't* going to jump in the river. He *wasn't* going to try and run out of the park. He was going for the big money!

"Run faster, horse legs! Faster!" he said, pumping his legs like well-oiled nuclear-powered pistons.

(As a soccer player, Quentin didn't have much in the way of mad dribbling, juggling, passing, or shooting skills. He couldn't bend it like Beckham. He couldn't pound the ball down the length of the field with a booming kick. The one thing he did have however was mighty horse legs that could gallop faster than anyone. So when a pesky forward bared down on his goal, he was the last defender. The one who came in out of nowhere and blew up the other team's chances at scoring.)

As the alien's blasts rained down around him, Quentin sprinted that much harder. Careening around the little kids train ride, he spotted the spaceship waiting – the interior blue lights again beckoning him in. As he neared the Havok, the aliens stopped shooting. He didn't know if it was to protect the ship or what, but he wasn't about to stop and ask why, especially as he could still hear them behind him, one rolling and the other running with a strange sound almost like a street cleaner.

Just when it felt like they were about to grab him, he put on the afterburners that smoked out so many forwards who believed they had a free shot on goal. Reaching the ship, he raced up the ramp and hit the red button on the side with all his might. The ramp snapped up, leaving the aliens on the outside, banging on it and shouting.

"Oh, thank . . ." he started to say. Then he heard what sounded like an electrical screwdriver outside. "Oh, shirt."

Quentin ran through the corridors and into the engine room before he realized that wasn't the cockpit and doubled back. Finally finding the cockpit ready and waiting, he jumped in the captain's chair and started hitting buttons again, this time with more ferocity and panicked randomness than before. After a few scared moments of no response, hitting an oval blue button at the top of the console did the trick! Suddenly, the engines roared to life and the two aliens scurried from under the Havok, each trying to smack out the flames that now ran across their backs.

"Whoa!" Quentin gasped, staggered at what he'd

done.

Scanning the console, a purple button flashed and he punched it. The engines roared even greater and the whole ship shook. When a red light appeared on a green switch, he thwacked it and a blaring noise wailed. Feeling as though his ears were about to explode, he hit the switch again and the blaring stopped. It was a delicate dance of hitting anything that lit up and when an alarm went off, hitting it back to the way it was.

Over on the left side of the panel, Quentin spotted a handle-shaped lever. Touching that caused a long joystick to appear from under the console and flash from red to blue to green. Instantly, he grabbed it and pulled back, hoping it'd do what years of playing videogames taught him.

"Let's roll, McFury!"

At first, the ship didn't do anything or go anywhere. But then the Havok began to pull angrily against the earth as though tethered by a thousand cables. The two aliens backed away and watched as the ship tried to lift off but would not, could not. Quentin didn't know that the green switch he flipped on and off should have been left on to defuse the extended landing feet of the Havok from the ground. By hitting the green switch on and then off, the defusing never occurred and the Havok now fought against the ground itself to get airborne.

"C'mon, you freakin' ship!" he shouted. "Get me outta here!"

The ship pushed upwards, trying to escape like a rabid dog on a chain. The hull of the ship creaked painfully as Quentin pulled harder on the stick, hoping that would somehow free them. It wasn't until he jerked the joystick back and forth though that things got interesting. As he moved it side to side, the Havok swung ever-so-slightly back and forth, even though it still refused to go up. So he decided to try the whole gamut of movement, shaking the joystick left and right, up and down, and round and round. And as he did, the Havok painfully pulled up from the ground.

The aliens watched in amazement. They assumed the Havok would peter out, stay landborne, and that would be that. But the Earth kid's failure to accept failure stretched out the land so much that with a final pull on the joystick, the Havok ripped free. With heaps of concrete stuck to its feet, the ship knocked away little hamburger-shaped bumper cars from underneath as it rose into the air. The ship was airborne!

Even though a newbie pilot, Quentin McFury gunned that ship off into the distance as though he'd been flying for years, eager to get away from any danger those aliens might still be able to throw at him.

Down below, the aliens were not pleased. They watched as the human flew off in their spacecraft. They were here alone. No backup. No transport nearby to come and get them any time soon. The tall one turned to the round one and spoke in their language, a language translated like this:

Tall Alien: Was that what we were looking for?

Round Alien: Yeah, I think so.

Tall Alien: (sarcastically) Great.

As the Havok disappeared over the horizon, they simmered in angry silence, each blaming the other. The round alien kicked a battered sign that fell over when the ship took off. The sign read:

"*Hamburger Havok – The Yummiest Bumper Cars in the World! Just Try to Ketchup!*"

CHAPTER ELEVEN
RAINING CATS & DOGS & SNAKES
(OR MAYBE JUST SNAKES)

"**G**reat," Quentin whined. "I've been talking so much my chimichanga's gonna be cold."

"No, it's not," Trinta said.

He took a bite and she was right.

"Everything you eat here is perfect always. So if you go off for a dance or use the bathroom or tell a really, really . . . *really* long story . . ." She pointed at Quentin before she continued, ". . . Your food will stay just as you wanted it."

Annoyed, Quentin steamed: "'Really, really, *really* long story'?"

"I did ask you to tell me everything. And I do know you – in our short time together – to be . . . loquacious. So the fault is mine."

"Yeah. Yeah, it is! But still . . . not cool."

Trinta didn't care and kept eating her salad. Each time she gnashed into a bit of grub-snake, it made a weird popping sound that made her dining companion gag a little. Or maybe that was because his eyes would drift past her as they moved, unable to lodge on any focal point and making him seasick besides. Suddenly, he snapped up and said:

"Wait a minute! You said 'loquacious'."

"Uh . . . so?"

"I'm not even sure I know what that word means. How would this language doohickey in me do that?"

"It plucks all the words that you've ever heard or seen within your language," she sighed, "and then matches that to what I'm saying. If I'm using language above your capabilities, it'll follow what I'm saying there. Instantly. It's very simple. It's done by a com . . . put . . . er."

"I *know* what a computer is. So this thing didn't make me smarter? It just rides along and gives me a boost word-wise?"

"Yeah," she said. "There are some mental-enhancers that do more than that. But it comes at a cost. And not just to your looks."

Trinta pointed to two humanoids below eating circular grisp sandwiches. They didn't seem too unusual, relatively speaking, to Quentin. But when he took another look, he noticed they had huge, bulging foreheads and that the rest of their skulls overflowed with protrusions and strange swollen eggs growing out of them.

"They're not supposed to look that way?" he asked.

"Nope. They're supposed to look mostly like you.

Except an even smaller head."

"Yikes. That's a monster pimple patch."

Trinta nodded and popped another bite of snake in her mouth.

"So outside of looking like a big bag of zits ready to blow, what's the drawback?" Quentin said. "Those upgraders probably know more than everyone, right?"

"But their bodies break down more, their emotions become dulled, and what sense of common decency they had before is . . ." she gestured with her ring finger going in a bunch of different ways. Quentin took it to be like the crazy sign. He didn't know she meant "*crazy-times-crazy-eight-super-duplex-crazy.*"

"So can I ask if you've had any . . . upgrades?" he ventured cautiously.

"No," she said. "You can't ask me."

"I can't ask you anything about anything and I've told you everything about me?!" he huffed. "That's bullshirt."

"What's this 'bullshirt' business?" she asked. "Makes me think your languo-upgrade didn't quite work."

"I say that instead of . . ."

"I know what you say it instead of. Why don't you just say the word? You're not going to get in trouble."

"I . . ." Quentin tried to gather his thoughts. "I . . . well . . . everyone . . . all the guys in school just swear all the time. They're all these . . . these punk cannonballers saying words they don't even really probably know what they mean. Just to be . . . shocking. Or cool . . . And so I . . . don't. Don't get me wrong. I love some good clever cussing in a song or something. Like the Pogues . . . or Kimya Dawson . . . or Los Campesinos! or

. . . whoever. But I just don't cuss. I want to be kinda different."

Trinta shrugged, his explanation not nearly interesting enough to warrant more than that.

Quentin took another sip on his literally never-ending soda. While giving a hearty sup, he swallowed hard, realizing she sidetracked questions about herself again. This one-way inquisition wasn't fair, but he knew crying "That's not fair!" wouldn't impress her enough to spill any of her beans. So he persisted on trying to turn the tables as their table turned.

"Can't you tell me anything about you?"

"I told you my name. On some worlds, that'd make us married."

"Are you telling me we're married?" He fluttered his eyes coquettishly.

Trinta tried to hide a smile, twisting it into a smirk in less than two seconds. But that wasn't quick enough for the young McFury to see that he got what he wanted and inside dance a little dance of joy. Because sometimes getting a pretty girl to smile is the biggest win in the universe.

While Quentin and Trinta ate and talked and spun around the room, down below, the Maitre'D – a large lizardy man with three arms, three legs, and two tails – emerged from a back kitchen and galloped over to the restaurant's entrance.

There, a Striker commander and her three Striker retrievers waited wearing their trademark golden vests and constipated scowls. The Maitre'D wasn't a man easily made anxious, but the sight of the retrievers put a hitch in his gallop and he nearly tripped right into them.

"Slow it, big fella," the Striker commander – Baiwyk Stanz – said.

A weathered Loreedian human in her mid-thirties, Baiwyk Stanz had been a retriever her entire adult life. She loved being given a new target, capturing that target, and bringing it back like any good hunting dog would. And if Baiwyk brought back her trophy a little beaten, a little bruised, well, you couldn't fault her for her enthusiasm.

She loved the simplicity of what was asked of her and the thorough brutality and efficiency she employed when carrying it out. She had the piloting skills to make an ace Striker pilot alone, but that didn't appeal to her keen sense of hunting in all dimensions. A ship-to-ship skirmish had its own adrenalin-pounding delight, but finding the most hidden of folks in an infinite universe – occasionally with a fevered ship battle thrown in – now, that had the makings of a good mission! Sometimes it would take a week, a month, a year. However long it took, it didn't matter to Baiwyk. For whenever Baiwyk was thrown at a target, that person was toast – often with butter and jam.

"You're in charge, right?" Baiwyk sternly questioned the Maitre'D.

The Maitre'D nodded nervously.

"We need your most subtle assistance. Anyone order anything from this menu?"

Baiwyk held up a tiny sparkly orange square to the Maitre'D. He peered into it for a moment as thousands of images instantly flashed through his eyes, ricocheting across his brain. All Earth dishes, the Maitre'D began to unconsciously salivate as hamburgers, sushi, pizza, butter chicken curry, shabu shabu, and a million other Earth meals popped and whizzed through his senses, all leading up to . . . the chimichanga. And on that image, the little orange square stopped, flashed three times, and shut itself off.

Baiwyk eyed the Maitre'D with a raised eyebrow. An eyebrow that conveyed exactly what she wanted: *Show me where – right now – and nothing too bad happens.*

The Maitre'D read her face without any translation needed and gestured upwards with his pointed nose. Following that upturned slimy snout, Baiwyk landed on the kid halfway between a boy and a man. The one with cheese on his face.

Trinta spotted the retrievers the moment they entered the place and intently watched as Baiwyk spoke to the Maitre'D. And she was very aware of Baiwyk spotting them. She did all this while looking directly at Quentin.

Not knowing that, all her uncomfortable staring made Quentin think he had something on his face. Which he did. And that cheese was removed with extreme haste. But once that cheese was gone, he couldn't figure out why she still stared at him with such intensity (and no blinking besides).

"Do I got a booger, too?" he asked. "Something in my hair? A zit? What?!"

As though coming out of a trance, Trinta blinked and said flatly, "I'm hungry."

Suddenly, her salad bowl's leaves undulated with turbulent green waves. At the bottom of the bowl, more and more shadows slithered across it. Quentin inhaled sharply. He was plenty repulsed by the hot dog grub-snakes to begin with and a whole heaping helping of them might be tasty to Trinta, but would definitely cause his meal to come right back up.

"You can run, right?" she inquired.

"Yeah, that's about all I can do," he said.

Before he could question why, Trinta jabbed her fork into the bowl and started flinging grub-snakes onto other diners below. As soon as she cleaned out a bowlful, she licked her lips like she could eat a whole roomful of snakes and instantly more slithered into the salad. As soon as they popped up, Trinta scooped 'em out and tossed them around the room, eliciting shrieks, yells, and squeals.

Quentin suspected this wasn't cool, but being the new guy in the galaxy he deferred to her cultural awareness of how one behaved here. (Although even he picked up fairly quickly she wasn't behaving well at all.)

More and more diners screeched as they got beaned with grub-snakes. One even cried out, "My diet!" as he ate the too-tempting grub-snake that fell into his soup. The pandemonium caused by Trinta's impromptu food fight was exactly what she wanted. Soon, dozens of irritated diners and their tables floated up, all screaming about her raining grub-snakes on them.

"I'm so sorry," Quentin tried to quell them. "She's not herself right now . . . I think. Not that I know what she's normally like but . . ."

Trinta kept chucking grub-snakes as more and more angry people surrounded them. Up at least fifty feet in the air, Quentin didn't like where this was going.

Enraged diners jostled them, shouting epitaphs he never thought he'd hear coming out of alien mouths. And even though he found Trinta's dining fork dangerous, it was nothing compared to the mini-scythes and laser-knives now being brandished at them.

Secure in the belief that whatever technology allowed them all to swim through the air would keep them there, Quentin didn't fear the angry diners would somehow knock them to the ground. But still, he knew there's nothing worse than a person angered while eating. And these folks were so incensed he was amazed they didn't give off smoke.

Down below, Baiwyk and her retrievers watched amused. This was going to be even easier than she thought. Sent out to get this young pup seemed beneath her to begin with. So Baiwyk figured she might as well get some laughs out of these hijinks, especially considering how this punk took out so many of her Strikers. She just had to make sure the kid wasn't so torn up by the angry mob she only brought back scraps. Missing a limb or two wouldn't matter. As long as the target's mouth worked, her benefactors always showered her with appreciation and praise. And, to be honest, her benefactors occasionally preferred their retrievals a little bloodied and torn.

"I don't know what she's doing!" Quentin yelled at the screaming mob. "It's not *my* fault she's gone crazy!!!" He turned to Trinta, "Stop it! They're going to kill us!!!"

Ignoring him and everyone else, Trinta continued

her unrelenting grub-snake hailstorm. Pretty soon, the entire restaurant closed in around them as they elevated higher and higher into the restaurant's cavernous reaches with diners trying to poke them with their utensils. A long-suffering married couple with triangle heads even threw food. But nothing would stop Trinta. Fifty plus feet beneath them, the retrievers watched and snickered, causing Trinta to figure now was as good a time as any to . . .

"Hold me," she said, turning to her dining companion.

With the entire restaurant's masses shouting at them – most for their death and dismemberment (not necessarily in that order), Quentin appreciated Trinta wanting a hug at such a moment. He'd have preferred it to be a more romantic situation, but he'd take it where he could get it, thinking: *Nice! In keeping my cool, I showed her what a great guy I am and—*

But before he could finish that thought, Trinta leapt across the table and wrapped her arms around him. Surprised by her sudden affection, Quentin boldly went to give her a kiss.

Now, he'd never kissed a girl before. (Not really. Once, he kissed a girl in church. When he was two. And he and Alison Simon didn't so much kiss as headbutt each other. Which was then followed by teary wails, a little bit of bleeding, and an entire crowd of churchgoers laughing at them.) So, here, fourteen years later, he desperately hoped the first real kiss in his life wouldn't end with any of that. No crying, bleeding, and/or recriminating stares. He was wrong. So very, very wrong as he winced in embarrassment from the recriminating stare he instantly got from Trinta, the kissee.

Trinta knew he had no idea what she was planning. But she didn't think he'd misread the signals so badly as to actually place his lips on hers! Thankfully for him, she didn't have time to be offended. For after she gave Quentin the Trinta glare, she got on with her business.

Noting the retrievers were directly beneath them and keeping their eyes on their prize even while guffawing, Trinta reached into her back pocket and pulled out a tiny damper patch, no bigger than a postage stamp. Shoving it on the table, it emitted a silent burst of electro-magnetic, anti-gravitational overload, immediately shorting out the entire system that made this restaurant such an extraordinary experience.

Holding Quentin tight, she curled up next to him as they fell rapidly. And not just them. *Everybody* dropped to the ground. Soon every shouted curse and insult thrown at the grub-snake tossing couple turned into cries for help, cries of surprise, and just plain cries.

The kid from Nebraska had never plummeted with a group of people before. Being at the top of the falling heap did comfort him some. Not enough for him not to cling too tight to Trinta though. And even as he clung too tight, she preferred that to the opposite in this case. Because if they were gonna make it out of here, they'd have to stay close to survive.

Down below, the retrievers had no time to get out of the way. They tried to scramble, but they bumped into the Maitre'D, which cost them the seconds needed to make an escape. People rained down towards them from above, along with tables, utensils, and food (including gobs of still-undulating gooey grub).

As the mass of screaming bodies hurtled towards her, Baiwyk reckoned that if she had ordered goose here that hers might be cooked.

However, Trinta didn't want to kill anyone, she only wanted an escape. Therefore, at the last moment, she hit her damper button again and the whole system came back online, mere inches from hitting the ground. This still had people slamming into each other and all of them landing painfully on the retrievers. But it softened the blow considerably, resulting in numerous injuries with nothing too critical. Once everyone had softly landed on top of each other on this invisible six-inch pillow of anti-grav, it made a teeming mountain of people.

At the top of the whimpering mound, Trinta pried Quentin's arms off her.

"Move it now, Bulldog!" she shouted.

Quentin opened his eyes, just in time to see her jump down the hill of people with a squeal from each person she stepped on. Trailing behind, he tried to move swiftly yet delicately to the bottom, apologizing to every person he had to tread on.

"Sorry. Sorry . . . So sorry. Very sorry about that . . . Oooooh . . . Sorry."

Gingerly stepping down the last few bodies, he looked up to see Trinta at the door, impatiently gesturing for him to hurry up. He jogged towards her, not seeing what the rush was all about or why she'd created the biggest dog pile ever or . . .

KKKKkkkkkkkrrrrrrRRRRRRRRRRAAAAAAAAAA
AAKKKKKKKK!!!

A blast from the bottom of the dog pile shot right past Quentin's shoulder and drilled the wall beyond him, sending off a burst of blue sparks. He gawked in shock – total SHOCK! – that anyone would shoot at him. Glancing back, Baiwyk Stanz – her body pinned down under mounds of other people – had wedged her right arm free, aiming a fraktor right at him.

Baiwyk fired again just as Trinta rolled the big green Host egg right at her. The blast tore into the egg (which screeched like a gutted cartoon pig), but it did nothing to stop the egg's momentum and crashed into Baiwyk's arm with the brittle loud crack of bone. Baiwyk didn't yell out in pain though. She didn't make a sound. And this lack of exclamation scared Quentin more than any scream of vengeance would have.

Trinta kept an eye on the dog pile for any more trouble as the teeming mass continued to moan and groan while futilely trying to untangle itself as her "date" for the night caught up with her.

"Let's go!" she barked before bursting out of the doors.

Quentin followed after, wondering what on Earth he had done to deserve this.

CHAPTER TWELVE
DRIVING LESSONS

A pproximately *338 days ago . . .*

Learning how to fly a spaceship beats the hell outta learning how to drive a car, thought Quentin. First off, there wasn't as much to run into in the sky. Especially not now with everyone gone.

He marveled as the Havok roared up through the clouds and then back down again. One moment, the Statue of Liberty was giving him the once over. Next, back up through the clouds and down again and there was Big Ben and Parliament.

"Look, kids, Big Ben . . . Parliament," he laughed to himself.

Of course, the building that he called Parliament wasn't Parliament but Buckingham Palace instead. Still, that was okay. Right now, he could rename every single thing on Earth and that would be its name.

He zipped across the rugged Siberian plains, past the Pacific Ocean, and over the Andes. He witnessed polar bears in the Arctic, zebras across Botswana, and a sperm whale in the Atlantic. But every time he took a pass around his little planet, he never saw another person. Not in Times Square, not at Tiananmen Square, not on any square damn inch anywhere.

Of course, had he flown over Denver International Airport, he would have seen a couple of people. Not humans per se, but the former owners of the ship he now piloted. And they weren't happy. They weren't happy one bit. They fumed knowing they'd look like idiots if the one person they were sent to grab – a boy no less, a fairly weak human *boy* – not only got away, but did so in their ride.

"I blame you," Dasimon Edbu – the taller one – said.

"And I, you," Weedoss Edbu – his potato-like brother – said in return. "If you hadn't left your fraktor on the ship, this'd be done already."

Hunched over a shredded Hummer next to two jet engines, Weedoss used his fraktor to fuse strips of the Hummer to the engines, piece by piece. Nearby, Dasimon sat languidly on a baggage cart, holding a small comm.cent in his branchlike fingers.

"I place a call and we're off this empty blip in three days max," Dasimon said.

"Yes. And then we suffer. We suffer embarrassment – not the worst thing. Then pain – a very bad thing. We were sent to do the simplest of tasks. And we will do that task. Especially as he's still in atmo."

Dasimon moved his mouth, silently mocking Weedoss.

"Now, come help me," Weedoss added, "before I turn my fraktor on you."

"Yaaaoooooooooooooooooooo!" Quentin screamed, belting along with the tooth-challenged Shane MacGowan to a Pogues song.

Orbiting his little blue and green planet, the ship's young pilot jammed out, running through the corridors like a kid whose parents left him home alone for the first time. The Havok had never had sounds like this in it. Before, the first few times orbiting Earth, Quentin did so in complete silence. But that silence shattered the fifth time around when he started flipping switches and a voice boomed throughout the ship.

"Haartin stepser aa finel zhuung appel," the voice said.

Startled, Quentin poked his head out into the corridor to make sure he was alone.

"Hellllllllloooooo?!" he shouted.

No answer came back. Flicking a few more switches, the Havok became bathed in the sounds of high-pitched Japanese pop music. The screen above the switches lit up and listed the artist and song in what looked to Quentin like Japanese. The ship apparently had downloaded all of the Earth's culture for reference. Noticing a scroll bar to the side of the screen, he ran his finger over it, hoping it would hit something a little more his liking. And it did. Right on old Pixies tune that put a gleeful snarl on his face. His ride now had tunes. And he knew how to use them.

So as the ship flew through the day into night into day again, Quentin rocked out until he fell asleep in the pilot's seat, exhausted, exhilarated, and an ex-planet-lubber. His lids fluttered as he slept, his world continuing to change and expand, beyond anything he ever knew.

There's something extra-satisfying about sleeping while in a planetary orbit. The movement lulls one into a slumber comforting and safe, offset slightly with the fact any moment you could crash. It was a sleep Quentin had on road trips with his parents.

On the way to visit the Black Hills to see Mount Rushmore ("just a bunch of big heads" was his eleven-year-old assessment), he remembered staring out the back window at the stars as they'd pass by. Then he'd watch for the shadows of houses and farms reflected off the lights of other cars driving into the night. Then he'd look back and forth at the silhouettes of the back of his parents' heads, occasionally capturing a glance at their eerily orange-tinged faces off the dashboard's light.

As his mom and dad would talk (about their neighbors, the weather, his annoying aunt and uncle who nobody in the family liked), Quentin would fade out, safe in the assumption that they wouldn't wreck. . . or leave him at a truck stop . . . or do anything else uncool. They would take care of him. Knowing this, his head would fall back against the dark grey upholstery, tilting to the right to gaze at where the starry sky and the horizon skipped back and forth.

Waking up with a start, Quentin fell out of the pilot's

chair and onto the hard metallic floor.

"Where am . . ." he spluttered before remembering exactly where he was.

Outside the cockpit, dawn sprinted forward as the Havok traveled eastwards. The sleep did him good, clearing his head and bringing his life into a strange new focus. A focus that centered around him finding his people. Wherever they were. Even though it didn't seem like they were here on this planet any more. Not seeing anyone anywhere, the words from that phone message resounded in his mind: "*Humans scooped and transported frommmm planet . . .*"

"Nobody's here," Quentin whispered to himself. "Nobody but me . . ."

Putting both hands on the console and leaning forward, he peered down, surveying the Sahara from miles above as he breathlessly passed over Africa and on to Asia. His tummy rumbled, loudly ruining the silent splendor. Pulling on his racing gloves, he considered zipping the ship down and getting something to eat at a—

"Wait . . . what the hell's that?" exclaimed Quentin.

Through the clouds, something moved. Something non-cloudy. *A plane?* he wondered. *Maybe a leftover weather balloon or . . .* Then to the far left, a flash of silver and red darted in and out of a cloud. *Nah, must be my head messin' with . . .* But then a flash of blue and silver popped through another cloud and headed straight for him. More than two miles off, it rocketed right towards the Havok. Grabbing the stick, Quentin angled the ship out of the projectile's path.

"Maybe it's flying 'cause of some glitch or

something," he mused. "A satellite that got shot off somehow or a . . ."

But when the projectile matched his turn and stayed straight on course for the Havok, Quentin knew whatever this was, it wasn't any sort of glitch. It was after *him*!

"Oh, shirt . . ."

Quentin jerked the stick down and the Havok plummeted down into the clouds. Instantly, the corkscrewed projectile followed him. With a burst of red flames shooting out the back, the projectile ripped right past the cockpit, narrowly missing the Havok. A tricked-out jet engine with a red sleek cockpit upfront, it screamed by with the long, sticklike figure of Dasimon riding atop.

"Great, the giant preying mantis can fly," Quentin muttered.

The small single-pilot ship – a sleek modified corkscrew dagger made from the parts of a jet engine, a Hummer, and bitterness – roared past again. Before Quentin could focus on that ship, another tricked-out corkscrew dagger zipped across the bow, disappearing as instantaneously as it appeared. This one had a blue and green cockpit with a chunkier design to house the hulking Weedoss inside. Quentin now knew the alien guys he left behind weren't content staying behind. They wanted their ship back.

The Havok emerged from the clouds over the ocean as Quentin scanned for any sign of those two aliens. He didn't know if they had weapons to shoot him from the sky or . . . *Do I have weapons*? he thought all of a sudden. *Surely, I gotta have some sort of lasers . . . or phasers ... or proton torpedoes ... or missiles ... or something.*

Disappointed no buttons on the console had any cartoon pictures of guns, missiles, or explosions on it, he chose to pin his hopes on the hours of videogaming skill that'd hopefully help him play keep away.

Of course, maybe they're just as scared of me as I am of them. Maybe we all just got off on the wrong foot. After all, I did throw a rock at 'em. And I did sorta steal their ride. Maybe they're actually friendly and ... Weedoss's blue-green corkscrew shot up under the Havok and flew fifty yards in front before giving a flirty "follow me" wiggle. *Yeah, maybe they are friendly,* he decided, too easily convincing himself. *Maybe they can help me find everyone and make everything alright. Maybe they ...*

In his corkscrew, Weedoss rejoiced that this skinned-up quarter-brain was so gullible to let him sit in front of his ship without blowing him out of the sky.

"He probably can't even feed himself," Weedoss said.

"So let's finish this and go!" Dasimon shouted back into the comm.

Weedoss's corkscrew seemed friendly enough as it flew ahead of the Havok. And Quentin desperately wanted to make friends. (Being abandoned will do that to you.)

As that corkscrew dagger led the Havok towards land, Quentin wondered where the other one was. He thought there should really be a scanner that ... there *was* a scanner! Right down to his left with a flashing green center symbol for the Havok itself. A tiny blip at the top of the grid obviously was the potato-lookin' alien dude's corkscrew and the blip directly behind him had to be the mantis one's.

From the leading corkscrew, Weedoss stuck an arm out and motioned for the Havok to follow, just like a highway patrol guy.

"Guess I'm getting an escort," Quentin said with an eyebrow raised.

But he *wasn't* getting an escort. You knew that. I knew that. And sure as shynola, the Edbu brothers knew that.

Their plan was simple: Make sure the ship was over land. Then set off a localized EMP blast that would shut down the ship's engines, causing it to crash. With the shields automatically activated every time the ship took off and a shagranium-plated hull, the ship could crash through an entire city and not be the worse for wear.

Sure, there'd be some small damage. But big damage, little damage, the Edbu brothers could fix almost anything. And as a bonus, their prey would rattle around the inside of the ship like a pinball, leaving the human kid in "good enough" shape for what they needed.

In the distance, Quentin spotted letters on a big hill and that pretty much only meant Hollywood. Los Angeles. (Nobody else really labeled their hills in such a way.) As he crossed from ocean to land, passing above a large Ferris wheel on a pier, his escort dropped a hovering ball out its backside, almost like a little dog dropping a little poo.

Without warning, the corkscrew then blasted away with a burst of flames. Before Quentin could wonder where it went, the silver ball exploded with a tiny puff and all the air outside went wavy. And when those waves hit the Havok, all of the ship's electrics went down.

"Not cool!!!" Quentin yelped.

The Havok nosed down and he grabbed the joystick. Thankfully, it still helped guide the gliding ship, but only so far as to where he was going to crash. The ship floated dangerously close to buildings as it kept drifting east with Quentin putting both feet on the console and clutching the stick close to him, trying to will the ship from crashing.

"C'mon, Havok, please, please, please, please, PLEASE!!!" he pleaded, spittle flying from his mouth.

The spaceship coasted on, only hundreds of feet from the ground, creaking as it stayed airborne. But when the Havok couldn't stay aloft any longer, Quentin did the only thing he could think of and steered it towards the top of a twelve-story building. With all his effort trying to will the ship where he wanted with that nearly immovable controller, the Havok hit the top of that building and bounced upwards, propelling the ship in the air a little while longer.

As Quentin held tight to the joystick, he clung to the hope that as long as he stayed off the ground, he'd be safe. Relatively speaking, anyways.

The Edbu brothers watched the ship bounce off the building and continue its wounded flight with mounting concern. The EMP pulse they hit the Havok with was designed by Dasimon to short out the ship's systems. It wasn't designed to take them out completely. In a couple minutes, everything would come back online. A couple minutes should have been more than enough for the kid to crash the ship. After all, even a formally trained pilot wouldn't be able to do anything other than crash in such a situation. However . . . if the Havok didn't crash and its systems came back online while still airborne, then the ship would continue on like it just got over a bad case of the hiccups.

"What if he doesn't go down?" Dasimon whined over the comm.

"We have more," Weedoss snipped. "We drop the rest on him if he doesn't go down this time. We fry the system."

"Why didn't you do that to begin with?!"

"Why didn't *you* shut the ramp to the ship when we got off so we wouldn't have to be here doing this?!"

Weedoss simmered as he swung away from Dasimon's corkscrew. Now flanking Quentin from half a mile back, they continued to watch surprised as the Havok bounced off a ten-story building and was thrown back up into the air, buying the boy more time. More time to . . .

Quentin thought of it like skipping stones. But instead of a stone and a pond, he had a two-ton spaceship and a city. So after bouncing off his first building, he picked another one down the block and aimed for it with all his might. The joystick barely moved, but sluggishly the Havok nudged towards where he wanted it to go.

I always wanted to visit L.A., he mused, *but not like*

this.

Pushing with both feet on the console as though wrestling a huge fish, the Havok dipped and bounced off the ten-story building, achieving a much bigger jolt upwards than before.

"That's how you make cake, yeah!" he shouted.

He knew that all skipped stones eventually ended up at the bottom of the lake with a sickening plop. But until he hit the ground, he was gonna do all he could to keep ship-skipping his way through the city.

"Traffic?" he said smirking. "What traffic? Bunch of whiners if you ask me."

The Havok trampolined off smaller and smaller multi-storied buildings, leaving Los Angeles in ruins, all with the ship still staying barely aloft. However, as Quentin bounced further and further into the city, the buildings grew higher and higher as his hopes and his ship sank lower and lower.

Maybe the ship's not dead dead, he hoped. *Just sorta dead. I mean, why would they kill their only way back? No way. They wouldn't.*

But as the Havok descended towards a hoity-toity four-story shopping center, his last strands of optimism fell by the wayside. His arms shuddering as the strength drained from them, Quentin pulled up on the joystick, knowing that there wouldn't be any more bounces after this next one. And as the ship smashed onto the roof of the shopping center and blipped back into the air, the returns were so diminished that the Havok simply sledded off the top of the building. Now, he searched for something soft to crash into.

Behind him on their corkscrews, the Edbu brothers watched eagerly, licking their chops. Dasimon's upper right lip even dared to raise up for a celebratory smile.

As the ship plunged down, Quentin braced himself to crash spectacularly. Despite plummeting towards the La Brea Tar Pits, sushi restaurants, and a car museum, he realized, all in all, he wasn't having such a bad tour of the town. *That is until I crash and die. Or crash and don't die and the aliens get a hold of me and rip me apart for stealing their ship.*

But just as the Havok was about to smash into the ground – only mere millimeters from impact – the engines roared back to life and the ship shot back up into the air! Quentin whooped with all the whooping his lungs would allow. He grabbed the joystick to no avail as the rest of the ship's systems had yet to come back on. But Quentin didn't care. He was just happy to be fully and unequivocally airborne again.

The scanner flashed back to life with two small blips coming up fast directly behind the Havok. The Edbus weren't done with him yet.

"Guess we're still playing tag," he muttered.

Rapidly, the two corkscrews roared by and once fifty yards in front of him, they dropped more than a dozen EMP balls. Quentin pulled on the joystick with all his might as the lights on the console flashed to life like the lights on a Christmas tree. And right before smashing into the EMP balls, the young pilot jammed the stick down. Thankfully, the Havok instantly followed his lead, diving with extraordinary force just as the balls exploded, sending their crippling waves off in every direction. Racing straight down towards the city, the ship barely stayed ahead of the electrical surge.

"Go, go, go, go, go, go, go, go, go, go, go, Havok! GOOOOOOOOOOOOOOO!!!"

Feeling impending doom nipping at his shippy heels, Quentin darted in-between the downtown buildings, hoping the waves might peter out from hitting the skyscrapers instead. Twisting the stick, the Havok shot around a tall round white building its pilot thought looked like a colossal tooth.

As he rode low to the ground past the carcasses of vehicles, Quentin could almost feel the EMP waves licking right behind him, nearly nudging the Havok, ready to take the whole thing down. This time for good! But the Havok took a hard right and zipped down another street, then another left, another right, and with a ferocious zooming back into the sky, Quentin threaded the needle between two skyscrapers and shot further upwards, safe and secure from that attack.

"Now, where are those . . ." he trailed off. Glancing at the scanner, Quentin watched the Edbu brothers fly off in two wildly different directions, lost amongst the buildings down below. "Probably looking for bloody blown-up chunks of me . . ."

Quentin didn't know how many EMP balls those guys had and, to be honest, he didn't really know how many alien guys there were either. But he didn't care. In accordance with his name, he was furious.

"You wanna play tag, let's play tag," he said. "And I'm it!" He narrowed his eyes and hoped he sounded more than a little bit cool.

Weedoss was upset that his brother hadn't built proper scanners into their corkscrews. He figured it was the least Dasimon could do since Weedoss did the heavy work of actually building their rides. Though Dasimon was good with the little things, Weedoss figured that little things required little effort, especially when compared to making working corkscrew daggers out of nothing.

"A two-mile radius on a 2-D display isn't a scanner," Weedoss muttered. "Might as well just call our eyes and ears scanners then."

But just when the hulking Weedoss was about to rip out the scanner and throw it out the window, a blip appeared. The scanner seemed to be malfunctioning because it showed the Havok right in front of him. Yet he couldn't see it anywhere. A few seconds later though, he couldn't see anything at all.

"You're it, Mr. Potato Head!" Quentin shouted.

The Havok came down hard on Weedoss's corkscrew, drilling it with one of the wings and knocking it into a convention center. The corkscrew tore right through the center before limply coming out the other side and crashing down on a taco stand.

"A shame," said Quentin. "I could really go for some tacos."

Not having a chance to salivate too long on how much he missed tacos, he pulled the Havok back up into the sky while glancing at the scanner for the second Edbu. Turns out Dasimon appeared to be on the run, miles away to the south. The Havok turned and headed towards Dasimon's blip.

"There we go," he said, spying Dasimon's corkscrew rip-roaring above what looked like a college campus.

"Here we go," Dasimon said into his comm.

There was a crackle in response. Then he heard weird mumbling from Weedoss.

"Shatterrrr hissss bonesss . . ." Weedoss snarled over the static.

Dasimon shook his head. *My brother, the drama queen.* He kept his corkscrew going straight ahead, waiting and baiting for his "hunter" to hunt him.

Quentin steered the Havok right at Dasimon's corkscrew, thinking he'd smack into him like he did the other one . . . until he realized he was doing the same thing as before. He wasn't chasing this guy. He was just being "escorted" to his own beatdown again.

Hell, even that stupid phone call was probably them bringing me to Denver, too! I'm not gonna be their dancing monkey any more!

Without a second thought, he turned the Havok in the opposite direction, back towards the downtown skyscrapers. As Quentin flew away, a small burst appeared on his scanner. Glancing as far back as he could in the cockpit, a series of EMP balls exploded in the tallest building on that campus he almost passed over.

"Now, if you wanna play games, you're gonna play *my* games!" he snarled.

On the scanner, Quentin watched hoping the other corkscrew would come after him, but it didn't head straight for the Havok. Of course, it wouldn't. The alien dude wouldn't go right back through the EMP waves he set off. The corkscrew instead took a wide circular path around before coming back towards its prey.

Quentin slowed and put himself high enough in the air so as not to be lost by his pursuer. When the corkscrew caught up to the Havok, he floored it. Suddenly, they were right in the heart of downtown, zipping in and out of streets, the heat from their engines scorching the asphalt. Dasimon stayed tight on Quentin's tail, even when they flew past the wreckage of Weedoss's corkscrew. But when Dasimon accelerated to ram Quentin and toss out the remaining EMPs, the Havok ascended and began bashing back and forth into the skyscrapers.

At first, small chunks from the bashed buildings rained down and ricocheted off Dasimon's corkscrew, causing little harm. But as the sci-freighter's unrelenting side-to-side assault on the structures gathered more force, huge debris avalanched down. Then entire floors of buildings toppled down on Dasimon's ship. And as Quentin smashed against the tall white building he once thought looked like a tooth, the whole thing came crashing down hard, burying Dasimon in the street as the Havok pulled up into the air and away.

Climbing higher into the sky, Quentin breathed easy for a moment. Just a moment. Because he knew he had to find his people. That was clear now. They needed him. He didn't know how he'd find them. He didn't know where to go or what he'd need to do. But he resigned himself to the understanding that he sure as hell wasn't going to find anyone else here on this empty planet.

"Let's go get 'em," said Quentin quietly.

Moments later, the Havok broke through the atmosphere and into space.

CHAPTER THIRTEEN
TIMEOUT

Quentin sat in the corner of the storage container like a child being punished.

I'm in timeout, he thought.

"Am I in timeout?" he growled huffily.

Trinta didn't look up from what she was working on. He wasn't even sure she heard him. He kinda hoped she didn't. Petulance doesn't play well on most people and definitely not on a teenager.

Trinta heard him, but kept on keepin' on. She tapped into a small, beat-up handset while circling the Havok. Scanning the damage to the ship, she wasn't surprised at how bad a shape it was in. The Havok took a lot of abuse just getting into these boxes, but even before that it was pretty much torn up from stem to stern.

Seeing how the boy flew it, Trinta was amazed it wasn't just scrap. From her hidden position during his battle with the Strikers, there were a dozen things she'd have done differently. Things any pilot is taught from day one to do. Tactics that, thinking about it further, probably would have ended up getting her killed. She reluctantly acknowledged to herself that the boy's inexperience and gut-throttling lack of technique is what aced out those elite fighters. Whether it was luck or stupidity, Trinta didn't care. She had to respect the result. Now, though, she just winced with each new breach to the hull she found.

"Is it okay if I take a nap?" Quentin groused from the corner.

"No!" Trinta shouted and returned to assessing the state of the Havok.

Quentin wasn't sure he'd be able to fall asleep anyway. After they burst out of the restaurant, his adrenaline was pumping through the roof. But the adventure wasn't over then.

Before they raced off into the night, Trinta decided to visit the *Jebel Museum of Storage Innovation* – one of the four storefronts surrounding the park. The museum rested right next to the restaurant where the retrievers were frantically trying to free themselves from the people-pile to come get them.

"You get the bike!" she ordered, hurrying into the museum.

Quentin had no idea what was going on, but she yelled so forcefully he did what she said immediately, if not smoothly. Rushing up to the black box bike-check corner, he stared at the scanner where Trinta had put her palm before.

"Uh . . . hello . . ." he said to the scanner. "I'm trying to get my friend's bike thingy . . . and I don't think we got, like, a . . . number or anything . . ."

Nothing happened.

Hearing Trinta rustle about in the museum with crashes and clanging, Quentin wasn't sure if she was fighting something for business or destroying things for pleasure. As he stood there feeling like a fool, he couldn't help fretting over the fact that very nasty folks were coming to kill him if he didn't hurry. Unable to think of anything else, he shrugged and put his hand on the palm scanner.

"It tickles," he giggled as it scanned him.

Instantly, the frict-bike appeared on a tray and lowered itself right to him.

"Uh . . . thank you," he said to the scanner, grabbing the frict-bike and scrambling over to the museum doors. He tried to peak in, but all he could make out were shadows and iridescent flashes. Trinta's violet silhouette would shoot across the room, then back again, intensely searching for something.

"You need some help?!" Quentin shouted in.

"Start up the bike!" she hollered back.

From inside the restaurant, the voices were getting louder and louder and their time advantage was coming quickly to a close.

Quentin mounted the bike, ostensibly waiting for Trinta so they could hastily escape into the night. But his other thought – a less noble thought – was that if anyone came out of those restaurant doors blasting, he could make a run for it. On his own. Without her. He wasn't sure he would. Like anyone, he didn't know for sure whether he'd be a coward or not until the time came.

He also imagined he could be utterly heroic, taking out their fraktor-toting adversaries with some ultracool bike action that would melt Trinta's icy heart. *Most likely if I tried that though, I'd probably run into the tree and impale myself on the bike, making her and everyone else laugh their butts off.* (Quentin hoped one day he wouldn't always imagine humiliating outcomes for everything he did. But he doubted it. High school just did that to you.)

"Rip the revs!" Trinta yelled as she ran out of the museum, carrying what looked like a little black lunchbox and a calculator.

Quentin revved the engines and when she jumped on, wrapping her arms and legs around him, they took off. The bike shot furiously up the wall towards where the boy believed the Havok to be. After a moment, Trinta tugged his shoulder and pointed in the opposite direction. He turned the bike around and they did a quick 180, which still boggled Quentin's mind, what with being perpendicular to the ground below and all.

As they rocketed away, he tried to focus on the task at hand: driving a vehicle he'd never driven before – along walls! – while an attractive woman had her limbs all around him like a "*sexy octopus*". (His words, not mine.) With her guiding them, they were soon back at the box in their "building".

"Didn't scare you too much, did I?" Trinta smirked, noting his very flush face.

"Uh . . . no . . . No! Uh . . . no . . ."

"Even if I did, part of the fun, eh?"

As she sauntered up the ramp into the Havok, he watched her go, content to stand in one spot and breathe for a moment. It had been a strange date. He wasn't sure she'd call it a "date". He didn't know what exactly to call it himself. He just knew he felt irrationally and unexplainably happy.

Trinta strolled into the cockpit and flicked the flashing yellow switches above her head – all thirteen of them. Suddenly, the entire inside and outside of the Havok were bathed in light. Trinta had a lot of work to do to get this ship up in the air again. And time wasn't on their side. It never was.

She didn't know where to start: the engines . . . the hull breaches . . . the slight tear in the co-pilot's seat . . . She felt overwhelmed before realizing she had to do what she always does when thrown a giant unholy mess: Just randomly start on something (anything!)

She wouldn't get it all done in fifteen minutes like she wanted, but if she wanted it to get done at all, she had to start somewhere. So she grabbed some tape and went to work on the slight tear in the co-pilot's chair.

Outside the ship, Quentin held his hands in front of his face to shield himself from the brightness. After going through a moonless night on a very dark planet into a very dark box, his eyes weren't prepared for the blindingly bright display Trinta put on. Even minutes after the lights had come up, he still felt like a blinded little mole rat.

By the time his eyes adjusted, he could just make out a pair of boots at the top of the Havok's ramp. A second later, Trinta's head popped down next to her boots with her now even-longer hair whispering against the ramp's grated floor.

"Hey, since you're not doing anything, plug up the hole, will ya?" she said, nodding towards the opening.

Not waiting for a response, she ducked back into the ship. Quentin appreciated she had such confidence in his abilities that she could set him a task and believe he could actually do it. Of course, he also felt sorta like her dog. *Like a dog you train to get beer from the fridge*, he fumed, not knowing why she made his moods swing so much.

"Why don't *you* plug the hole?" he snarked.

Despite the bruised feelings, he clomped over and peered outside to the long shadows of gargantuan blocks of abandoned artifacts of people's forgotten pasts. A gust of wind shot tufts of his hair back, bathing his face in a wash of dust. He closed his eyes and enjoyed the breeze, no matter how sooty it was. At least he did until Trinta yelled:

"Now!!!"

Surging with the anger felt when his parents would yell at him to do chores, Quentin snapped his head back in to let Trinta know he wasn't her chore slave, but smacked his skull on the top lip of the hole as he did.

"Ow!" he yelled.

Rubbing his wounded head, Quentin hastily grabbed the largest sliced out sheet of metallic wall and slammed it over the gap. He wondered if he should ask Trinta if he oughta fuse it, but figured he'd done his share by leaning it over the opening. *It's good enough*, he thought. *If Purple Rain wants any more done, she can do it her own damn self.*

As Trinta paced around the Havok, she stopped every few moments to examine the readings bouncing back at her. After a couple minutes rounding the ship, every databurst sent back resulted in the same response: a shake of the head and then a roll of her tongue across her bottom teeth, trying to will herself into the belief that it wasn't so bad.

Meanwhile, Quentin bounced up and down, trying to keep himself awake. Trinta found this annoying but felt she could suffer it silently. However, when he started jogging in place, she discovered she couldn't suffer anymore silently or otherwise.

"Stop it!" she snapped. "Just go over there and sit down!"

So he went into the corner and sat down, then said something about being "put in timeout" and then asked if he could go to sleep, to which Trinta replied he couldn't.

A couple hours later, the sleepy Earth boy sat slumped against the corner, his eyes most definitely closed, a whiffling snore sniffling from his nose. Napping peacefully, his eyelids fluttered slightly as a low buzzing filled the room.

By the time his eyelids went from fluttering to open, he was just in time to see the Havok enveloped in a burnt sienna haze. At first, he thought his eyes were having trouble focusing, but that wasn't it. The brownish shimmer surrounded the Havok in strange patchy blobs, expanding into tiny shimmer bubbles before receding back tight to the ship. Standing up and rubbing a terrible crick in his neck, he zombied over to Trinta.

"What's goin' on?" Quentin inquired, yawning.

"The hull's healing," she said.

"Hull's healing, huh?" he asked, smiling to himself. "How?"

"The museum's displays of early nano-construbots included a few kaylania-bots. So I took a phalanx and multiplied 'em. Set 'em to work. Sight to behold."

Quentin couldn't disagree. It's not like he actually saw the bots, only the haze of the swarm so teeny were they. The bots slowly regenerated the ship's exterior with a buzzy hum, reminding Quentin of the locusts that used to haunt him to sleep in those humid Nebraska summers, only quieting before thunderstorms.

What the bots did was truly impressive. Ripped stretches of the strafed hull slowly grew new metal skin before a bot swarm would attack another blight on the Havok. Trinta oversaw it all proudly.

Misreading the moment, Quentin put his arm on her shoulder as though they were an old couple watching their millionth romantic sunset. Trinta snapped her shoulder back, tossing his arm off with such sudden and angry force that he shivered slightly.

"Sorry," he muttered. "Don't know why I . . ." He hastily changed the subject. "So what's the plan? And who were those guys who tried to get us? Is the ship going to get fixed alright? It'll fly again, right? Hey, are we safe here?"

"A lot of questions, Bulldog," Trinta said.

"A lot's gone on," he snapped. "And I've been quiet when you told me to and I sat in the corner like you told me to! So I don't think it's too weird to ask you a couple questions! Alright?! That's not too crazy, is it?! Is it?! IS IT?!!!!"

Trinta took a step back and eyed him curiously. She had to remember he wasn't a moron. Just a touch new. She nodded deliberately, the way a mother would to settle down a child having an irrational tantrum.

"I don't have answers," she said. "I don't have a plan. I have some thoughts."

Quentin folded his arms and waited for her "thoughts".

"First, we gotta get the ship right," she said. "After that, there's no other plan. Unless you want to live here."

"No."

They stood awkwardly for a moment, Quentin shifting back and forth on his feet.

"Especially as we ruined their one restaurant," he said.

"Good point."

"Who were those guys?"

"Don't know."

"Is that normal?"

"Not really. One of us must have pissed off somebody somewhere."

"Not me. I'm adorable."

Trinta guffawed heartily. The first time ever in front of him. He felt pleased.

"So what happens after the hull gets fixed?" he asked.

"I jurg up the engines, get the systems up to minimum workage . . . then we see how far we can get before the ship falls apart."

"Oh, I like to call that 'the Usual'. Too bad we're not back on Earth. We could just take it into the Junker Monkeys. They always fixed up my dad's car. And his car was a piece of—"

"*Earth*?" Trinta interrupted abruptly.

"Yeah. Earth. What? Is that bad?"

"I thought you said you came from some place called Nebraska. That you were a . . . a Bulldog."

"Yeah. On Earth."

"You're an Earther?"

"'Earther'? I came from Earth if that's what you're asking."

"Yes, that's exactly what I'm asking," she said, stroking her chin.

"But wouldn't I be an 'Earthling'? Isn't that what everyone calls us?"

"Why'd you want to be called that? Sounds like something you'd call a pet," she said. Then she realized maybe his word *was* better.

"Guess you got a point. But Earther sounds goofy, too. Maybe we could be called—"

"Regardless . . . You're from Earth?"

"The only one. As far as I know."

Trinta's mind percolated rapidly. She suddenly had a much greater appreciation for what he was, maybe not as a person but as an item of worth. She'd heard chatter for a while now about the intergalactic interest in what apparently was this boy.

"Well, that changes . . . things," she said. "Gives me

an idea of where to go next."

"Back to Earth? That's cool. My parents aren't there so if you want to stay over . . ."

"No. Somewhere else."

"Where?"

"Not exactly sure. But I've got an inkling . . ."

"Well, it seems like we might just have a plan. Woohoo . . ."

The buzzing bots around the ship gradually came to a halt. Then they all hurried towards Trinta and streamed as a tiny, barely visible line into the scanner in her hand. Externally, the ship now appeared to be right as rain. In fact, Quentin had never seen the Havok look so good, almost sparkling. Not only did the bots repair the hull, they threw in a wash for free.

"So what now?" Quentin inquired.

"I try to get the engines back online. Maybe a couple hours work. Maybe a couple days."

"That's a pretty big jump in estimates."

"I'd also say 'maybe a couple weeks', but I figure we'd be dead by then."

"Oooookay . . . Can I help?"

"I doubt it, but you might as well tag along. Might need another pair of hands, even if they're your tiny doll hands."

"Thanks."

Trinta headed back up the ramp and right as Quentin went to follow, a noise from across the room stopped them. Trinta swiftly hit a button on the ramp and the Havok's lights all shut off, leaving them enveloped in darkness. They turned to the covered hole in the wall where a sliver of light shined through.

"Did you fuse the wall back?" she whispered.

"'Fuse' it? No. I just leaned the panel back on it. I don't know how to fuse—"

Trinta put her hand over his mouth, silencing him instantly. She knew she should have fused the wall back herself. She just assumed it wouldn't be a problem even if he did mess it up. Nobody could track them there. The frict-bike left no traces since it covered up its path as it moved along. And anyone looking for them would go first to any of the three-dozen ship docks across the planet before they'd even think of searching *in* the boxes themselves.

The glow leaking in then went from a bright white light to a soft green as the Earther's heart beat so hard Trinta could hear it.

"Do we have a plan?" he whispered.

"What is it with you with the plans?" she harshly whispered back.

Quentin bit his lip, staring at the slit in the wall. He felt guilty for not doing a better job securing it. He felt bad that he lost any of the goodwill he accumulated with the tall, lovely alien girl. But mostly he just felt scared.

So when the panel shot off towards them and a hulking figure moved inside from the shadows, one could forgive the Earther for screaming like someone threw a baby opossum at him.

CHAPTER FOURTEEN
MOVING THROUGH TIME
AND A LITTLE BIT OF SPACE

*A**pproximately 336.5 days ago . . .*

Breaking Earth's orbit, Quentin gazed down at his little planet, not sure he'd ever be back.

"So long, Earth," he said. "Try to stay out of trouble while I'm away."

He passed the moon, noting with some melancholy that the US flag had fallen to the ground. America. Earth. Nebraska. North Platte . . . No! North *Quentin*! None of those names meant anything anymore. And even if they might, he doubted he'd find anyone who'd understand him even if they did.

Hell, not everyone on Earth speaks English. So how does that work for the universe? I'm gonna sound like a monkey to these people. Or I'm gonna have to do a *lot of charades. And I <u>hate</u> charades.*

After a couple weeks of flying through the stars (technically he wasn't actually flying "through" stars – that'd be highly dangerous as well as partially suicidal), Quentin zipped out of his galaxy altogether. (Although he wasn't sure when exactly that happened as there wasn't a sign reading: *Now Leaving the Milky Way.*)

Approaching a ravishing emerald green planet, he really realized he was boldly going where no one (of Earth descent) had gone before. He wasn't great with astronomy but he knew none of the planets in his solar system looked like that. Hoping to find friendly people here and perhaps info on where his fellow Earth folk might be, he burst through the planet's atmosphere, only to find that the whole planet consisted of rippling, pulsating leaves. Nearing the surface, a sixty-foot brown serpentine fish-worm munched forth out of the waves, leaping into the air and then disappearing back under.

"Don't know how I talk to that thing," he said.

Taking the Havok back out of orbit, his stomach growled.

"Alright, Mr. Hungry, let's get you some grub."

For all Quentin knew, there might have been a magic food generator on the Havok. But he wasn't going to trust that for his dietary well-being. Not by a long shot. That's why he made a point of making one last stop before leaving Earth on his mission. (Well, that and he was totally starving.) Just as he broke his planet's orbit, he doubled back quickly and found his way back to

North Platte.

Parking the ship in front of the Huge Saver supermarket on A Street that he'd been to a million times since he was little, Quentin raced in and filled up cart after cart of food (a lot of the junk variety). Once stocked up, he wheeled the overflowing carts of groceries into the Havok's cargo area.

"This oughta last me 'til I find everyone," he said.

Flying over to his home (and accidentally knocking the chimney off Steve Z's house in the process), the Havok landed roughly in the McFurys' big backyard. Quentin ran inside and grabbed as many t-shirts, jeans, underwear, and socks as he could. Not knowing when the Edbu brothers or an entire fleet of bloodthirsty aliens might appear to get him, he raced all the clothes back into the ship and jetted off without a second thought.

As he passed over his house, a couple of sun-worn Frisbees on the roof caught his eye. He had forgotten all about those Frisbees. He wondered if in time he'd forget all about this – his home, his town, his everything – the same way. He then wondered if "Frisbees of My Life" would be a good name for a song.

Breaking orbit again, he realized it'd be a pretty frak-awful name for a song.

But one thing he did *not* forget about were delicious fudge sticks. Perfect for a road trip, even when there were no roads. So popping down to the cupboard (actually, a small converted storage hold previously full of spacesuits), he opened the door up with a satisfying clink. There, the food stared out, beckoning him to devour it all.

"Hello, Mr. Jerky," he said. "Hello, soups. Hello, cereals. Hello, Little Debbie's." And with a sneer he added, "Hello, *beannnns* . . ." He didn't even know why he grabbed beans. He *hated* beans. (And generally when he ate beans, they hated him, too.)

For this visit though, Quentin seized a handful of fudge sticks and a big stick of jerky. Admittedly, not the best lunch ever. 'Course he wasn't even sure if this was lunch, what with no delineation of time any more.

Just times when he was awake.

Times when he was asleep.

And times when he ate.

Times when he ate jerky and fudge sticks.

And drank Dr. Pepper.

Not a bad teenage life really.

A spaceship pretty much runs on its own. Just like driving a car is basically about accelerating, stopping, and steering. Yeah, there are windshield wipers, air conditioning, and a host of other functions as well. But for the most part, the driving itself is a pretty simple thing. It's the same for a spaceship.

Spending a lot of time on the Havok though, Quentin figured he oughta get to know all of its bells *and* its whistles. Every day, he'd stare at the massive console extended in front of him and on a piece of paper he drew a breakdown of it, labeling all the switches. All three hundred and seventeen. And each day, he'd hit a switch – on particularly adventurous days more than one – and write down what it did:

Switch 19 – Havok does Figure 8 so fast I yurt a

little in my mouth.

Switch 33 – Brings temp down to a freezing 19 degrees F.

Switch 34 – Brings temp up to a butt-sweating 109 degrees F.

Switch 35 – Makes the temperature just right.

Switch 49 – Gives engines an extra burst. (In fact, that switch shot the Havok forward so fast Quentin had to pull the ship hard left to keep from ramming into a comet. That was a *"one switch only"* day as he almost had his very first heart attack.)

Switch 73 – Nothing. (That he noticed anyway.)

Switch 74 – Nothing. (That he noticed anyway.)

Switch 75 – Nothing. (That he noticed anyway.)

Switch 89 – Lights on. Lights off.

Switch 99 – Landing gear down.

And so on.

Each day had its own dollop of homework where he tried to memorize what each switch did. Or at least the most important ones that might save his life. Due to this, he felt if he had to run away from some threat, he might do okay. But still he wondered if the Havok had any weapons. And if so, how cool were they and would he figure out how to use them before something bad got him first?

Three months of not brushing his teeth at first was pretty fantastic. It was such a chore to take a brush across his teeth to clean them. And the spitting?! It was really too much to ask back on Earth. So up here on his own spaceship, he didn't even bother. He had no one to impress. No one who'd be put off by his foul breath.

That is . . . until his repellent breath began to disgust even himself.

"Eeeuughgh," he said, catching a whiff. "It's like my mouth is farting."

Thus, Quentin popped down to the med-chamber (or the "pill room" as he knew it then) eager to see if there was any mouthwash or toothpaste.

He'd noticed the med-chamber on his third day in space but hadn't gone in since. Didn't see a need. Didn't have any headaches or sicknesses or anything worth going down there for. But now, he figured there had to be something simple to take care of his horrid halitosis and it couldn't hurt to look.

The trouble was that all of the pills and other medical items were labeled with squigglies and dots. Considering how testing the ship's switches proved so useful, he figured he could do the same here. Unaware that some pills might perform internal operations that could very well kill him if taken on a healthy body, the Earth kid blithely rummaged through the little trays and compartments. Finally, he came across a small square strip of hopefulness. A tiny silver tab with a tongue emblem on it that looked exactly like breath-freshening strips back home.

"This has gotta take care of my turd-breath," he convinced himself. "What else could it do? It's got a picture of a tongue on it."

Seeing nothing better to do on a Thursday in space, Quentin McFury popped the tab on his tongue and waited for his breath to refresh itself in a tingly manner. The tingliness happened, but there was no refreshing breath to be found. In fact, the slight tingling grew fevered and raced up his tongue, blasting its way to the center of his skull. Grabbing his head in pain, Quentin fell to the ground.

"Urrrghghgh . . ."

His teeth clenched hard, his uppers and lowers engaged in a bizarre mouth war. His ears vibrated in pulses from the inside of his skull out. His eyes fluttered as his head rapidly shook back and forth. Quentin cursed his own stupidity and his own recklessness fueled by tedium and bad breath. As his whole head bulged, the Havok's young pilot wobbled upright and tried to make it down the corridor.

"Maybe if I drinnnnnk sorrrrme wattttteerrrrr . . ." he mumbled.

And that's when he passed out on the cold metallic floor.

When he awoke, Quentin McFury was a changed man. He didn't know what happened exactly, but when he stood up and was able to read a sign in the corridor that he never understood before, he knew it was something big. The sign said: *Central Corridor – Watch Head Feet, Especially During Flight.*

Gingerly walking down the hallway, still feeling woozy, words appeared everywhere. Above the doorway to the pill room read: *Med-Chamber.* A sign next to the cargo area read unpredictably: *Cargo Area.* There were even scribblings on the walls, graffiti-esque doodles that contained such clever jottings as: *Edbu to Rule, Edbu Forever,* and *Dasimon Eats Criblars.*

"'Criblars'?" questioned Quentin. "What the hell are 'criblars'? And how the hell can I read all this now? Did

I hit a switch? The English switch?"

(We know there was no switch. We know he took a languo-upgrade. He just didn't take it right.)

Surprisingly pleased by this turn of events, he didn't fully grasp his new world of understanding until testing switches three days later. When turning Switch 191 on the far right side of the console, the music display flashed and the screen jumped from playing a Styx song about sailing away to voices talking. Understandable, English-speaking voices. It was comm chatter from a transpo-hub to a series of ships, all giving advice on how best to dock.

"Slow from a vector 6A entry and hover before dockpad until the mech-trap brings in," the man said.

"Always good advice," Quentin joked, nodding seriously.

Under the switch he hit, there was a knob. He turned it and the man's voice disappeared, replaced by a woman's voice: "This is Versa Stilen. If anyone with bonus engine trill to share, me give other in return."

Turning the knob again, he hit upon a robotic voice proclaiming, "The Marrmorr Sequence provides resilience beyond reason. Leaving bolt seeds to the hazard clouds should not be attempted without realizing the potential pain yields. But if yonder . . ."

Quentin wasn't listening any more. He wasn't really listening to begin with. Even though he comprehended most of the words, he didn't get what they were talking about. (Mostly because he licked the languo-tab instead of placing it on his forehead as everyone else in the universe knew to do, thus short-circuiting its effectiveness.) But that was beside the point.

He'd been aimlessly drifting through this chunk of the universe, filled with nothing but empty rocks and gaseous giants that housed no living souls. Now, scanning through the signals, Quentin heard the delightful cacophony of thousands of different voices, all out there reaching out to others. It filled him with some trepidation. It filled him with some doubts. In the end, it filled him with hope.

"Hello, everybody," the boy whispered. "It's me . . . Quentin."

Days later, more and more chatter rang out over varied signals, which convinced Quentin he was approaching something big. His eyes confirmed it when he spotted a huge space station nearly seventy miles long, two miles tall, and as wide as Texas. Immense illuminated structures rotated on colossal half-balls across it, all different colors shimmering. There were planets not far off, but you'd never know it from all the gaudy glitz and glowing bursts of lights emitting from the space station. Spaceships lined up around it for as far as the eye could see. Around the space station, flashing words circled it, beckoning. Instantly, even this planet-lubbing Earth kid knew what it was.

"That's no space station. That's a mall."

Guiding the Havok towards it, this vibrant spinning carnival made the North Platte Mall look like a tiny cow turd in comparison. And even if he probably couldn't buy anything, he'd be more than happy to window- (or holo-) shop. Maybe he'd even make some new friends, especially since it was a mall and that meant there had to be other kids there.

'Course they'll probably think I'm a total dork, he fretted. *But who cares? Getting made fun of would at least be dealing with someone somewhere.*

As he drifted up to Docking Station 19631123.5 as instructed, Quentin bounced in his seat, ecstatic to soon be in the presence of people again. He even pulled on his fingerless gloves, thinking they'd make him look so cool everyone would want to be his friend and help him. But it wasn't to be.

For just as the final docking mech-locks were set to bring him in, the mall's scanners swept over the whole ship. After a few seconds, the mech-locks retreated back into the dock, leaving the Havok awkwardly waiting in limbo for a hug that would never come. The comm beeped and seconds later a crisp nasal voice spoke haughtily:

"Your admittance declined. Reasoning forthgo: Funding inadequate and unknown specied status."

Quentin was rejected. Rejected by a voice that sounded like every snotty rich kid everywhere filled with an inappropriate sense of power and entitlement. A voice filled with disdain and smugness wrapped in one crappy package.

The Havok's pilot leaned back and sighed defeatedly. Staring at the dock in front of him, so close, yet so denied, he wished that the joystick had a trigger that would . . . Suddenly, a small flashing blue button sprang out of the top of the joystick! The light twinkled and begged him to press it. His finger slowly descended through the thick air towards it, unsure what would happen.

"No, you snotty little crapball," Quentin muttered,

"I'm gonna *decline* you!"

And before reason fully kicked back in, he accidentally fired. If he waited three more seconds, he wouldn't have. He'd have realized a series of things: First, that it's stupid to blow things up solely because they won't let you in. Second, that what he was shooting at probably didn't even house the jerk he wanted to hurt. (Which was correct, as the snotty kid was in a different solar system altogether, working to save up for a moon-wrecker.) And finally, Quentin McFury would have realized that while no good deed goes unpunished, every bad, rash, stupid deed reaps harsh punishments.

The blasts the Havok shot out weren't much. Just enough to cause a kerfuffle. The short flurry of low-energy laser bursts ripped up the cylindrical docking bridge, sending sparks and debris everywhere. When it cleared, the dock wasn't in great shape, but it was the space equivalent of a minor fender bender. Nothing too bad.

Still, gargantuan intergalactic malls do not like to be shot at. And so when Quentin heard a thump on the hull and spotted a chubby blue-starred fighter in the distance rapidly tearing towards him, he hit the thrusters and flew out of there as fast as he could. Luckily the mall's security response was limited to this one patrol ship as the rest of the mall's security force was dealing with a Level 3 break-in at the Clone-a-Bear shop.

As the Havok flew off, leaving the mall's patrol ship in his space dust, Quentin made the wise decision to never come back to this mall again.

". . . Sternsogg Brihol, wanted by Sigowev Planet Sheriffs, double violent and flees with wreckage-strewn . . ." a stern genderless voice on the scanner said.

Two weeks after his mall experience, Quentin rested his arms on the console and gazed out into space. The radio scanner played in the background, randomly cycling through broadcast conversations, newscasts, warnings, and weather reports. He liked how it jumped from one transmission to the next, giving him another taste of a universe he never knew existed.

This would then segue into thoughts of how small he really was in the scheme of things and how small and insignificant he always would be. Out here in the middle of the universe (well not so much the "middle" as infinite doesn't really have a middle), Quentin considered himself a flying infinitesimal ant. But be the right ant at the wrong time and you can change everything, whether you want to or not.

". . . Eclipse mounting on the third tier revolution provide the rampant fireworks of visual stunningness to . . ." a new voice said along with screeching music.

While staring at the console, Quentin felt a certain malaise as he wearily picked at a button that read "Rip Thrust". And although he could now read the buttons' functions, they still didn't make much sense to him. Using his fingernail, he tried to scrape off the bumpy words. But the words weren't there really. The languo-upgrade took those unreadable squiggles and translated them visually into your language as very teeny-tiny raised text. Consequently, with nothing solid to peel off, his fingernail just kept squeaking across the button. And he didn't care. He could probably do this for an hour. Maybe longer if he really fazed out.

Behind him, a conversation played in the background, talking about boring things with boring words and boring attitudes. As his eyes fluttered, bored by the boring boringness of bore, his ears perked up slightly.

"All of them?" a gruff female voice asked.

"And still but one," a male voice said, clearly someone seeking her approval. "Near onto all."

"And Earth?" the female voice asked.

Shooting out of his seat, Quentin frantically stumbled to the scanner, pressing his ear to it. He wanted to absorb every word of what followed after the explosion of that word: Earth! His eyes opened wide in case something might actually burst out of the scanner. But nothing did. All that came out was a sigh and the male voice saying:

"It is done."

"Good. Now, I want all to—" the female voice said before the scanner then continued its random jump to another signal.

"ANIMAL PLUCKING OF SIZES, COLORS, AND KINDS, ONLY SOULISTICO'S," an annoying salesman bellowed.

"Noooooooooooooooooo!!!" Quentin cried out.

Desperately trying to find the previous channel, his mind raced: *Maybe there are others like me out there! Maybe they know what happened! Other people . . . Or maybe they're the ones who did whatever happened to Earth . . . everyone . . . my parents . . . Mom . . . Dad. . . If they're even alive . . . I need to find those people talking again and . . .*

It had been so long without hearing that word. Earth. Almost a year. As he desperately scanned from one transmission to another, Quentin's eyes watered in frustration. He wasn't even sure if the signal was even still up for him to grab on to. That conversation could be done and gone. But that didn't stop him. And as the hours dragged on and the scanner went from one wrong signal to another, Quentin began to question whether he heard the word at all. Maybe someone said: "Trearth" or "Girth" or "A'erth" or something else entirely like "pickle" and his mind turned "pickle" into "Earth". Maybe . . .

But as he continued his fruitless search, Quentin found sparks of something he forgot. A spark of recognition of where he came from. A spark of hope that he could find his people and find out what happened to them. But moreover, a spark of fight. He wasn't going to just sit back and avoid everything. Since the mall incident, he'd avoided several planets with life on them. Not anymore. Now, he was going to jump into this universe feet first and let the cards fall where they may.

Unfortunately, before he could become Earth's first interplanetary ambassador, three Strikers zipped towards him with terrifying haste, with a squadron following close behind. The sound of the scanner cycling through signals muted a beep that had been echoing. A red-lighted switch flashed above his head and he eyed it strangely. He'd never seen that one before. Hitting it, a crackle snapped over the speakers and the confident, steely voice of a Striker pilot boomed down, haughty and bullying:

"Shut systems down, twarpo, and capture prepare!"

Quentin quaked hearing those words. He'd never been pulled over by a cop before and this felt like a more ominous version of that. If he'd known how destructive the Strikers could be, he'd realize it was a much, much, much, MUCH more ominous version of that.

"Look, I'm sorry about your stupid mall," he said into the comm.

"Shut systems down, twarpo, and capture prepare now!" the Striker repeated.

After recently hearing his planet's name, in addition to not sleeping right for days, Quentin wasn't in the mood to roll over for the first bully in his path. While his belly may have been empty of food, it was full of anger. So Quentin hit the red button and responded:

"Or . . ."

It was a simple question. It had a simple answer. The Striker Leader said:

"Or blow your ship millions of the pieces and pick you parts out for dessert."

Quentin could tell the Striker Leader (aka Bripsy) was grinning maliciously, fully assured that this kid would give up, weeping buckets all the way. And if it was the day before, good old Bripsy would have been right. But not today.

"Well, then I guess you better kiss my – ," Quentin hit the afterburners and tore away speedily.

But the Strikers were on him faster than he could have ever imagined and fired several rapid bursts of warning shots. Then, the comparatively friendly laserfire soon grew to explosions that ferociously rattled the ship.

"Be grateful we hold back," the Striker Leader said. "Now give or be frittered!"

"Yeah, I'm grateful," muttered Quentin. "Grateful not to be dead. Grateful not to be blown into 93,573 pieces. Not yet anyway."

ShrrrrrrrrrrrRRRRAAKKKKKKKKKK!!!

Explosions rocked the ship, but the battered Havok held together barely . . . just barely. Grabbing the stick, Quentin pulled up on it with all his might, until his muscles shook and stretched so much he worried they might snap. His once thin, finger-sized fingers turned red, squeezed out like plump sausages from his "driving gloves".

"I am *NOT* going to die today," he growled.

KrrrrrrRRZZZZZZZZZzzzshhHTTTT!!!

"Ooookay, I might totally die today . . ."

And as you've heard this part before, let's catch back up to Quentin and Trinta as they . . .

CHAPTER FIFTEEN
THE CHEEVE RISES TO THE TOP

When the sheet of metal crashed to the floor, Quentin froze, not moving one single muscle. He'd like to think he did so consciously. Not to give away his position. (Well, not anymore than his baby opossum scream already did.) And, speaking of opossums, not moving *was* the smartest move. But he didn't plan to do that. He wasn't thinking anything more than: *Holy shirt!*

The bulky outline of an immense figure entered the box with two small green circles lit up where eyes would be. Slowly, the green glowing eyes scanned across the darkened room.

Staying statue still, Quentin glanced over to where Trinta stood only moments ago . . . and saw nothing. Granted, it was dark, but it wasn't *that* dark. She was gone. Standing out in the open like a neon pink giraffe in a hockey rink, the green eyes settled menacingly on

Quentin. He tried not to blink . . . not to breathe . . . not to think.

"I know you're there," the shadowed figure grumbled gravelly.

Quentin didn't say anything. He hoped the man would lose interest and . . .

"I see you right there, boy. Nice strands on top."

In the dark doubly so, the Earther scrunched up his face, more confused than ever.

"Ya got good hair," the man said in response to the boy's expression. "Now, you all alone?"

"Uh . . . yeah. I think so."

"You 'think' so?" the man scoffed. "That means you're not, lil' boy."

"Uh . . . no. I just . . . um . . . I thought that since *you're* here . . . and *I'm* here . . . then I'm not really alone, am I?" blustered Quentin, convincing no one. He tried to change the subject and go on the offensive: "But who cares who I am? Just who the hell are *you*, chock-a-block?!"

"I'm Cheeve," Cheeve sneered menacingly. "And me telling you my name should do you two things. First, it should make us feel all friendly-like. And second, it should scare enough hell out of you to realize anybody so free with his name must fear nothing or have some 'plans' for ya. Or maybe a lil' of both," Cheeve chuckled while lumbering over to him.

Thoroughly unsettled, Quentin kept doing nothing. He didn't know where he'd run to if he tried. Maybe into the ship? Maybe grab the frict-bike and jump out the hole before the huge intruder could grab him? Maybe he could scream for Trinta?

In the end, he did nothing. It seemed safer that way.

Trinta, however, was a little more proactive. That's why she disappeared before Cheeve stepped inside the container. It's not just that she was quicker than Quentin, but also quicker-witted. If he had lived her harried life up 'til now, maybe he'd be faster on the uptake, too.

So as Quentin and Cheeve continued their chat outside, Trinta fruitlessly sought something that would help them out of their current predicament. A weapon would be nice. But she wasn't gonna be picky.

"I imagine your friend is looking for something to take Cheeve out with," Cheeve said casually. "But I wouldn't advise that. For two reasons: First, you don't have anything in that gut-wreck ship that'd hurt anyone. The fraktor you have needs a new pulson says my scans. And second, the element of 'surprise' is real lost on me at the moment. So why don't she be a good girl and come on out here with the rest of us?"

"You really dig lists, don't you?" Quentin asked.

"Wrong question, kid. You should have asked – 'Her who?' Then you could have kept the useless '*I'm alone*' sham going for another thirty seconds. It wouldn'ta helped but you may have earned a little more respect with the lady."

Trinta hit the lights and walked down the ramp with a scowl just for Quentin.

"See what I mean?" Cheeve said. "She looks pretty peevy with you."

"Don't know why," Quentin muttered. "*She* broke the gun." His eyes darted down to avoid Trinta's icy glare.

The "room" now well lit, Cheeve took off the two green glowing monocles that allowed him to see in the dark and dropped them in his shirt pocket, keeping both eyes focused on Trinta.

"Nice long gal, you are," Cheeve said salaciously. "Very long . . ."

Quentin and Trinta's first real look at Cheeve told them what they already suspected. He was dodgy. A massive, chunky humanoid with long orange and black hair with patches missing, to Quentin he looked like the mutant hybrid of a past-his-prime heavy metal rocker and a Jack O'Lantern.

Wearing a long yellow jumpsuit that fit around his absurd bulginess (small thighs but ginormous calves, thin upper arms but huge lower arms), Cheeve oozed skeevy danger, the kind of danger that implied death plus infection. A danger only intensified by a series of disturbing instruments hung from his tool belt, each tool splattered with dried blood.

"So, kids, ya might have some explaining ahead of yas," said Cheeve.

"Explaining to whom?" Trinta cocked her head with a steely-eyed glare.

"You heard before. Me. *Cheeve.* Don't pretend like you no hear. I don't like pretending."

"Who cares what you like or don't like?" she scoffed.

"I like her," Cheeve snickered in the boy's ear.

"Don't care," Trinta said. "Now, *Cheeeeeeeve,* who are you and why should we care? Give me a reason not to end your smarmy chatter right now."

The hulking Cheeve smirked. He smirked so tight

his lips might twang if you touched them. He stared at her for a moment before answering. In that moment, he licked his lips and flared his nostrils ever-so-discreetly, successfully making an enormously intimidating impression.

"I'm Cheeve Mamis. I run the security ops here on Jebel."

Quentin almost said something terribly unbrave like "Oh, shirt" but held back. He was slowly learning that saying nothing often beat saying anything that could be used against you.

Still, despite his advancements in discretion, hope drained from the young McFury, being as he was trapped here in the storage box with the head security guy for the whole planet and no weapons and no plan and no nothing. He bounced ideas around his head, trying to come up with a scheme that'd not only insure their escape, but also impress Trinta, his eye not entirely on the ball.

"So, who are *you*, Thricer?" Cheeve asked Trinta.

Hearing that word, she gave a slivered shiver of a wince.

"Don't see too many Thricers around much anymore. Wonder why . . . Oh, that's right. You . . ."

"Say, Cheeve," she said, cutting him off. "If you're in charge of security, why'd you come in here alone? I know loads about security set-ups. Enough to fill a whole storage planet ironically enough. And I know of no security – and certainly no *head* of security ops – that'd enter a breached box like this without backup. Especially with suspected irritants inside. That's just industry standard. So, where's your backup, Cheeve?"

The hulking Cheeve nodded, impressed. He motioned for her to continue.

"So either you're not what you say you are . . ." she said.

"Wrong."

"Or you *are* what you say you are, but you aren't as – let's use the word – 'respectable' as you should be."

"She's good," Cheeve fake whispered to Quentin. "Don't ever let this one go."

"We're not actually . . . uh . . ." Quentin said, trying for no clear reason to explain the non-relationship he had with Trinta.

"Yeah, I *know*, big fella," said Cheeve sarcastically. "She's beyond your wildest dreams and your even wilder reality. But that's beside the point. I'm not here to lecture blotchy boys on how they can't get gorgeous gals. That's not my role. That's the role of . . . life. Cheeve's here in the here and now for the opportunity. And if I can't find opportunity, I make some."

He stepped towards them. Not in an overtly threatening way. But when that husky mass moved, implied threats followed.

Instinctively, Quentin stepped back without knowing it. Trinta did not. Trinta didn't even blink. She knew you couldn't let your eyes off this behemoth for a millisecond. Even a blink could give this monster enough edge to do whatever damage he wanted.

"Sit back. No need to worry, kids. Cheeve likes ya. Likes ya both."

"Great," said Trinta flatly. "Now I'm not worried . . . at . . . all."

Mustering up courage, Quentin asked, "So what can

we do you for, Cheeve?"

"Do me for?" Cheeve smirked. "Excellent question. He's so helpful. Cheeve wants everything of worth from your 'ship'. You can keep the 'ship' and do whatever you want with it. But you got anything of value, that's mine. No questions."

"And why is that?" Trinta asked. "Because you're 'security'?"

"No, because Cheeve says so. And Cheeve said no questions."

"And what if we go to your bosses and tell them you're stealing from us?" Quentin dared.

"Oh, no!" shouted Cheeve, feigning fear. "Don't tell on me! Please don't tell on Cheeve! Cheeve be good now! Cheeve run away so frightened! Don't be bad to Cheeve!" Switching quickly, his eyes narrowed with a ferocious glimmer and he spat out: "My 'bosses' do not care. And even if they did – even if they really, really did – *Cheeve* would not care. And that little fact – you know, the one about *Cheeve* not caring – yes, that should make *you* care. Care enough to not piss me – that is, Cheeve – off." Clapping his hands, he then said merrily: "Now, let's see what you've got for Cheeve."

He barged up the ramp, a moving mountain of malice that knocked the two shipmates off their feet.

After giving each other matching "What-do-we-do-now?" looks, Quentin and Trinta shrugged and trailed after the gargantuan beast barreling through their ship.

A moderately-sized science freighter, the Havok wasn't designed for carrying gigantic loads from one system to another. What it was good for was carrying and protecting small yet important shipments of a scientific nature. Built specifically by the Edbu brothers to sustain all kinds of damage while protecting its highly prized (and sometimes unstable) contents from all ravages, the Havok helped keep precious cargo stay precious. And the precious cargo came in all sizes and in all places.

You just had to know where to look. And Cheeve liked to look.

"*Gibbidida, bop-gode-keijaimagiddidie wilwhee-bop-bop booooo*," Cheeve sang while skipping along the corridor.

As he clunkily flitted down the hallway, his long, disgusting fingernails clicked along each wall, plucking out panels. The panels fell to the floor like wind chimes clattering to the ground. And behind each panel was . . . nothing.

Usually, these cupboards would not be laid bare. They'd be overflowing with vials and tubes of harvested eggs, molds, amoeba, and all sorts of other living materials. Or drugs – experimental or not so much. Or quasi-tronic life-forms – tiny and pure, waiting to be freed into expectant (or unexpectant) worlds.

So the fact that there was nothing – ABSOLUTELY NOTHING! – for Cheeve . . . Nothing after nothing after nothing . . . Clang upon clang upon clang on the metal grated floors . . . This unleashed a volcano of rage and bile, threatening to consume them all.

"Joke or trick or lie or scam or . . ." Cheeve muttered incoherently.

At the end of the corridor as his tantrum bubbled forth, Quentin and Trinta watched transfixed. At first, it was entertaining (not to mention surprising as Quentin never knew those cupboards even existed). And then it went from "entertaining" to "kinda hilarious" as Cheeve turned redder and redder. Undoing the last several cupboards – each as empty as the last – his irritation blossomed to explosive annoyance. And after the last cupboard mocked him with its barrenness, Cheeve had had enough.

"Looks like the kiddie Easter egg hunt ain't goin' so well," Quentin whispered to Trinta, who got enough of the gist to snicker.

When Cheeve first found the Havok in the storage box, he was understandably surprised. He didn't expect to find a sci-freighter in there. And when he detected someone had already broken into that container, he salivated. Hearing the racket inside only whet his considerable appetite further, knowing that someone had done his hard work for him.

All he'd have to do is snatch the sparkly bits and baubles of technoscience waiting for him and cash in. ('Course he'd have to get rid of his thieving precursors somehow. Usually stating his official security role on the planet worked wonders, leading most would-be thieves to run away scared. But some thieves clung to the age-old rule of "finder's keepers". And in those situations, Cheeve gleefully loved dissuading these people of their beliefs with sickening mayhem and violence.)

"Absolutely NOTHING?!!" Cheeve screamed, his gargantuan back to both Trinta and Quentin. "I didn't expect much on a sci-freighter like this. But I expected something. *Some* thing. Not a *no*-thing. And a no-thing raises my ears. Because ab . . . so . . . lute . . . ly . . . *no*-thing ain't just suspicious. It's insulting. It's a slap to the face. And my face is so, so sensitive."

Turning, Cheeve sneered at them. His body hunched over in a way Quentin recalled seeing on nature shows. And in those programs, a very large animal with very sharp teeth would hunch just like that right before eviscerating a much smaller, cuter, and cuddlier creature. The Earth kid didn't feel too cute or cuddly, but he knew which animal he was in that analogy, especially when Cheeve stomped down the corridor towards them, snarling viciously.

Quentin closed his eyes right before Trinta stepped in front of him and held out her hand. Surprisingly, Cheeve came to an abrupt halt, his face only inches from her extended palm. His snorting nasal breaths disgustingly steamed her fingertips as though she'd come in from a hot shower.

"This isn't a robbery," said Trinta matter-of-factly. "This is a negotiation."

"Negotiation?" Cheeve said, his lower teeth ferally pulling on his upper lip. "Here's how Cheeve negotiates. You give me stuff, I hurt you only a little bit on my way out. You don't give me stuff, I hurt you a lot before you die."

"You aren't very good at negotiating, are you?" Trinta said. "It's kinda cute. You see, I cleared the whole ship out minutes after I got on this thing."

"Yeah, *when* did you get on my ship?" Quentin questioned, his curiosity trumping his fear of Cheeve for the moment. "And *how'd* you get on my ship, too?"

"Ignoring the runt here," Cheeve said. "You, girl, are

obviously the smart one. Maybe the *too* smart one."

"No, just smart enough," Trinta said.

He didn't have to call me a 'runt', Quentin silently stewed.

"So just so I know," Cheeve said, leaning in to the Thricer, his teeth snapping just a hair's breadth away from her nose. "How much pain do you think it'll take for me to get what I want out of you?"

Trinta half-grinned and cocked her head prior to answering: "None. No pain at all. We work out what I want, this all goes down easy and peasy. You try to pain it out of me, I won't say anything. If you know anything of Thricers, you know that."

"What if I just hurt the runt kid?" Cheeve said, grabbing Quentin and slamming him into the wall.

"Then I watch and have a laugh myself," she said.

"So he's nothing to you?"

"Less than nothing. I jumped his ship for the ship. He's just the monkey that was on it."

"Hey!" Quentin protested weakly.

Neither Trinta nor Cheeve even glanced the boy's way.

Believing she, in fact, didn't care for this "runt", Cheeve threw Quentin harshly to the floor, the boy groaning as he banged down on his elbow. Rubbing this latest injury, he glowered up through his hair at the two "grown-ups" discussing business.

"So what do you want to *negotiate*?" asked Cheeve.

"You seem like a guy who can pick up groceries, right?" Trinta said.

Cheeve nodded and motioned for her to continue.

Trinta said breezily: "I want a phezing engine block,

an oxy-gen 470 filter, and a bar of Greenteal Chocolate."

"Don't want much, do ya?" said Cheeve sarcastically. "And let's say I can make all that happen – which I can – what do I get in return? How do I know you even have anything worth anything?"

"Because a ship like this, an Edbu brothers ship, is never without at least three dozen phester nano-rerriums. And that means a lot of something to anyone who has them. Money, power, etc."

"And you're saying you have three dozen?"

"I'm sayin' nothing until you come back with what I want."

"And why don't I just pain you to see if you'll talk? And then if you don't and die horribly – unfortunately, of course – what's to say I don't tear the ship apart and find what I'm looking for?"

Trinta smiled. A smile so big and so wide that she forcefully informed Cheeve she was in charge and had something over him. Something huge. And that smile drifted across as one part pride, one part hard negotiation, hitting him exactly as she wanted it to.

"Who's to say the stuff's even here?" shrugged Trinta. "I've been down and around. It could be . . . anywhere. It could be in the kid's pockets or it could be down in the mini-park. Nice park, by the way. Very parky. Or it could be two thousand miles to the west in another storage box the size of my thumb."

Right then, Cheeve knew he had very little wiggle room. *You're up on me now*, he bristled. *Only for the now though, Thricer*. Therefore, he decided to get the gal what she wanted. But only because it was what *he* wanted. Because if she had three dozen nano-rerriums, that'd instantly make him a major player in this galaxy. Even three nano-rerriums would change his life for the better forever.

Cheeve nodded and offered her his enlarged elbow.

Trinta hit it with hers and they had a deal.

"Now, don't try and trick me with anything but what I asked for," she said. "You do and you'll never get even a glimpse of what you might have had. Not even a glimpse of a glimpse."

"I'm only partially insulted you'd suggest that," Cheeve said.

"Yeah, and you're partially impressed, too."

Cheeve couldn't help but grin. Turning to leave, he peered down at the kid on the ground and said to Trinta: "Nice pup. Docile and everything. Just hope it's potty-trained."

Cheeve then clomped out of the Havok and down the ramp.

With that huge beast's footsteps drifting away, Quentin stood up haughtily. Before Trinta could say a word, he stormed off into the cargo bay and shut the door with a whoosh. It wasn't a door slam, but it was all he could do under the circumstances. A muffled yell soon followed. He wasn't really hurt or anything. At least not physically. The dent in his pride was pretty huge though. So huge that Quentin yelled again for good measure:

"Arrrrrrrrrrrrrrrrrrggggggggggggggghhhhhhhhhhhh!"

As he left the box to run his errands, Cheeve chuckled to himself, "Kids . . ."

CHAPTER SIXTEEN
BALLS

A little over an hour since Cheeve had gone off to pick up Trinta's "groceries", Quentin still sat and pouted in the cargo hold. He didn't know why she was so mean to him. He knew why Cheeve was. He was just a jerk. But the lovely tall girl's dismissiveness hurt him more than any of that bully's physical abuse.

Well, that's not totally true, the teen thought as he rubbed his bruised elbow.

Before his death-defying adventure with Trinta and the mag-nets not so long ago, the cargo hold resembled a crappy scrap yard. Now, it resembled an even crappier and scrappier junkyard with strewn pieces of sharp metal jutting out and wrecked containers spread everywhere.

Quentin didn't care though. He just sat and pouted, sitting and pouting so much he didn't even notice the cargo hold's new nano-construbot made doors.

"Frakkin' aliens," he muttered.

Grinding his teeth, he parsed over every idiotic thing he said and did during their encounter with Cheeve and beat himself up over it. He desperately wanted to be cool. And he wasn't.

"But what the hell else was I supposed to do?!" he grumbled. "Not like I could beat the dude up. He's, like . . . giant-huge . . . And I don't know what he's looking for. I don't know anything about any of this!"

That was all true. But these facts didn't make him feel any better. Facts always get trumped by emotion. And the emotion he wallowed in was a good old-fashioned dose of teenage humiliation, amped up by looking like a wussy weasel in front of an attractive gal he wanted to impress. Getting tossed to the ground like an unneeded pillow impresses no one.

As he argued with himself, he heard Trinta rummaging about the ship. He wasn't sure what she was doing, but swift metal snapping sounds accompanied whatever it was. *Maybe she's welding or doing something else to make me feel like even less of a man*, he simmered. *Maybe she's killing a robotic octo-boar and cooking it for dinner.*

"I had a chance there," he said as he stood up and paced. "I was almost cool and then I lost it . . . If it wasn't for Cheeve . . . I was totally . . . Freakin' Cheeve!"

Angrily Quentin kicked a small metal cube. His foot bounced off of it with such a speedy recoil that his instantaneous shriek startled even himself. Falling to the ground, he grabbed his foot in pain, sure that he must have shattered his pinky toe.

"Don't kick metal things, you dork-nozzle!" he

yelled.

A head appeared in the window of the cargo bay's door for a second, but it promptly moved on. Probably Trinta checking on the scream and then laughing at him. *Everybody's laughing at me,* he seethed. *Same as always . . .*

Gingerly, he rested his throbbing foot up on a shopping cart. Head hung low, he peaked from out of his fallen hair to see something he'd never noticed before. Colors. Balls. A bunch of vibrantly colored balls. All sizes. All kinds.

The cargo bay was a room filled with dark grays and blacks and a few shades in-between. What the room didn't really have much of was color. So when he spied a whole host of colors in the corner, he couldn't help but be a little curious. Raising his eyebrows inquisitively, he limped over to the balls. (Honestly, he felt the pain in his toe wasn't as bad as he originally thought, but liked the limp for the drama of it all.)

"So let's give *these* a kick then," he said with a sly grin.

It had been a year since he kicked a soccer ball. He missed soccer. He missed running down the field, dribbling the ball (even if poorly), and kicking it on to a teammate. He liked his team and the idea of team. A group of guys working towards a common – if sometimes literal – goal. And for the duration of any game, they were all there for each other. They experienced every win (not very many as they were pretty horrible) and every loss (very many but each accepted with proper humor and bitterness) together.

Even though outside of the games and practices nobody hung out with Quentin (and he never really wanted to hang out with them), his teammates were something akin to friends (or brothers) when they were on the pitch.

One of Quentin's proudest moments happened when he drilled an opposing forward who pushed his teammate Jaime Alejandre down. Jaime wasn't the biggest of guys, so it didn't take much. But when that Norfolk forward gave Jaime an elbow as he dribbled past, knocking Jaime to the grass, Quentin instinctively punched the forward in the chest with both fists, laying the dude out instantly. The red card that followed was worth it.

Jaime wasn't hurt bad, but the team loved their mouthy, quick defender for that one act. They even cheered Quentin hoarse when they got back to the locker room after the 5-0 loss. On the bus back to North Platte, they celebrated and patted him on the back like they had actually won. Even Coach Daniels gave him a serious nod that signified, "*Well done, son.*"

Of course, after that, the most popular guys on the squad still ignored him when they passed him in the halls. Quentin harbored no ill will towards them. It was high school. That's all. Just high school. And even now, he sadly missed even those jerks.

When he drew his foot back to kick those balls all across the cargo bay, Quentin hoped with childish glee he'd see a brilliant display of ricocheting rainbows.

"Rrrrraaaaaaaaarrrrrrrrrrrrrrr!" he growled.

But when Quentin booted those hundreds of balls of

various shapes and sizes with every bit of force he could muster, the balls did not fly all around the room. Instead, they reacted far differently than what his foot expected. They just slunked up in the air a few inches as one connected collective group of balls before limply falling right back down. Not an impressive bouncing ball fiesta. Not at all. Thankfully, the balls didn't cause Quentin's foot any more pain as they draped themselves around his foot like a wet blanket.

"What the . . ."

He stared at the balls pretty vexed. A square metal box with a smashed up corner where the "balls" must have spilled out of caught his eye but gave him no answers. As Quentin grabbed the orbs, they all clung together, as if connected by tiny invisible threads.

"Maybe it's one of those weird beaded hippie doorways," he said. "I can hang it in the cockpit and everything'll be real groovy."

Feeling the orbs radiating warmth, Quentin suspected it had to be more than a beaded curtain. He moved them all together into one giant ball of balls and dropped it, hoping that it might bounce a little. It did not.

These balls are officially not meant for any sort of fun, Quentin fumed. *Like everything else on this ship, they're here to annoy me and make me look stupid. That's it. Nothing more. Nothing less.*

That's what he thought until he noticed a tiny black ball in the middle of the pile. No bigger than a golf ball, it stood out amongst the dozens of red, green, blue, yellow, orange, purple, and other colored orbs. But *that* was the only black one.

Before he realized it, he reached in and touched the black ball. Instantly, he regretted it. Regretted it big time. The ball immediately fused with his finger and he couldn't pull himself away from it. At first, it was mildly amusing.

"C'mon!" he said as he lifted his finger up and the long clump of balls followed it. "Ha, ha . . . funny. Now, c'mon . . . C'mon, c'mon, c'mon . . ." He tried to pry the ball off with his other hand, but the balls weren't going anywhere.

After a few seconds, things got very interesting. Very interesting indeed. All of the balls lit up. First very dimly and barely even perceptible. (In fact, Quentin wouldn't have noticed if he hadn't had them all right next to his face trying to see what the hell his finger was sticking to and how it was sticking.) The balls started glowing brighter and brighter, radiating more and more heat as they did. Not hot enough to hurt, but enough to scare the enchiladas out of Quentin.

"Uh, Trinta?" he called softly.

He wasn't sure he really wanted her to hear him, hence his putting out that small call of her name. Just in case she was passing by and might want to step in to check in on him. She wasn't "passing by" though and the balls surrounding the little black one began to grow smaller, then bigger. They then wrapped themselves around his hand and up his forearm like a freakish, undulating glove. The rest of the balls hung off like a bunch of heavy strange grapes, grapes Quentin had no desire to eat now or ever.

"Trinta!"

Now he yelled, *definitely* hoping she'd hear and help

him out of this mess.

"Trinta! Please! Trinta! Help, please!!! Trinta!!! TRINTAAAAA!!!"

But she didn't hear him. She was having problems of her own.

Trinta didn't have anything to offer Cheeve. (Not really anyway. Not anything she was going to give up for him unless she absolutely had to.) She knew the kind of things he'd be expecting and she knew they didn't have any of that. No nano-rerriums . . . No weaponized culture cultures . . . Nothing worth anything at all. She knew because she had had the same disappointment when she first arrived on the Havok.

Searching the ship for treasure was one of the first things she did after leaping onboard with her frict-bike back at that mall. She didn't scour the ship for science treasure necessarily to steal it, but she did like to know everything about a ship for the sole purpose of knowing how it could help her in a jam. And this wasn't just a jam, this was a jam with peanut butter and dog hair.

The one thing that helped her in this mess were the facts. The fact that a ship like this should absolutely have what she said it did made her bluff beyond believable. It'd be unthinkable that it'd be empty, especially as whenever a ship such as this dropped off a series of items, it almost always picked up another set in return. Such ships were never ever empty. But this one was. No sign of anything worth anything. And not only was that weird. It was troubling.

Trinta wondered for a half second if maybe Quentin was putting on an act. Maybe he wasn't an Earther or as fresh into the universe as he seemed. Maybe he was some kind of trickster supergenius. *If he's playing me*, she thought, *then fair play to him. He deserves whatever he scams out of me, Cheeve, whoever*. But she knew in the end, he wasn't anything but what he was – a kid. Which left them in the same predicament as before with nothing to give to Cheeve when he returned.

She considered telling him that she hid some weaponized f-cells in the museum, but that idea lasted only so long as it took for her to realize he wouldn't go without taking one of them with him. And that person would die when Cheeve didn't find what wasn't there to be found. Then that enraged muscled psychopath would come back and take out a little more aggro on whoever was left. Sad that that was the best-case scenario.

Trinta had to think and think quick. But nothing was coming up. The more she struggled to plot and scheme, the tighter her brain centered around the pessimism that they were toast.

So Trinta searched for a smaller task to take her mind off the overwhelmingly mind-crushing dilemma. This was done with the hope that such mental chicanery might shake loose a butt-saving idea. And the first thing Trinta saw was a host of cupboard doors littering the corridor where Cheeve left them.

Click, snap. Click, snap. Click, snap. The panels went back up one-by-one as Trinta gave herself in to the task. Tried to push Cheeve, Quentin, the still broken Havok, and everything else out of her mind. Like doing dishes after dinner, she fazed out. Occasionally, as fingers nimbly picked up the panels and snapped them back into place, her mind would drift. Images, thoughts, sounds, smells . . . all would flash across her mind and then off again.

The raining people of the 3G&B. Click, snap. *Violet grass floating above an auburn sea.* Click, snap. *The lilting hum of a jarred engine rebooting.* Click, snap. *Spinning lighted pinwheels, thousands of them.* Click, snap. *Quentin's goofy grin.* Click, snap. *The crackle of a ship passing through the rings of Biwhi.* Click, snap. *An oval green house on a dark red cliff.* Click, snap. *Yellow lines.* Click, snap. *Fingers twisting around a bottle, then drinking. Drinking deep.* Click, snap. *Father.* Click, snap. *Billions of people in a fixed silent scream forever.* Click, snap. *A small burgledog, wings flapping in the air. Cuter than cute.* Click, snap. *Cheeve's snarling mouth overflowing with mismatched moldy teeth.* Click, snap. *A small azure-jeweled box, resting on a shiny black table . . . waiting to be opened.* Click, snap. *The small azure-jeweled box . . . her purple fingers delicately pulling the top off . . . seeing inside a . . .*

"Uh, Trinta . . ."

Hearing her name in the distance faintly, Trinta snapped out of her stupor and let out a sigh for missing out on an idea so close she could almost grab it. Regardless, she figured she oughta check on the pouty little Earther, just in case he had his head caught in a grate somewhere.

But just as she started towards the cargo bay, she heard a clanging outside the Havok. It was their "door" being shut back up. Cheeve had returned. Earlier than

Trinta ever anticipated. That didn't bode well. But not much did lately. All boding was bad any more. That's why Trinta didn't like boding. Didn't like it all.

"Oh, sweet kiddies, papa's home!" Cheeve shouted. "Dinnertime!"

His last syllable rattled through the Havok like a feral mouse looking for rancid cheese. And Trinta still didn't have any bright ideas. Didn't have any dim ideas either. She only had the ol' standby: some unnecessary violence that hopefully she'd be on the winning side of.

Provided Cheeve brought the phezing engine block, everything else they could make do. If he had that, she could toss the block to the Earther while she did the heavy lifting of close quarters combat. Then maybe the floppy-haired boy could surprise her and put them in a position to run away before she got her butt too kicked. Or maybe she'd be able to take out Cheeve and none of this would be an issue. Maybe.

Heading down the corridor to get to Cheeve before he got too ornery, she heard Quentin holler for her. *He can deal,* she thought. *He's a big boy.* She glanced in the cargo bay window briefly and continued on towards Cheeve.

"Hope I keep all my teeth," she muttered as she trotted down the ramp.

Seeing her, Cheeve smiled. It wasn't a warm smile. It was a smile that made her question everything: *Should I be doing this? How'd I get here? Can't I just leave him with the Earther and make a run for it? What if I die?* In the end, she trampled down those fears, those questions to her dignity and honor. And just when she was about to see how much bullshirt (as her Earther boy might say) she could drag Cheeve through, she went sprawling to the floor, reeling from a vicious punch to the face.

"I got the stuff *you* want, girl," Cheeve said. "Let that be a taste of what you'll have more of if you don't have what *Cheeve* wants."

Trinta always believed there were two ways to fight. One way involved being reserved, calm. It was a way of fighting that kept emotion bottled and was purely about tactics. An uppercut to scatter the brain. A sweep of the legs to slow the opponent down. A two-finger punch to the ribs to give a taste of the pain buffet coming if the person didn't relent. She felt a reasoned, emotionless fighting style can sometimes be exactly the right thing at the right time for everyone. It made sure no one got too maimed or killed. (Which every person with even half a soul, including the Halfsouls of the Penerl System, could agree on.)

But when a fighter chose emotion for the reserve to draw upon (specifically anger, hate, frustration), that fighter had the power to make extremely bad things happen. In the right hands – in *her* hands – they became the fuel to a fair fight when otherwise she might be beaten into a purple pulp. So, when Cheeve dropped her with his hello punch, he gave Trinta the biggest gift possible. And it only got better as, head down, she spotted the phezing engine block, the oxygen 470 filter, and the bar of chocolate next to Cheeve's boots. He actually brought what she asked for. Wiping the blood from her cut lip with her sleeve, Trinta nodded to herself confidently.

"Get up, girl," Cheeve said. "Don't make me play

kickbody."

Trinta had disliked Cheeve from moment one. But in the last minute he went from "disliked" to "hated" and this made her grin mischievously.

As she stood up and locked eyes with him, Cheeve felt the tiniest of shivers in his grotesquely enlarged and mottled spine. He didn't know what the shivers meant. Trinta did though. It meant even though she might get her butt kicked, she wasn't going to get it kicked without kicking some of her own. Her eyes even lit up as she realized her chances of making it out of this had grown to a solid 13.1%.

And that was all she needed.

CHAPTER SEVENTEEN
KNOCKING OVER BLOCKS

"Hello," the strange figure of multi-colored, multi-sized balls said.

Quentin didn't know how to respond. Usually when he'd receive such a friendly greeting, he'd say "Hello" back. Or sometimes "Hi", "Hey", or "Howdy". Or if he was feeling particularly crazy: "What's shakin'?" But never in his sixteen years had he been granted such a salutation by a bunch of balls. He wasn't prepared for it. Not one bit.

"Hey . . . uh," he stammered. "What's shakin'?"

"Not much," the balls said. "You know."

Detaching from the Earth boy, the balls reformulated themselves and assumed a humanoid shape, essentially mirroring Quentin, only several inches shorter. At the top sat a head of clustered green balls with two white ones where the eyes would be. At the mouth, a series of small red balls came together and created an eerie rictus grin. The torso gelled together with larger orbs, all of an orangish hue, while the arms (green like his face) jutted out with nimble little hands of smaller finger balls at the end. For legs, two long trunks of sparkling globes the size of pool balls stretched out, ending with feet made of two large spheres at the front and two smaller ones at the back. Every once in awhile the balls would swivel around and change color, giving the figure a constant sense of flux.

"I'm Quentin," said Quentin.

"I know," the figure said. "I'm Roddy Gabb."

"Uh . . . hey ya, Roddy . . . Gabb, is it?"

"Yes. Roddy Gabb."

"And who . . . uh, what . . . uh . . . yeah . . . um . . . uh, I . . . hurm . . ." Quentin stammered. He didn't know what this . . . thing was and he was damn curious. But he didn't want to offend him (or her or it). This was a first impression he was dealing with! Thankfully, Roddy understood where he was going and took care of his questions for him.

"I'm Roddy Gabb. I'm a viadroid, here to be adjacent to your life."

The kid from Nebraska raised his eyebrows. He was pleased. Very pleased. Because if he understood Roddy right, he was saying—

"So, you're like my robot?" Quentin asked eagerly.

"I don't know if I agree with the 'ownership' angle, but yes, I am here to assist you on a daily basis."

"That sounds . . ."

"And I wouldn't say that I'm a 'robot', just to clarify," Roddy interrupted, slightly irritated. "I am a viadroid. And I'm not even sure that really defines who I am as a person."

"A 'person'? But you're not really . . ."

"I just want you to know that, first off, I'm not what *you* say I am. I'm what *I* say I am. And to say I'm just a 'this' or a 'that' is not cool. You know that."

"Oh . . . I see. So you have like an artificial intelligence and – "

Roddy cut him off again: "'*Artificial*'?! I have an intelligence. There's nothing 'artificial' about it. Was I generated by another being? Yes. Was I brought into this universe in the same manner as you? No, and thankfully not. That'd be unimaginably gross. So let's just all be cool and say we're all equal. We're all just people tryin' to get by."

Quentin was flummoxed. Absolutely flummoxed.

"It's like the first day of school, Quentin," Roddy added. "This is us just meeting. So let's simply feel each other out and learn a little about each other. It's like in second grade when you threw up on Gigi Johnston. We don't want to start off that way, do we?"

"Wha—" Quentin spluttered out. "How do you . . . How do you . . . ."

"How do I what?"

"Know . . . know about . . . *that*? There's no way you could . . . know . . . know that. Unless everyone's been watching my life from space or something." Quentin gasped, horrified at *that* possibility. "Everybody hasn't been watching me from space, have they? They haven't seen everything I've ever done, have they?!"

Cocking his head curiously, Roddy said, "Uh . . . no."

"Or . . . or when you glommed onto my hand . . . you didn't suck all my memories and stuff into you, did you?" said Quentin.

Roddy nodded, respecting the Earther's intelligence for adding up what happened.

"Why'd you do that?!" Quentin barked. "Why'd you take my memories like that? That's not cool."

"You didn't tell me not to."

"How was I supposed to do that? You just jumped up and started humping my arm."

"Didn't you read the manual?"

"What manual?"

"You should have just thought to shut off the memory upload."

"Well, I didn't know that! I thought you were a bunch of balls! You have all my memories now, so *you* gotta know I'd have no idea!" He paused and took a deep breath before continuing: "So you know *everything*?"

"About you? Yes."

They eyed each other awkwardly for a moment. Roddy shrugged.

"I don't judge."

"Of course. Because you're a robot."

"No. *I* just don't judge."

"Oh."

Silence. Good ol' awkward silence. Nothing like a boy and a robot, not making eye contact with nothing more to say.

Outside the ship, Trinta crouched smiling a bloody smile, eager to show Cheeve the power of not pissing someone off can sometimes be the difference between a win and a loss.

Glaring at him first, she then looked past him, towards the container's opening. Outside, day began to break and the shimmering dust swirled around in the crosswinds the long tunnels the blocks of skyscraping boxes created. That opening would now serve as the goal in a new game Trinta called: *Push the Big Cheeve Through the Tiny Hole.*

"So I see you got what I wanted," she said.

"Yeah. Yeah, I did. Now, where's my end of the deal?"

"First, I want to see that you didn't get me anything cut-rate. You're making out like a bandit here and you know it."

"I know nothing, girl," Cheeve snarled. "I don't know that you don't have nothing at all. And only because I knew three towers down had all the engine materials Cheeve could want and seven blocks up had an oxy-gen filter and that I always keep some chocolate on me are the only reasons I agreed to your deal. I did it because it could be done with little Cheeve sweat. But I'm ready to sweat if you want me to. Very ready."

The grotesque man talking about his sweat sickened even Trinta's strong stomach.

"Can I take a look?" she asked coolly. "Not at your sweat – my groceries."

He gave her a look that questioned her questioning his integrity. After a moment, he reluctantly gestured for her to inspect his wares with a "Pfft" of disbelief.

Her lip still smarting, she strode past Cheeve – already smelling plenty sweaty despite what he said. She surveyed the items. Everything was there. Not in great shape, but they were what she asked for. She didn't specifically ask that they all be new or clean (or not partially eaten), so she shouldn't really complain. But she did anyway.

"The chocolate has a bite out of it," she said.

"Right now, you're lucky *you* don't have a bite out of ya. Now, where's my stuff?"

With this question, she had the perfect opportunity for a clever rejoinder prior to taking a swing at him. But she didn't want to give up a three second advantage just to appear clever. Instead, she wanted to surprise him with a punch to the face that would break something. Ideally, his bulbous nose. Yet when she threw both fists right at the center of his feral face, she didn't connect. Even with her accelerated speed, her hands were stopped millimeters from crushing his nose, held in Cheeve's mighty, meaty mitts.

"To be real honest, a part of me hoped this'd go gritty," he snickered.

This sentence Cheeve spoke was exactly what Trinta considered a bad idea. There's no reason to talk when you're fighting. Especially if you have the upper hand (or in this case, *both* of her upper hands). But in those fleeting seconds when he chose to gloat, Trinta found a way to make her incapacitated hands work for her.

Using her held hands as a lever, she jumped up and spun around, kicking Cheeve square in the face with both of her booted feet. Unsurprisingly, Cheeve let go and staggered back, groaning and covering his mouth as though trying to keep all his teeth in.

As she landed on her feet, Trinta didn't have time to take pride in her work. Grabbing one of the cut panels from the container, she slammed it against the security

brute repeatedly, each smash yielding another chortling Cheeve moan. She wasn't sure how much was too
much, but a man like him seemed like he could take a
lickin' and keep on tickin'. So she gave him five extra
smashes before she snatched the oxy-gen filter and
engine block and raced towards the ship.

Reaching the ramp, she realized Cheeve wasn't hurt
at all.

"You forgot your chocolate!" Cheeve yelled.

Trinta didn't even bother turning around. She had
chores to do.

Not knowing Trinta was in a battle for their lives,
Quentin stepped out into the corridor, eager to
introduce her to Roddy. He hoped she'd know how to
deal with Roddy better than he did, as the two of them
clearly weren't clicking. The viadroid followed behind
him from the cargo bay, half-rolling/half-walking
towards the corridor.

Right as Roddy neared the doorway, Trinta ran in
and threw the heavy engine block at Quentin. He
caught it with a grunt. When she tossed him the
incredibly light Frisbee-like oxy-gen filter, he fumbled
it hopelessly. Before he could figure out why she was
throwing things at him, Trinta sprinted back out the
way she came in.

"Find the block in the engine and replace it with the
new one!" she shouted.

"But I don't . . ."

"You *don't* have a choice! Do it!"

And then she was gone again.

Roddy strolled up behind Quentin, only catching a

glimpse of Trinta's hair before she disappeared down the rampway. They heard growling and loud crashing outside.

"Who was that?" Roddy asked.

"Trinta."

"Oh, the one you . . ."

"Shut up."

Quentin picked up the filter and looked at it and then the engine block. He scrunched up his face, not sure which one fixed the engine.

"Do you know what these are?" he asked Roddy.

The viadroid didn't say anything.

"Well, do you?"

"I thought you told me to 'shut up'," Roddy groused.

Quentin threw up his arms in frustration, which was quite difficult with both hands full. He then took a deep breath and put on his most contrite face for his new robotic pal.

"Sorry," he said. "Now, do you know what these are?"

"Yes."

"And do you know where they go?"

"Yes."

"Is it because *I* really know where they go, but I just forgot? Or maybe I have to lose myself to it and instinctively I might know where they go?"

Roddy, by default, had a blank stare. But right now, for this woebegone Earther, he gave the blankest stare a viadroid had ever given anyone. For a moment, Quentin worried he broke his new robot pal with that one stupid question. Then he realized it was the same dead-eyed stare he'd provoked all his life for asking the wrong question at the wrong time.

"So I'll take that as a 'No'," the teen said.

"Smart boy."

"Well, guess we oughta do what she said then."

As Quentin strode heroically towards the cockpit ready for action, Roddy cleared his robotic throat. Turning around slowly, the Havok's young pilot realized he'd gone the wrong way.

"Right. That way." Zipping off in the other direction, Quentin muttered, "I don't know how you know all I know and know it better than me!"

Outside the Havok, all hell was breaking loose. Cheeve was very, very angry and only beginning to unleash a small amount of that rage on Trinta with a flurry of punches, kicks, and vicious headbutts. Occasionally, Trinta would get in a good jab or a kick to the ribs, but for every time she landed something, Cheeve would swat her with the force of a ten-ton truck dropped from a mile up.

In fact, the man's large forearms only had to glance off Trinta and she'd reel back, knocked loopy. Luckily, each punch that sent her backwards away from him gave her precious seconds to regroup mentally and figure out how best to avoid the next violent onslaught.

"You call this a fight?" taunted Trinta, running behind the ship and lurking in the shadows.

Trinta wasn't big on gabbing during a fight, especially when breathing wasn't coming easy. That is, unless it slowed down the action. *Still breathing hard.* Giving her time to recover a little bit. *Still breathing hard.* Giving her time to figure out a plan. *Still breathing hard.* What she didn't count on was Cheeve's speed. *Still breathing hard.* After carving out maybe thirty or forty seconds of "rest", she heard his voice behind her.

"No. I do not call this a fight. Cheeve calls this an hors d'oeuvre," he said, smacking his lips. "And maybe your little boy will be the meal."

He stormed towards her at full speed, aiming to crush her into the Havok's landing gear. Thankfully, Trinta still had her quickness, leaping up a second before impact and causing him to smash into the ship instead.

Noting the sizeable Cheeve-sized dent in the landing gear, Trinta decided to scamper off again before he got his few wits back.

Inside the engine room, Quentin and Roddy shook from Cheeve's battering against the Havok outside.

"That didn't sound good," Quentin said.

"Didn't feel good either," Roddy added.

Behind the consoles where Quentin first met Trinta, the engine's side panel was off and Roddy gingerly pulled out the fried engine block from deep within with a hand of tiny balls. A gnarled confluence of melted cables and grease, it looked like a charred electronic heart. Roddy handed the greasy thing to Quentin, who took it with all the joy of being handed a dead opossum. (He was *really* creeped out by opossums.)

"Thanks," Quentin said flatly.

Roddy grabbed the new block carefully and speedily reconfigured his "hand" to fit through the tight cavities of the engine's chambers. Working on any engine required patience and nimble fingers, two factors that suited the viadroid admirably. What would have taken at least an hour for Trinta to change out took him only a few minutes as he manipulated his fingers and arm into a thin stream of balls to lock the block into position. A quick click and a plugging of several cables into several ports and Roddy slunk his "hand" back out with a snapping of his fingers.

"Wow," Quentin said, impressed. "You know your stuff."

"I know *some* stuff," said Roddy, correcting him.

"Do you know where I could put this?" Quentin said, holding up the fried block.

But before Roddy could answer, the Havok shook again. Whatever was going on outside was big, ugly, and not taking into account the ship's recent injuries. Quentin tossed the used block down with a clang as Roddy eyeballed him like he was a litterer.

"Let's see what's goin' on," Quentin said, flying out the door.

Roddy followed after, shaking his head in disapproval.

Down the hall, the Earth boy shouted: "I'll clean it up later, I swear!"

Reaching the cockpit and looking outside below, it was worse than Quentin feared. Trinta wasn't just losing the fight. It looked like she didn't even know she was in it. Wobbling back and forth, her eyes drifted up to the cockpit window. But there was no eye contact to be made. Her eyes were glassy, the left one almost totally swollen shut. She'd seen better days. Yesterday was one of them.

"She doesn't look so good," Quentin said.

"No, she doesn't," Roddy said, sidling up behind him.

They peered over the dash, unable to find Cheeve anywhere.

"Maybe she beat him," Quentin said hopefully.

He was about to rush out and help her when Roddy stopped him. Scanning tight onto Trinta's retina revealed to the viadroid Cheeve's hulking figure just before he came into their own view, stepping out from under the ship. She hadn't beat Cheeve. Not by a long shot.

"Best we wait," said Roddy evenly.

"Yeah . . ." Quentin said, not wanting her to get killed but not really sure he could help either. He stood frozen, watching with an indecision that kept him firmly planted on the side of self-preservation and some might say cowardice.

Cheeve danced a mocking jig towards Trinta. He definitely had suffered some slung arrows from her fighting arsenal. His nose, for instance, wasn't as center as it used to be. (Although despite the blood, it looked slightly better off-kilter.) He also had a tiny limp from where she stomped his foot with both feet and a gash on his arm where she raked one of the metal sheets across him. The real problem though was that Cheeve didn't seem too bothered by any of it, his body moving like a fighter just getting into his groove. Whereas Trinta now moved only slightly better than a crow-picked scarecrow blowing in the wind, Cheeve moved with purpose and power.

Unable to stand any longer, Trinta collapsed to the ground in a heap. Cheeve creeped up on her prone body clenching and unclenching his fists. Quentin watched those fingers turning into fists, those fingers each individually holding more potential for destruction than anything in Quentin's whole body. Unsure what to do, the Earther did nothing. He watched helplessly and did . . . nothing.

"I hope the boy lasts longer than you," Cheeve said.

Cheeve raised his fists, about to crush Trinta when a shout brought him to a halt.

"Knock it off, you ugly booger!"

Quentin actually meant to swear there. He wanted a yell that would stop Cheeve and make him quiver with fear. A manly yell filled with an implicit threat only explicit swearing can achieve. Somehow though, instead of one of the more admirable and vile vulgarities that swirled in his head, he came out with "ugly booger" instead.

Closing his eyes with embarrassment, Quentin didn't see Cheeve turn to face him. The nostrils in Cheeve's crumpled nose flared and his eyes widened with fury. And as ridiculous as Quentin felt his "booger" declaration to be, it did what he wanted: Save Trinta. (For the moment anyways.)

"Ah, there's the whiny pup," snarled Cheeve.

The enraged face of Cheeve sent a hot-freeze shiver down the Earther's spine. Even Roddy shuddered involuntarily. Eyeing Quentin and easily visualizing three dozen horrible things he could do to him, Cheeve licked his lips before going all evil talky:

"I'm going to rip off parts of you, runt . . . and I'm

going to use those parts . . . to excruciate you. The pain will make you weep blood. First, I'll tear off your longest finger and use it to stab holes in your body. Then I'll wrench your arms off and smash them against your ears . . . and you'll pray for it to deafen you to your own screams. Then I'll take your left foot and shove it all the way up your . . ."

As Cheeve stepped towards the ship, ready to take his speechifying up a nasty notch, a steely voice spoke with disdain:

"Now, you're just gettin' gross. Leave the Earther alone!"

Quentin and Roddy couldn't see behind Cheeve's colossal frame but they knew it was Trinta. And when Cheeve turned around, they all saw it wasn't the same Trinta who had been sprawled out just minutes ago. She stood proudly, full of fight in her eyes. She still looked like crap, that's for sure. A black eye, split lip, dislocated shoulder, and a huge gouge on her leg were only the starting points of how hurt she was on the outside. And *inside*, inside her body was nothing but bruised organs and internal bleeding. But right now, at this moment, she was on her feet. And that counted for something.

"Earther?" Cheeve said with a glint in his eye.

Damn, Trinta cursed herself. If she wasn't so beat down, she wouldn't have let out that information. In fact, there were times in her relatively short life so far, where much worse off than now, she'd never let slip anything nearly so damaging. But here, she did. And it gave Cheeve the biggest grin he'd ever had, smiling as though he swallowed a whole planet full of canaries.

"I had a feeling you had something worth more than some nano-rerriums," Cheeve said. "But I had no sparkle of this. The last Earther . . ."

Why the hell does everyone know about me? Quentin wondered with concern.

Cheeve turned and appraised Quentin like a dessert behind glass. He had a real sweet tooth for this little candy, now dreaming of the system he'd purchase with what he'd make off the Earther. His grotesque green tongue protruded out as he salivated over what he'd come across: a bold new future where he had everything he ever wanted and more. Power. Riches. Respect. All right there for the taking in his meaty paws. As his tongue flitted over one of the more protruding fangs in his moldy mouth, he shook off his stupor and marched towards the Havok to claim his prize of all prizes.

"Hey, Cheevy," Trinta said. "Gotta say you're one of the weakest Kearners I've ever come across. A real Kearner would have finished me off a long time ago. Maybe it's because you have a proper hoity-toity job and you're all into 'security', but it's like you're feeble inside. Sort of like you're a little baby. Not a Kearner baby. Oh, no! Maybe like one of the babies from my friend the pup's world."

Those words were more than an insult for Cheeve. They physically got inside of him and stirred up a pot of incense so intense that for a moment he even forgot his own name. He turned and faced her with an explosive rage in his eyes, eager to snuff out her very existence and take the Earther in for his reward.

But as Cheeve grinded his teeth, ready to pounce on

the Thricer and tear her apart, Trinta peered up to the cockpit. Locking eyes with Quentin, she glanced down to her right hand. Her hands were out as if ready to take on Cheeve if he ran towards her, but her right hand did a quick gesture of a gun firing and then the hand flying away.

"Why's she just standing there?" Quentin asked.

Trinta frantically glared right at him and waited until his eyes were locked again on her own. Slowly, she moved her eyes down to her right hand that continued to do the firing/fly away gestures barely outside of Cheeve's view. Finally getting what she wanted him to do, Quentin nodded seriously.

Just as Trinta gave him a wink of acknowledgement, Cheeve rushed towards her and barreled her over, both of them crashing to the ground.

Quentin turned to Roddy: "So she wants me to blow him up and fly out of here? That's what she wants? She did the shoot-shoot thing then a little flying thing, so that's what she means, right?"

Roddy shrugged. He didn't know.

"Can't really ask her now, I guess," Quentin muttered.

Looking back out he was semi-relieved to see Trinta had rolled Cheeve onto his back and was kicking him repeatedly in the face. Cheeve's head slammed back against the metal walls with the clang of gongs. More than actually hurting him, it continued to stun Cheeve and kept him from attacking momentarily. Which was all-good by Trinta, because if those roles were reversed she'd be Trinta-butter by now.

"What do I do?" Quentin asked Roddy.

"I don't know."

"Is the engine even up and working?"

"It should be fully online in a few minutes."

"'A few minutes'?! Aren't you robots supposed to be all precise and stuff?! Like 1.3 minutes or something?! Right?! Right?!"

"Everything doesn't have the same precision as me," Roddy snapped. "I don't like to give specifics because it doesn't take into account all the factors. But if *you* want to work out exactly how long it will be I can give *you* a formula and – "

"Alright! Sorry! Not the point! I need to . . ."

Quentin put his hand on the joystick and instantly the weapons system came online. He targeted it in front of them.

"Maybe I don't need to do anything since she's beating the . . ."

But before he could finish his sentence, Cheeve hit Trinta in the face with a fist like a bulldozer rocket. It was brutal. They could hear the crunch from inside the cockpit. And once she went up in the air from the force of the blow, she fell down with a sickening crunch twice as fast. Her eyelids went shut and stayed shut before she hit the ground. She looked broken.

"No . . ." Quentin gasped. "No, no, no . . ."

Cheeve picked Trinta up and tossed her limp body towards the ship. Her body rolled over and over and over several times before it came to a rest against the ramp with a painful clunk.

"Noooooooo!!!" Quentin cried out.

Cheeve gazed up at all the ruckus. He saw the "pup" and unleashed an evil smile. An evil smile with a few less teeth than before, but still . . .

"That . . . bastard . . ." muttered Quentin.

He'd never seen anyone he cared for hurt like Trinta was. He felt sick to his stomach. But he felt something else, too. His old friend. Anger. That, plus a desire for revenge. He knew he couldn't beat up Cheeve in a million years. Even if there were physical upgrades to be had, Cheeve would probably still always come out on top. But at this moment in this situation, Quentin did have some power.

"Now, pup, Cheeve must grab his treasure," Cheeve said.

But before that hulking monstrosity could move one step closer, Quentin fired an unrelenting burst from the ship's cannons at him. Unfortunately, Quentin missed his target. By quite a ways. Like not even really close. He instead hit the wall behind Cheeve, leaving a giant gaping hole in their storage box.

Cheeve chuckled at his good fortune, but as he did, the whole storage box creaked a loud metallic whine. And the whine only grew louder as it reverberated all the way down through the lowest boxes of the storage skyscraper and all the way back up to the top where more and more boxes were still being built. Cheeve had lived on this planet for years and never heard anything like it. And that scared Cheeve.

"Uh, how soon can we get goin'?" Quentin enquired, his voice trembling.

"Another minute or two probably," Roddy said. "We should have partial power for now. And I'd advise we use it in the estimated time of: immediately!"

"Ya think?" Quentin responded sarcastically.

Roddy lowered his head, hurt by the snotty retort. But as much guff as everyone had been giving him, Quentin didn't feel bad in the least. Especially considering they'd be crushed under the load of thousands of boxes of knick-knacks and other heavy assorted sundries if they didn't move and move now. He fired up the engines and they came alive with a soft hum. They didn't roar to life as they usually did, but it was something.

"Go get Trinta and let's get the hell out of here!" he barked.

Roddy rushed out of the cockpit as Quentin hit the thrusters. The ship shook slightly prior to elevating gingerly the way a good ship should. As Roddy clomped back in the Havok, Quentin shouted down to him:

"You got her?!"

All Quentin heard was a muffled "Yrrp" which was good enough for him. As he hit the button to prep liftoff and the ramp closed shut, outside Cheeve stormed towards the cockpit with one of the tools from his belt now in his hands – a refraktor that sent out fraktor spray in all directions. Pulling the trigger on it, an off-balance Cheeve shot a series of blasts that singed the top of the cockpit. Before he could get off another shot, Quentin hit the thrusters and the ship lifted into the air and tilted upwards, causing Roddy to crash back down the corridor.

"Sorry!" yelled Quentin back to him.

The building's structural creaking grew louder and louder like the whole skyscraper of boxes was groaning in pain as it began to sway. Even though Quentin shot a gaping hole in the wall, it still wasn't big enough for the ship to get through. It was big enough, however, to witness the buildings outside move back and forth. They weren't moving though. It was just Quentin's strange perspective hovering in the air in a box in a swinging building that jumbled everything up.

"Focus and go, big man," Quentin said to himself, shaking his head.

He fired at the wall again, ready to burst through as soon as he had enough room for the Havok to make it out. Firing blast after blast and ripping open a wide enough space, Quentin floored it. Thankfully, the engines roared to life just as the whole building started to collapse.

As they stormed out of the box, the Havok smashed into Cheeve, knocking him out of the building with a high-pitched squeal that reverberated off of the skyscrapers as the hulking beast fell down into the darkness. The Havok flew diagonally up into the air away from the collapsing building, boxes separating from other boxes and ricocheting towards them. Some bounced off the hull, thumping the Havok down for a moment until Quentin could readjust.

"C'mon, Havok!" he shouted.

More and more storage containers smacked against the ship, several cracking open as they plummeted down, their former contents caroming against the cockpit's windows. Suddenly, there went this galaxy's biggest book, the size of the North Platte library! Then there went a huge glass statue of a strange-hatted dictator with a duckbill! CRRAAAASHHHH! There went thousands of cans of the untasty drink Pizzy Super Dee! All smashed, crashed, and slashed into the

Havok as it desperately tried to climb above the falling detritus. All until Quentin smacked a fiery red button next to the stick and the Havok shot straight up through everything, clanging and banging the entire way.

"Yeeeeeeeeee-heeeeeheeeeeeeeee-hooooooooo!!!" he screamed.

The Havok climbed higher and higher, far above the skyscraper it was once a part of. Down below, the rest of the building crumbled and fell against another mountainous tower of boxes that then toppled over. And then that building tumbled into another and the whole set of neighboring buildings teetered and fell outwards like a beautiful flower, all created from the flotsam of packrats.

Once into the atmosphere, Quentin set the ship on a course to break orbit as soon as possible. Where they were going he had no idea, nor did he care. Right now, he only wanted to make sure Trinta was okay. Rushing into the corridor, he bumped right into Roddy.

"How is she?" Quentin asked hurriedly.

"I don't know."

"What do you mean you don't know?"

"I didn't get her. I was telling you I couldn't find her when you started up the ship. I barely got back on myself."

"What . . . you mean . . ."

Quentin felt faint. He thought he might actually drop to the ground and become a sobbing puddle of tears. He reached back and steadied himself, holding on to the doorway as tight as he could. Running his hand through his hair frenetically, Quentin couldn't accept the fact that Trinta was gone.

And it was good that he *didn't* accept it, because a moment later, she limped out of the med-chamber and hobbled towards him, each step shakier than the last.

"Well, that was . . . something . . . Hey, who's the robot?" she said, right before collapsing into Quentin's arms.

CHAPTER EIGHTEEN
THE MEASURE OF DREAMS

She didn't look good. Before she crumbled unconscious into Quentin's arms, Trinta staggered forward like a mangled wind-up toy. A mangled wind-up toy covered in bulging bruises and bloody gashes.

So he was glad to see her later slumbering peacefully in the sleeping quarters. The room had two beds, one short and squat for Weedoss Edbu and the other long and thin for Dasimon Edbu. Being a taller guy himself, Quentin had been using Dasimon's bed. But under the circumstances of chivalry and concern, he happily gave over his better-fitting bed to the taller, more unconscious Trinta. He thought about taking a bunk, too, but didn't want to do anything that might wake her. She needed her rest. He was just happy she was still alive. And on the ship.

Retreating to the cockpit, Quentin plopped into his seat with a large oomph. Hunkering down for some shut-eye himself, he failed to notice the unmoving Roddy in the corner where he had formed himself into a pyramid of balls with a head at the top. When Roddy cocked his head quizzically, the Earther shot out of his chair.

"What the hell?!!" Quentin shouted.

"Sorry," the viadroid said. "Didn't mean to startle you. How's Trinta?"

"I don't know . . . She's sleeping. I think that's a good thing. No, wait! You're not supposed to sleep if you have a concussion, are you? One kid back home did and he died. Or my dad told me that . . . Did she have a concussion?! Should I wake her?!"

"Just let her sleep."

Quentin nodded, grateful Roddy was there to calm him down.

Back on Earth, he always wanted to make decisions and be treated like an adult. But now that he had to make decisions (BIG TIME GROWN-UP DECISIONS), he couldn't be more relieved to have a pile of balls help him out with the responsibility.

As they put Jebel behind them, Quentin aimed the ship towards another galaxy as fast as they could go. He didn't know if there'd be anyone on their tail for the destruction they caused, but he didn't want to stick around to find out. He felt relieved that by taking out the chief security officer their escape should be slightly easier.

"Where are we going?" asked Roddy.

"Dunno. Figure we'll run as far away as we can from there. Wait 'til Trinta wakes up and . . ."

"So she's the boss?"

"Uh . . . no," Quentin huffed. "No, she's not the boss. I don't have a boss. It's *my* ship."

"I'm sorry. Didn't mean to . . ."

"She's just a . . . a . . . what do you call . . . you know, a person that illegally gets on a ship or something? A, uh, a . . ."

"A 'stowaway'?"

"Yeah! She's my stowaway. That's all. I'm in charge. It's *my* ship. Not *her* ship. Not *your* ship. *My* ship!" Quentin pointed to his chest with those last two words, in case Roddy or anyone else was confused as to who the "my" referred to. Of course, he knew it was only technically his ship in as much as anything stolen is officially in the ownership of the thief. Regardless, he'd been feeling disrespected for days and was sick of it. "So the plan is we wait for Trinta to get up. Then we'll discuss where we all want to go . . . and then *I'll* decide. That's how it works. I'm like the . . . the . . . president of the ship. It's a democracy, but I'm in charge. Okay?"

"Do I have to call you 'President Quentin'?"

Irritated at first, the Earth teen then smirked knowingly. He *was* being a little ridiculous. He knew it. And as he scrunched up into his chair, ready for a nap he craved more than anything ever, he gave Roddy a playful nod, saying:

"Yeah. Either that or Supreme Leader Quentin T. McFury. Your call, Roddy. But for now, your supreme leader is going to catch some zzz's."

As the boy closed his eyes and drifted off, he heard Roddy mutter:

"'Night, Supreme Commander."

Shortly after shutting his eyes, Quentin dreamt one of his most popular recurring dreams of the past year. Alone in the McFury family room in the basement, the sun set outside, lighting the room up with a warm orange hue. Often, that auburn shaded room coaxed Quentin into a pre-supper nap with the TV on some old rerun of some show made before he was born. But here in this dream, he played a videogame, frantically jumping up and down while hitting buttons. Usually with these dreams, his parents worked their way in and life felt normal again.

However, this time when his mother's voice called down crisp and clear for him, it wasn't her voice. His mother's voice was . . . Trinta's. This disturbed him. This disturbed him very much.

"Quentin honey, we're ready to eat," called Trinta/Quentin's mom.

Weirded out, he let the controller fall gently on the soft carpet and trudged towards the stairs. With each foreboding step up, he didn't know what he'd find, but he had enough of an idea to know he'd hate it. And hate it he did.

Reaching the top step, the kitchen table beckoned him forward, fully laid out with his favorite dishes. Tacos, Spanish rice, ribs, everything. There was even a large cake with huge heaps of frosting coating it with his name in bold dark red letters. But there at the head of the table weren't his parents as he knew them, but Trinta in one of his mom's outfits – a white blouse with navy blue pants – and Roddy in his dad's garish green button-down shirt. The sight of the two of them in his parents' clothes next to all the food he loved so much almost made him throw-up.

"Sit down, son," Roddy said. "I made you a cake."

"After all, it's your birthday," Trinta said. "It's all your birthdays."

"*All* my birthdays?" the Earther said. "What does that . . ."

Out of nowhere, candles emerged from out of the cake and lit themselves up. The light cast from the candles almost blinded him with its brilliance. But just as fast as the candles appeared, the flames began to snuff themselves out one by one. Quickly, Quentin tried to count the candles.

"What does it mean? Is that how old I am when I die? What does it mean?"

Roddy put his arm around Trinta and they laughed warmly. Gazing lovingly at each other and then to their "son", they repeated proudly:

"Our boy, our boy, our boy, our boy . . ."

As each candle went out, the room grew darker and darker. It wasn't just the room either. Outside the patio windows, the skies fell black, too. Like the whole world was dimming out of existence. And as the last of the candles snuffed itself out, everything clouded over in shadow.

"Hello . . ." the Earth boy blindly called out.

Enveloped in such all-encompassing darkness, he wasn't even sure he was still alive. Or still in a dream.

He was alone. That's all he knew. He felt as though wrapped up in a big black blanket. Except this blanket provided no comfort, just brittle coldness. As he started to shiver, he listened to the only noise there was – his chattering teeth. He desperately wanted out of this nightmare. But no matter how many times he told himself it was only a dream, he couldn't wake up.

Trinta slept soundly in her bunk. And by "soundly", it meant she slept with a lot of sounds. Every few moments, she'd grunt and kick out. Then she'd stop and remain motionless, almost breathless, for twenty minutes or so. Then she'd cry out with pained moans and screeches into her pillow before quieting again. Her ravaged body needed all the rest it could get, but even in dreams she couldn't fully find respite. And where Quentin's dreaming was fairly linear – if not a little odd – Trinta's dreaming jumped from one bizarre interlude to another.

At first, giant orange and blue snakes chased her up flights of neon stairs to nowhere. No matter how many steps she jumped ahead, the snakes would bounce right behind her, improbably slithering up and up. And every time she tried to kick one, it would dart out of the way and bite her left big toe. *Always* the left big toe.

Finally reaching the last flight of stairs, she found herself staring down at an upside-down green waterfall. The water fell upwards into the sky, crashing into a set of clouds with unfathomable fury. Sprinting for her life, she dove into the waterfall just as the snakes tried to wrap themselves around her legs. When she hit the water and was swept up into the watery skies, it all went black until she burst out, reappearing as . . .

. . . An elongated pink noodle. She was now a pink noodle sitting on a gigantic silver spoon that protruded out of a giant red gas planet. Noodle Trinta sang with no words she'd ever known, only pure unadulterated gobbledygook. The music accompanying her was one part lullaby, one part heavy metal anthem.

"*Goggle-de-google, retaggle-de-baggle, spaggle-spaggle-tragora . . .*"

As she sang, Trinta admired the stars surrounding her – doodly, twinkling stars as though children had drawn them, all sparkling different colors, all much bigger than the pinprick glitters of white that usually dotted the sky. After awhile, Trinta's warbling faded to only husky breaths in tune with the continuing melody. Shutting her eyes, she . . .

. . . Flashed upon remembered and misremembered times of her life . . . each one punctuated with a random devastating punch to the face by Cheeve. As Cheeve – dressed like a Cavecian butler with a bowtie made of insects – hit her, she glimpsed memories/mismemories of . . .

. . . Being nine and dancing in a pretty green dress and dark red boots. Everyone watched as she danced around the room like an erratic fool, but she didn't care. She smiled from ear-to-ear and back again, twirling faster and faster as the music accelerated into a mad jig for the end of the world: that world anyway . . .

. . . She flashed back to Cheeve – this time dressed like a doctor in a robe of white and green stripes. He laid her out with a fist to the face and she flashed on . . .

. . . A barren yellow room with high ceilings and long angled windows with dark lavender clouds visible outside. Trinta didn't know who she was or why she was here. Staring out in one direction, she couldn't move at all.

Maybe I'm a table, she thought. *Or a sofa. Think I'd*

rather be a table than a sofa. Don't want all those butts sitting on me. Or maybe I'm a . . .

Suddenly, enormous metallic doors opened and a rush of children ran in. All Thricer children full of glee, they skipped into the room and jabbered animatedly as though waiting for a party to start. The gleeful chatter stopped abruptly as a hell-shattering rip erupted from above and they all looked up in horror.

Trinta couldn't see what it was, but she heard the screams. She heard *every* scream. And before she witnessed the unrelenting carnage, the dream went black . . .

. . . Now dressed in the azure flowing robes of an Abdilliam monk, Cheeve slugged her with a vicious uppercut and she flashed to . . .

. . . Blues, the darkest of blues. Not water. Not the sky. Not anything else, neither gas nor solid. Or was it all of these things? So much blue in every form surrounded her in an immense cocoon of blueness. Slowly emerging out of it towards her . . . were a pair of brown eyebrows . . . then a slightly lighter colored violet nose. Then open eyes, staring out to her . . . *through* her . . . The face was a man's . . . more than familiar to her . . . yet in the dream he was somehow beyond identification.

Staring at that face for what felt like years, it fell back into the blue and another face slowly emerged. This man's visage was slightly older than the previous one. But this one's face was fuller. Like he'd had a few more meals in his life than the man before. Trinta tried to place him, but again, it escaped her mind. Maybe he was . . . Slowly his face drifted back into the blue, lost again to the cocoon.

Finally, another face bubbled up. White eyebrows, white hair, haunted blue eyes. Those eyes fell on Trinta with a bitter sadness. His lip trembled, unable to speak. He tried . . . but the lips would not open . . . the words would not come. And though at first Trinta had no idea who this man was, her mind sparked and it all came flowing back like a shot from a fraktor and she whispered:

"Dad?"

. . . With a thunderous flash, Cheeve appeared again, dressed just as he was back on Jebel. He snarled and punched her hard. She blacked out to . . .

. . . Well, nothing. This time, she didn't go into another dream. She slept on, unencumbered with any more fleeting illusions. Her body demanded this true, pure sleep though still fresh on her slumbering whispered lips rang out the word "Dad". And though she didn't move again during the rest of her rest, her mind conjured a new destination for them to go once she awoke.

If she awoke.

Back in the cockpit as the Havok flew absolutely nowhere special in record time, Roddy did not sleep. He did not dream. He did not dream of electric sheep. He merely watched the stars and planets they passed while everyone else slept. He didn't mind.

In the relatively short time he'd known Quentin, there was a lot to process. Sifting through the memories attained from the merge, the Earther kid turned out to be a mass of contradictions. What this boy thought of himself and how he lived his life was unlike anything Roddy had been prepared for. And he'd been prepared for quite a lot. Hell, there were entire species that only used one word to communicate and had no facial expressions that he was completely equipped to deal with. But this Quentin . . . this Earther . . . had more emotions running through him than he ever thought possible. How this boy could overflow with being so cocky and so self-loathing in the exact same moment confused the viadroid completely.

If this is the way all Earthers are, he thought, *it's no wonder he's the only one left.*

Roddy glanced over at the sleeping Quentin, drool slowly dripping from his mouth down onto his T-shirt with a dragon and the words "The Clash" on it. Tapping into the kid's memories as though they were his own, he realized that this was a music band on the boy's planet.

Stringing a long arm of balls to the other side of the room, Roddy flipped through the ship's database. Keeping the volume at a level he knew wouldn't wake Quentin, he started up a Clash song called "Straight to Hell". As it played, he didn't "get" all of it, what with there being cultural things going on in the lyrics beyond Quentin's full Earth awareness. But as they passed a comet, Roddy couldn't help but get caught up in the music. The lament of it all.

As Joe Strummer sang about there not being any asylum for anyone, Roddy nodded his head rhythmically. There wasn't any asylum for these kids. There wasn't any asylum for him. Only space. And no matter what you did, there were always repercussions.

And no matter what you *didn't* do, there were always repercussions. Even a bally robot knew that.

So with a tinge of regret, Roddy extended his long arm of balls over to the comm next to the music controls. There, his tiny little finger of beads hesitated a moment prior to touching the comm screen. He knew he didn't have to do this. He didn't *want* to do this. He wanted a better reason than it was his "orders" or his "programming". He wanted to know more about who this kid was before betraying him. But in the end, he knew they could shut him down or countermand his independence even from the furthest reaches of space. And that's why his tiny finger of orbs touched the screen. Instantly, a tiny little animated drop of water spread out across the screen and the message was sent. He did his duty. He just didn't feel good about it.

"Nice song," Trinta said behind him.

The long stretch of multicolored balls reaching across the room immediately snapped back into Roddy's body with a swiftness that surprised both Trinta *and* the viadroid. Molding his body into the shape of a squat rectangular box that matched his head, Roddy eyed Trinta, unsure of what she saw and moreover what she knew.

Her hair now shaved off tightly, Trinta appeared to be in better spirits (primarily in being more conscious than un-.) Still, she basically consisted of bruises, lumps, and wounds only kept together by her battered slightly violet skin. Her left eye was still so swollen it couldn't stop winking.

"I scare ya, pal?" Trinta asked Roddy.

"I didn't know you were there."

"Obviously, no need to be scared. I'm not that scary. Although after the beating I took, maybe I am. Hi, I'm Trinta."

"Roddy Gabb."

Quentin slept on, unaware of the conversation behind him.

"Where we goin'?" Trinta leaned against the doorway, staring out at an orange planet in the distance.

"Don't know. He just put us on a course to get as far away from Jebel as fast as possible."

"Good plan. You know, he's not as dumb as he looks."

"No . . . I guess he's not."

Trinta watched Quentin sleep. She didn't mind the boy. He wasn't her ideal guy or anything. But he wasn't the worst guy either. He was alright. *Too bad about him being an Earther though*, she thought.

"He's just new out here," she said. "That's all."

"Yes. I know."

"Course you do. You . . ." Trinta mimed Roddy sucking all of Quentin's memories with a slurping sound. She smirked at her little joke. Roddy enjoyed it, too, but she couldn't really tell. All he did was nod.

"You're a Thricer," Roddy said, somewhere between a question and a statement – something that deserved a new punctuation mark to be created and called a "queriod".

"Yep."

"One, two, or three?" asked Roddy.

"One," she said.

"Okay, good."

The Havok continued coasting through space as the Clash played on in the background. Trinta and Roddy didn't have anything else to say and the music became welcome filler for the silence. Even the occasional whiffling snore from Quentin found itself greeted with a chuckle by both Roddy and Trinta as the ship traveled onwards.

It's not that either Trinta or Roddy felt awkward with each other. They just didn't know what to make of the other one. Not yet anyway. Both knew time would be the only thing to shake loose those feelings. Traveling through space put you in close contact with others in unusual circumstances that quickly defined who you were and who you were surrounded by, so they were in no hurry.

"Time for a course change," Trinta said.

Trinta stepped in front of Quentin, careful not to wake him, and entered in the name of a new location. If necessary, she could have put in the coordinates, even though that's not needed in today's spacecraft. Simply put in a word and your route was mapped out, only awaiting the pilot's confirmation. Confirmation Trinta instantly gave for passage to the planet Borstan. She'd never been there before and would never visit again after this trip. She wasn't entirely sure why she put it in, but she knew it was right.

"Don't you have to run it by the supreme commander?" Roddy said.

Trinta turned back to see that the viadroid had put himself in a human-esque body and extended both his arms sarcastically towards the drooling Earth boy. They both chuckled, just enough to wake Quentin up.

Squinting at them under the fog of his own sleepiness, it took him a moment to remember who they were.

"What's going on?" Quentin asked.

"Course correction," Trinta said.

"Cool . . . Where we goin'?"

"To see my father."

"Great. Like the new hair, Sinead. I'm goin' back to sleep."

Quentin then scrunched back up in his seat and did as he said, dozing right off again.

CHAPTER NINETEEN
FATHERLAND

Gliding above the lovely, rolling hillsides of long, lush dark green grass, the planet Borstan captivated Quentin deeply. It was kinda how he imagined all of Ireland to be. Except his vision of Ireland overflowed with leprechauns, castles, and U2 on every hill. The Borstan hills had none of that. Many though were dotted with white domed structures, each the size of a very, very small house.

But if those are homes, the teen reasoned, *they gotta be, like, one bedroom homes. And what's the point of that here? They should all have castles instead. Maybe I could get a castle here.*

Approaching the base of one of these hills, Quentin noticed Trinta acting a bit jittery. Not even "jittery" per se. Just acting more like him. She was less graceful. Less sure of herself. Almost nervous, with her eyes drifting frenetically, never setting still. She rubbed her thumb across her fingertips as though to make sure they were still there. She whirred with unrelenting activity, her head not in the game. And he totally understood why – she was going to see her dad.

Since Quentin didn't get along with his father, he figured it was the same for her. Or maybe there was something worse her dad did. Something unforgivable. Or maybe *she* did something. He was curious as curious could be, but every time he tried to pry, Trinta not only rebuffed him, she often left the room. That still wasn't enough to keep his curiosity at bay.

. . . *Earlier, in the cockpit, seven hours from Borstan.*

Quentin devoured a Little Debbie Swiss Roll lustily. He teethed off the ends and unrolled the tiny chocolate and cream blanket to chew on as Trinta watched in disgust.

"Wrrnrntt sorrmme?" he asked, mouth full.

"I'd rather eat Cheeve's butt," she said.

Turning away, she tinkered with a small silver disc. The cockpit was silent for thirty-seven seconds.

"So why are we goin' to see your dad?" he asked.

Trinta kept working on the silver disc like he wasn't there.

Turning to Roddy, Quentin said, "You heard me, right?"

"Leave me out of it. I already know too much about *you*."

Roddy rolled out of the cockpit and went down to the engine room.

"Is your dad a jerk?" Quentin inquired. "'Cause my dad's a jerk. *Was* a jerk, I guess. Whatever. Did yours always compare you to other kids? Because mine did and it drove me – "

Trinta took the silver disc and stomped out of the room. The young Earther almost followed, until he heard an angry, smashing clang and wisely decided to hold back.

. . . Earlier, in the sleeping quarters, four hours from Borstan.

Trinta lay on the bed, hands behind her head, staring at the ceiling as Quentin came in sipping a cup of hot cocoa.

"Sorry about the whole dad thing," he said. "But I just want you to know if you need someone to talk to about . . . bad dads . . . I'm here."

Trinta didn't say a word.

"Not that I'm an expert or anything," he added. "But sometimes it's cool to talk to someone about parent crap. I wish I had somebody back on Earth to –"

"Quentin," she interrupted.

"Yeah?"

"Go talk to Roddy about *your* crappy dad then," she snipped frostily before getting up and thumping into Quentin on the way out. She made sure she hit him just hard enough to spill his hot cocoa.

"Yaaaa, my hand! NOT COOL!!! NOT!!! COOL!!!"

. . . Earlier, in the cockpit, thirty minutes from landing on Borstan.

All three of them peered straight down. Trinta had turned on the translucents and they surveyed the lush grasslands passing by underneath. Nearing her father's dome, the ship's red warning lights flickered and a stern holographic face appeared.

"I am Securitan Hagland. Name of person you are visiting?" the hologram now known as Securitan Hagland said.

"Blanker Bedinbur," said Trinta.

"Relation?" Securitan Hagland asked flatly.

"Daughter."

The hologram then scanned Trinta up close, gold lines racing across her face, then sputtering to a stop.

"Permission granted," Securitan Hagland said. "Only one hour. Pleasa-day."

The hologram shimmered and disappeared. They flew on silently as the ship locked in on her father's location, navigating them across the planet towards his dome.

"Tight security, huh?" Quentin said. "Sorta like a gated planet . . . or something."

Nobody said anything.

"So your dad . . ."

Not waiting for another word, Trinta stormed out. Roddy immediately followed, pulling himself altogether into a giant ball and rolling off, leaving the Earth boy alone again.

"I was just gonna ask if we should call him by his first name or Mr. Bedinbur. Everybody's so frakkin' touchy."

Stepping off the Havok, a breeze drifted over them, smelling of freshly cut grass. It reminded Quentin of his last summer on Earth, mowing lawns to save up money for a car. He suspected Borstan sadly didn't have such enterprising young men as its grass reached up above his waist. It felt like thousands of tiny emerald fingers tickling him as he followed Trinta up that hill.

To be out of the ship and in nature made Quentin irrationally happy. Playing upon his nostalgia, the lush green grass reminded him of childhood days, cheerfully playing in the park. With such memories fresh in his head, he trekked up the hill with a bounce in his step.

"Maybe we can roll down the hill after," he said jovially.

Trinta ignored him. Trinta was not jovial. There was no bounce in her step. It was a trudging one-foot-barely-in-front-of-the-other march towards an inevitable and unwanted encounter. There was no happiness for her on this planet. And even though seeing her father would bring up childhood reminiscences, it wouldn't bring any sort of smile to her face. Maybe a grimace. A gritted-teeth grimace that conceded no one gets to choose their parents. It was this reluctant acceptance of the universe's random allocation of children to crummy parents that provided the slightest comfort. Her parents could have been worse. Although she wasn't sure how.

Suddenly, the Havok rattled to life behind them and lifted up into the air. Quentin turned around and ran back to the ship, frantically trying to stop it.

"Somebody's stealing my ship!" he screamed.

Before he could react, the Havok then terrifyingly dove towards Quentin, screaming right up to him . . . stopping only a foot from his face and hovering there.

"Shirt . . ." he muttered. Peering into the cockpit, no

one was at the controls.

"C'mon, Bulldog, we got somewhere to be!" Trinta shouted.

He turned to see her holding up the silver disc she'd been working on. She moved her hand up and the Havok then raced into the sky. *Ah, she must have made a remote control for it,* he figured. He didn't like that the way she shared this information almost made him poop his pants, but he hid his anger and played it cool.

"Ships can only stay on the planet for fifteen minutes," she said. "Otherwise there are repercussions."

"Like what?"

"Like total destruction of the ship and its owners."

"Those cussions are pretty repur."

Trinta shook her head and continued striding upwards.

"Sorta like a '*This zone is for the loading and unloading of passengers only,*'" Quentin said in his best airport disembodied voice.

Nobody acknowledged him as they kept traversing through the long grass.

"I like the ship remote," he hollered. "Hope you remembered to lock it!"

The dome shone brightly as the harsh orange sun glared its reflection off of it. Completely smooth, the dome looked like a massive white salad bowl had been flipped onto the top of the hill. Climbing up to its summit was no problem for Trinta or Quentin, but the grass kept getting caught in Roddy's orbs until eventually he just made himself long leg stilts of balls to take sweeping steps up and above the grass.

As they reached the dome, Quentin couldn't see any doors or any windows. He gently put his hand on the dome and although it was very, very smooth, it was also very, very *hot*!

"Arrrrghghhg!" he screamed.

"Well, what'd you expect?!" Trinta snapped.

Quentin waved his hand in the air trying to cool it down.

"So where's the door then?!" he barked. "Your dad couldn't afford one?"

Before Trinta could respond (which was good because she was going to punch the Earther *really* hard in the chest), the dome slid open and retreated all the way back into the ground. This now revealed a small room with five white chairs. At the head of the chairs sat a short man, no more than five feet tall and pale-ish purple. This was Blanker Bedinbur.

Blanker stared out at the three of them vacantly . . . until his eyes rested on Trinta. Then he stood up and gave her the tiniest of nods. Trinta returned an equally small nod, barely acknowledging him, and walked up onto the platform. Quentin and Roddy followed, Roddy bringing himself back down to his smaller humanoid shape so as not to tower over them all by a good twelve feet.

Once Blanker sat down in his chair, the rest did as well. When they were all seated, the dome slid back over them with an abrupt whoosh, leaving them all in an awkward gooey silence that filled that tiny, tiny room.

Fifteen minutes later, Blanker still stared at Trinta. She stared back. No one had said anything. Nothing at all. No one had muttered, coughed, cleared their throats, shuffled their feet, or made any noise what-so-ever. Quentin felt like he was in a dentist's waiting room. (Then he changed that to an orthodontist's waiting room. He wasn't sure why he made the change. Maybe it was because orthodontists are generally crueler than dentists and there was definitely something unidentifiably cruel about this room.)

Quentin couldn't work out how Trinta's dad could live here. He wondered if Blanker was some sort of monk vowing to live a life of poverty in very tiny rooms. Blanker's red shirt and pants did have a monk-ish feel to them. And his wiry salt and pepper goatee carried the specter of age mixed with wisdom.

"So, Trinty . . ." Blanker finally said.

It was only two words but it carried novels with it. Novels of a past only shared by parent and child with all the attendant emotional carnage and lingering resentments it beheld. And while father continued to stare at daughter, she averted her eyes and shook her head in contempt.

Shrugging, Blanker turned conspiratorially to Quentin: "Always she's been like this."

Quentin wasn't sure how to respond. His allegiance was to Trinta, that much was certain. But since she'd been ignoring him and treating him like a constant annoyance, he decided he didn't need her permission to talk.

"What do you mean?" asked Quentin.

"Vindictive," the older man said coldly.

Trinta closed her eyes tight. She couldn't believe she chose to come here. She couldn't believe that he was talking, calling *her* "vindictive". Keeping her eyes shut and her face emotionless, she refused to show her father any reaction. He didn't get the right to know his words still mattered. Not now.

"So who are you, boy?" Blanker asked Quentin.

"I'm Quentin. Quentin McFury."

"And how do you know my girl?"

"We're, uh . . . friends? I guess. 'Shipmates'? I don't know."

"So you're not here to ask for my permission to marry and to make her some children?"

The boy blushed beet red. He probably could have laughed off the "marry" comment but something about the way he said "children" really unnerved him. It seemed so unseemly.

"Uh . . . no . . . I, uh . . ." Quentin stammered.

"Don't tell me the robot's going to ask for her hand then. I don't want to see her marrying some cut-rate viadroid."

Hearing this, Trinta unfurled the slightest of half-grins. That was pretty much how the Bedinbur family communicated – with tiny nods, half-grins, and other microscopic facial gestures that always masked as much as possible. For them, family was a war of attrition where emotions were protected with all they had.

"So what are you here for, girl?" Blanker queried wearily.

"I need your help," she said.

"Figured that. Figured you weren't here for a hug

and a tuck-in." He leaned back in his chair smugly. "So, you're asking for my help? I never thought the day'd arrive where . . ."

"No. I *need* your help. I'm not 'asking' for it. I'm telling you what I need. And you as a doting, loving father hearing this will feel a pang in his bleak and decayingly wretched heart and will offer help without question or a second thought."

Quentin vaguely recalled an English class where some Russian writer said how all happy families are alike and all unhappy families are unhappy in their own ways. But Quentin didn't think there was such a thing as a "happy family". As for the families he considered "happy", he found out otherwise when every family disappeared and he went through their things.

So seeing this terse, spiky interaction with father and daughter helped Quentin feel normal, even though he'd never been further away from normal in his life.

"Maybe I will help," Blanker said. "I suppose I owe you certain fatherly dues."

"Yes, I suppose you do," Trinta stated sternly.

"But you know there's only so much I can do. The leash is pretty short. And it's not like I spent every minute here waiting for you to show up. I love you, girl. But my life ain't all about you. When you become a parent you'll figure that out. And maybe you'll lose that bitterness you keep preserved in that unbreakable jar just for me."

"Don't worry. I'm not ever going to be a parent," she spat out.

"Don't do that because of me."

"Don't flatter yourself," she said. Even though they

all knew he was the reason.

"Well, with these two fellas," Blanker said, "I can't say I don't disagree with not doing it immediately. Wouldn't want our line to continue with either of these . . . inferiors."

Quentin frowned, hurt by his comment. Blanker obviously wasn't a terrific guy, but still the words stung. What really infuriated Quentin was that both he and the robot were placed on equal footing.

"So let me tell you what *I* want," Blanker said tightly. "And then I'll see if I can help you."

"But you might not be able to help us."

"Yeah, you'll just have to take that chance. I know you're asking if I'm trustworthy. But I am your father. That should count for something, right?"

Trinta didn't answer.

"All I want . . . is to hug my daughter," Blanker said. "That's not so much, is it?"

Trinta swallowed hard, like holding back the need to be sick. It *was* "so much". *Too* much. She didn't want to do it. Not at all. Not with what he put her through. Not with what he did to their family. But finding strength, she got up slowly and trudged over to him.

As she waited there coldly detached, Blanker stood up and put his arms around her. Not a big hug nor particularly warm, Trinta endured it, gritting her teeth as though she were hugging a porcupine with all its pricks lit on fire. Thankfully, the embrace lasted only a few seconds before Blanker released her, but not before whispering in her ear. Trinta jerked her head back as though the words were poison and sat back down abruptly, like she needed a shower that could wash you entirely inside and out.

"So, what can your doting father do for you?" said Blanker chipperly.

Nodding at Quentin, Trinta said, "He's an Earther."

Blanker's eyes went wide. Wider than they'd gone all day. Wider than they'd gone in years. In fact, he might have sprained his lids from the distance they went outside of his normal lid action.

"An Earther . . ." said Blanker, practically chewing the word. Sitting down slowly, he eyeballed the boy up and down, almost impressed. "An Earther . . ."

Quentin turned away. He hated being ogled like some sort of endangered species. (Even if that's exactly what he was.)

"Really?" Blanker asked, scrutinizing the young guy with wonder.

Trinta nodded.

"Yeah, I'm an Earther!" Quentin said. "So what? What?! Why is that always such a big freakin' deal?!"

"Now I can see it," Blanker said. "He does have some spark."

"He's the *last* Earther," Trinta said.

Blanker took his eyes off the Earth kid and narrowed them tight on Trinta, demanding confirmation she was telling the truth. She gave him the famed Bedinbur Very-Tiny-Nod-of-Assertion.

Blanker muttered: "She's still going . . ." He turned back to Quentin, sizing him up. "And he's it?"

"Apparently," Trinta said.

"Do you know what happened to my . . . people?" Quentin asked Blanker. He still felt weird saying "my people". But if he was the "last" one as they were saying, they were his people and he had to know what happened to them.

"No, not entirely," Blanker said. "But I'm pretty damn sure who has them."

"Are they still alive?" he asked. His heart fluttered, not ready for the answer.

"I . . . I don't know," Blanker said. "Maybe, maybe not. When did they get scooped?"

"'Scooped'? I don't know. Over a year now."

"A year? Wow. That's a long while. Not good. Not good at all. Why'd you wait so long to do anything, son?"

"Why'd I . . . Why'd I wait '*SO LONG*'?!!" Quentin seethed. "What the hell are you talking about?! All I did was take a nap and then the whole damn planet was gone! And since we didn't have any spaceships lying around, I had to steal one from the guys trying to kill me! So I guess I'd have found you sooner if I just stopped at the first INFORMATION MOON and asked where 'Blanker Bedinbur' was! Stupid me for not getting your daughter to stowaway sooner! (And I *still* don't know how she did that!) So, yeah, you're right, Blanky . . . WHY did I wait so freakin' long?!!"

That felt good. Quentin hadn't had a real good rant in forever. And with everything he'd been dealing with and everything he'd been through, it was extremely satisfying. Sneering at Blanker, he caught a glimpse of something dark and malevolent in the older man's eyes that made him regret it all. Before he had a chance to run, scream, or cry, Blanker leapt at the boy and threw him hard to the ground.

"What are you – " were the only words the Earth kid

got out as Blanker spun him face down and wrapped an arm around his throat. Blanker's other arm reached down and grabbed him by the nostrils. Never in his most depraved nose-picking days as a kid had fingers gone so far up his nose and he rightfully squealed in excruciating pain.

"No one talks to me that way, boy," said Blanker evenly but not evilly. "No . . . one . . ."

Through this, Trinta didn't move. Didn't try to stop Blanker. Didn't join in and give the annoying Earther a bonus kick. Nothing. Roddy also watched silently, observing with interest if not concern.

"I'm . . . I'm . . ." Quentin muttered, turning red as his neck was squeezed hard against Blanker's rigidly unyielding, muscular arm.

"Trying to apologize, boy?" Blanker said. "I do appreciate that. Trinta knows how I like a good proper apology for an unthinking discourtesy. Shows character."

"I'm . . . I'm . . . _NOT_ sorry, you crapworm," gasped Quentin, his breathing growing more and more labored.

Blanker respected the kid for standing up to him. Especially during a full-on beatdown. That didn't stop Blanker from twisting his fingers until Quentin's nose gave a crack though. When Quentin's eyes started to bug out and he neared going unconscious, Blanker released him, tossing his limp body to the floor.

"Mouthy kid when he wants to be," Blanker said to Trinta.

Scrambling into a corner, Quentin hurriedly took in deep breaths. As he frantically massaged his aching nostrils, unsure he'd ever sneeze right again, the older man took his seat again as though nothing happened. And despite Quentin's hard breathing and strange nose scrunching, it did seem as though nothing had happened as Trinta, Roddy, and Blanker all sat quietly like folks having a little meeting.

"So can you help me?" Trinta asked Blanker.

"Nope. Couldn't if I chose to, kid. Sorry."

Trinta winced at her father's words.

"But it was good to see you again," he said calmly.

"You can't do *anything*?" asked Trinta. More emotion spilled into her voice than she wanted because she knew this was her only chance. Blanker's only chance, too.

"No. Even if I could get you the coordinates, I wouldn't give 'em to you. She'd chew you up and rip you apart three times over. And that's if she *didn't* know you were mine. If she knew that, she might just turn you into another bleeding fountain for her ice garden. It's not even your fight, Trinty. That was mine. And I lost."

"But . . ." Trinta blurted out then stopped. She knew she couldn't sway her father's mind here. No reason to try. If there was anything he taught her, it was to fight the real battles and avoid the ones that had no chance for victory.

"Plus, we aren't exactly outside of prying eyes here, so . . . no, kid," Blanker said. "No on top of no on top of no. I got nothing for ya. And I'm sorry. I really am."

Trinta's left eye watered up. She wished with all her heart that they'd never come here. And that this man wasn't her father.

"I'm glad I waited these years for you," Blanker said. "Warmed my heart to see ya. Take care of yourself, kid. Live every day with the cold fire in your heart. And know you're always my girl."

The dome covering them slid backwards and revealed a dusky sky. With Borstan being a smaller planet with a faster revolution, their short chat with Blanker turned into a lost afternoon.

Wobbling a little in the knees, Trinta rose up slowly. Quentin didn't know if it was due to her dad not helping her out or some other father/daughter issues or just everything . . . but he knew Trinta wasn't herself. She could barely make eye contact with her dad, glancing at him once then turning and trudging off the platform. Roddy soon followed.

As Quentin went to go, Blanker grabbed him by the arm and said:

"Take care of her. Take care of yourself, son. In that order."

Quentin nodded and shuffled off as the old man gave him a wink. A wink that felt like a vote of confidence in a weird way that he didn't quite get. A wink that said he was okay by Blanker.

Watching Trinta disappear down the hill, Blanker hollered these departing words: "Thanks, Trinta. Thank you, my little swirl. Miss you always."

As they stepped off the platform, the dome closed slowly back over Blanker. Quentin watched the man stand proud and defiant. Defiant of what Quentin didn't know. And despite the fact that the older Thricer had probed the insides of his nose with ridiculous vigor, he respected the guy. He didn't know what went down between him and Trinta, but he wanted to believe this guy wasn't necessarily a bad guy.

"What a tiny place to live," Roddy said.

"Yeah, where does he eat?" Quentin asked. "Where does he sleep? Where does he go to the . . ."

Before he could finish, the dome finished sliding over the room with a loud reverberating clang. Suddenly, a cacophony of dozens of hefty metallic locks riveted into place where the dome met the ground. Each lock secured with a sound like the ringing of a bell from a lost cathedral.

Trinta continued stalking off, not looking back for anything as she descended the hill. The other two looked back though. And Quentin soon wished he hadn't.

"That doesn't sound right," he said.

The dome vibrated and the hum carried over the nearby hills. As the humming increased in volume, the dome walls shook violently. Without warning, the dome crumpled in on itself with a thunderous grinding wail, the walls magnetically pulling in on themselves. With each inward crash of imploding metal, the already small dome became smaller and smaller, like someone crushing an aluminum can. It would have been fascinating to behold, if not for the fact someone was inside this "can". Someone who now yelled angry, piercing screams of anguish.

"Arrrrrrghghghhhhhhhggggggghhhhhgnnnnnnnn!!!"

"Oh, God . . ." Quentin sputtered. "We've got to . . . we've got to help him! We've got to . . . We have got to do . . . something! Help!"

Trinta didn't turn back, didn't stop. In fact, her pace picked up, racing off as the dome got smaller and smaller. Quentin couldn't believe what he was seeing but couldn't turn away. Roddy did though and swiftly followed Trinta down the hill.

The dome's terrifying reduction continued with each crumpling crush eliciting a smaller and smaller groan from within until there was no living sound at all. Eventually, the crushing halted with a jiggering final crinkle, leaving only a flat white sheet of metal.

Staring out to the dusky vastness of the dozens and dozens of domes on hills extending far into the distance, Quentin shook uncontrollably. Each of those domes could do that. Every single one. Hurriedly, he ran to catch up with his friends, hoping to get off this planet and never return again.

CHAPTER TWENTY
FOLLOW ME NOSE

"Seven minutes until irritant eradication," Securitan Hagland's voice boomed frostily, echoing across the hills of Borstan.

Trinta marched through the grass, going nowhere but at a very brisk and determined pace. Roddy had returned to traversing the untended meadows with his elongated robot legs and Quentin raced after both, struggling through the brush and panic to catch up.

"I think we oughta be going!" the Earth teen shouted. "The voice says we really oughta be going, right?! That's what he means, right?!"

Trinta's eyes, red from holding back tears, darted along the landscape as she stopped, unsure where to go next, unsure what to do next. Not sure she wanted to do anything at all.

Taken aback by such naked emotion from her, a still shaking Quentin ran up and put a hand on her shoulder: "It's going to be . . . okay . . ." He searched for the right comforting words even though he himself was pretty damn far from comfort. "I don't know how, but it will . . ."

"I can't believe it . . ." she muttered.

"I know. Me, either. That was . . . so brutal. I'm so sorry he's gone. No one should – "

"No! I can't believe he didn't help me!"

"What?!" exclaimed Quentin. "That is cold."

"I did him a favor. And he did nothing for me. *Nothing!*"

Her callous response to her father's death left him staggered. But, currently, nothing made too much sense. However, he knew now wasn't the time to ask a lot of questions.

"Four minutes until eradication implementation," Security Hagland declared.

Where is his voice coming from? Quentin wondered. *Are there speakers in the grass? In the sky? Is it telepathy?* Getting his eye back on the ball, he grabbed Trinta by the shoulders and hurriedly demanded:

"Where's the remote?"

She reached into her pocket and pulled out the silver disc. Then, without warning, she drew her arm back and chucked it over a hill.

"Not cool, Trinta," Quentin said. "Not cool."

"Two minutes until . . . no, *three* minutes until eradication," Securitan Hagland's voice thundered over them.

"Watch her, Roddy," said Quentin, sprinting over the hill. "I'm gonna get the ship!"

Following his orders, Roddy moved towards Trinta.

"What're you gonna do, ballsy?" she challenged the viadroid, eyeing him angrily.

Quentin crawled through the grass as bugs bigger than his head squirmed over his arms. One creepy-crawly yellow and blue one climbed up his back and across his neck before he knocked it off. Frantically on all fours, he rummaged through the overflowing pasture, desperately trying to find the remote.

"Now, it is two minutes until . . . well, you know . . ." Securitan Hagland said.

Grabbing fistfuls of grass and shaking it, clawing it, desperately reaching out for anything, Quentin wondered how bad eradication would be. Maybe it'd be as gentle as the anesthetic he had before he had his appendix out years ago. He hoped that'd be the case. But having just witnessed the gruesome end of Blanker, he doubted it.

"C'mon, remote, where are you?!"

Just as he was about to give up (which is the universal key to finding anything lost), his fingers flittered across that silver disc. (Thankfully, the scuttling goo-bug humping the remote scurried away once Quentin grabbed it.) Holding the remote aloft and pressing the center button, he heard the Havok's familiar rattling hum as it appeared from over the horizon. Racing back up to the top, he motioned with his hand for the ship to land at the bottom of the hill. . .

. . . The bottom of the hill where Roddy now forcefully restrained a kicking and punching Trinta! Using his orbs as a full-on body cuff, Roddy wrapped himself around her tightly. Her kicking boots repeatedly punctured through the wall of balls momentarily until Roddy would wrap around her again.

Startled to witness this skirmish between his friends, Quentin forgot to reposition where he had aimed the Havok.

"Oh, holy shirt . . ." he muttered.

"One minute until eradication!" Securitan Hagland bellowed.

Realizing there wasn't time to alter the approach too much, Quentin tried to tweak the landing as best he could as the ship barreled towards Roddy and Trinta. Noting the impending crash of the Havok into his precious body, Roddy tried to move away with Trinta still wrapped up. It looked like a horrible sack race, especially when they tripped as the roar of the oncoming spaceship crescendoed. When they hit the ground so did the Havok . . . nose first a mere seven feet away, covering them with clods of dirt and grass.

"Sorry!" yelled Quentin.

He galloped down the hill and speedily helped Trinta and Roddy up. They then all crawled across to the ramp of the askew ship stuck diagonally in the ground like a thrown javelin.

"Let's go, folks! Let's go!!!" Quentin shouted.

After pushing Trinta and Roddy onboard, Quentin jumped into the corridor and slid straight down the tilted hallway into the cockpit with glee. Once there, his fingers darted across the console and he grabbed the joystick with force, rapidly shooting the Havok backwards into the air.

"Eradication commencing . . ." Securitan Hagland

started to say.

"Oh, can it, pruney!" Quentin barked as he hit the engines and the Havok flew off with a mighty bellow.

Tearing out of orbit in record time, the whole ship shook its hearty rattling hum as it did. And not needing any praise for a job well done for the first time in his life, the young Earther leaned back and breathed a satisfied sigh of relief.

Hours later, Quentin still sat at the controls, staring out at the great expanse. He had no idea what went down on Borstan. In the same situation, he figured he might have behaved the exact same way Trinta did with Blanker. Might have then tossed the keys to the car and jeopardized their own existence, too. But to be honest, he had no idea what this situation was. And he needed to know. He'd never seen someone die before.

So when Trinta made her way into the cockpit with shoulders slumped and sat sullenly across from him, he knew he shouldn't press her. And he tried not to. He really did. But as minutes passed and Roddy entered and took his place in the corner and more minutes passed and all there was was silence, silence Quentin's mind kept turning into the echoes of Blanker's bloodcurdling screams, he couldn't be silent any longer.

"What was that down there?" he questioned softly. "What the hell happened to your dad?"

Trinta focused on a star in the distance and wished the damn ship could go further faster. Or back in time. Or something other than keep her enmeshed in the weird and soul-shattering sense of loss she felt.

"What happened?" asked Quentin again.

And again, Trinta didn't respond. The Earther turned to Roddy, who rested in the corner like a stoic, oversized beanbag, trying very much not to get drawn into this. It didn't work though.

"Roddy, what happened there? What was that all about?"

"I don't know," Roddy said.

"You don't know?! You're a robot! Aren't you supposed to know everything?!"

"No, that's ridiculous," Roddy huffed. "In a universe in which the most recent measurements pigeonholed it as 'pretty damn infinite', it's unrealistic to expect anybody to know everything about everything. Even *me*! But at least I know a hell of a lot more than you!" He then formed himself into a six-foot wheel and rolled out of the room.

"Look . . . I've never . . ." Quentin turned to Trinta, grasping for words. "I don't . . . I . . . what the hell was that?"

His question wasn't for curiosity's sake. It was an honest, trembling question. Trinta said nothing though. And Quentin was okay with that. As the silence warmed back over them, he felt he'd get an answer at some point . . . probably . . . hopefully . . .

An hour later, Trinta could almost allow herself to speak. Not much. Only enough to calm the boy.

"What do you want to know?" she said curtly and with no emotion.

"That . . . that 'house'," Quentin said. "Why'd it do that? Why didn't you help?"

"Because it wasn't a house. It was his prison. And if I

could have helped him, I would. But it did exactly what it was designed for. And there's nothing I could have done to stop it."

"Why'd it do that?" he asked, greedily soaking up answers even though he knew he shouldn't question her too much. "Why then?"

"You only get one visit. You're kept alive in that room until the one visit. And once you okay your last visitor . . . you're done."

Quentin processed it all slowly.

"So why'd we go visit him then?" he asked.

"Because I thought he could help us with your situation. Guess I was wrong."

"So . . . he's . . . kinda dead . . . because . . . because of me?" Quentin felt queasy, like his stomach dropped out of him. "That's not cool." His skin went tingly. Lightheaded, he felt even worse about what he'd witnessed. "That's not . . . I didn't ask . . . I didn't . . . That's horrible . . . absolutely . . . horrible . . ."

"It's not your fault," she said. "Not really. And it's not as simple as – "

"Yeah, it is! *I* killed your dad! I can't believe this . . ." he gasped. "He'd still be alive if it wasn't for me. I think I'm going to be . . ."

But before he could finish, Trinta slapped him across the face. Hard.

"Calm yourself now!" Trinta said sternly. "You did NOT kill him! *I* chose this course. This is on me. Me alone. I'm the one that lives with this. I'm the one who took this chance on a dream . . . a stupid dream. So don't take this on yourself, Quentin. It's not yours to take."

Quentin took a deep breath, his eyes watering from her slap, her words, everything.

"Besides," she continued, "if he wasn't in that prison in the first place, he never would have had that outcome. And I'm the one who put him there. So, do yourself a favor, Bulldog, and don't steal *my* guilt and *my* grief. Just leave me alone."

Quentin didn't know what to say. Clever enough guy that he was though, he did as she said and left her alone. Exiting to the corridor, he hesitated a moment as he heard tiny heaving gasps. Although not sure if she was crying, he *was* sure she wouldn't want his shoulder to cry on. Nor would she want anyone to know she was weeping. All he knew was that she wanted to be alone and so he left her as such.

One question still nagged at him though: *Why did Blanker say "Thanks" to her? Why?*

The next day, the Havok drifted aimlessly nowhere. Quentin rested on his bunk in the sleeping quarters, feet hanging way off the too-small bed as he chewed on a stick of jerky. He'd come to really hate the taste of jerky yet still enjoyed the way his teeth tore it apart. Made him feel feral. Of course, gnawing on it like a dog with a bone, he swiftly turned fire engine red when he noticed Trinta staring at him from the doorway.

"Uhrm . . . hrrm," he said, speedily chewing up the giant bite in his mouth.

Her green eyes now grey, her silent face sank as though it lost all its facial muscles. She plopped down on her bunk.

Extending his half-eaten snack to her, Quentin

offered, "Jerky?"

Trinta gazed at it strangely, then shrugged and ripped off a bite. Bunching up her lips, she gobbled it down, surprised it wasn't that bad.

"You okay?" he asked.

"No. Not really. But that's beside the point, I guess."

Hunched and weary, she rested her arms on her knees and ran her hands through her new tufts of growing hair.

"I really thought he would . . ." Trinta said. "I don't know."

"He would what?"

"He would . . . Look, this wasn't all about you helping your people. I won't even pretend that. But I thought he'd give me a lead or something. He knew how to get to her and – "

Quentin interrupted, "Her who?"

"She's called the Mother. He used to work for her."

"Work for the . . . 'Mother'? What's she? Does she have, like, a ton of kids? She doesn't live in a shoe, does she?"

"No. She's a nomadic Dowager Empress, ruling wherever her ship takes her. She's as brutal as she is hideous. And she's a collector."

"Collector of what? Beatles memorabilia? Antique spoons? Beanie Babies? Bells? (My mom collects bells. It's really weird.) What?"

"Cultures . . . people . . ."

"Like . . . one day she's all into your culture and paints herself purple and eats your wormy salad sort of thing or . . ."

"Yeah, or. She collects the actual people. Whole

civilizations."

"How? What for?"

"For her amusement. For turning them into weapons. For power. For dinner. For whatever she wants."

"How can she do that? Isn't there some sort of police force or army or something? Or is she like the head of an evil empire that controls the entire universe?"

Trinta smiled, remembering Quentin was a babe in the stars here.

"No, there's no police force," she said. "And no empire or anything like that. Why? Is that how it works on your planet? There's one police force or one guiding empire for the whole planet? Everybody's under one government?"

"Uh . . . no . . . not really . . ."

"And out here, the rest of the universe is slightly larger than your little planet, right?"

"Only slightly," said Quentin wryly.

"So why would it be different out here? There are pockets of power. Pockets of extreme law. Pockets of extreme lawlessness. Mostly there are just regular places with a little bit of everything: corruption, bureaucracies, even a few decent planets that sort of somehow work alright. But for the most part, it's everyone working each day as it comes with whatever set of rules that are thrown at 'em. It's not about survival. It's about something less simple. It's mixing up what you want and what you need so much that you aren't sure which is which, but you do what needs to be done to get it."

"Sounds like high school," Quentin said. "So, what

are you wanting or needing?" Or should it be some new combo word like 'waeding' or 'neenting'? I prefer 'neenting'."

"Me? I just want to get in a few kicks before I go."

Trinta snatched the rest of the jerky from his hand. He didn't mind. *If jerky helps, by all means, take it,* he thought.

Trinta wasn't going to be "okay" any time soon, but she was feeling a tiny bit better. Even though her crying wasn't something she was proud of, it let her grieve, exhausting her from feeling anything else. A good numb.

"So what was your plan?" Quentin asked. "Your dad would tell us where this Mother is and we'd go get my people back?"

"Sort of. He worked on one of her escape holes back a ways back. I also had a few other things in mind. Some . . . self-serving things. But that was the gist."

"So what do we do now? Nothing? Can't we find her another way? Could we just drive around looking for her? Would Roddy know where she is?"

"No. The odds of us finding her without the beacon code is three hairs off impossible. The beacon code would give us coordinates to . . . Hell, forget it. Even this backdoor my father could have got us into wouldn't guarantee anything."

"How would your dad have the code?" Quentin asked.

"He was doing a job for her back in the day . . . before he . . ."

She stopped, her words dropping off like a lost signal and leaving them in silence.

After a few minutes, Quentin said, "So looks like I'm kinda screwed, huh?"

"Yeah, I guess so. We can keep looking, but we'd be better off building our own planet of cheese."

"Well, I *do* like cheese," he said.

Grinning, Trinta laid back on her bunk and rested her head in her hands. Staring up at the pipes above carrying fluids throughout the ship, she wondered how she got here. She knew how she got here. Closing her eyes, she knew it was a long story. (Too long of a story for this time around yet maybe long enough for another tale some day.) What amazed her were the strange points of concurrence that led from one step to another. She didn't believe in fate. But she knew as well as anything if one small thing had been different on the path she took to get where she was, she wouldn't be *who* she was. And at times like this, being who she was was the only thing that kept her going.

Quentin sat on his squat bed, head down. Sneaking peaks through his curtain of hair, his eyes secretly studied the lovely Thricer with a mixture of concern, worry, and smit. He couldn't help he was smitten. Watching the bereft Trinta, he wanted to fix everything and make it all better for her but knew there wasn't anything he could do. It was frustrating enough to be a powerless teen boy in high school in a Nebraska town, but to be so powerless in the middle of the universe with a too-tough-to-show-her-own-anguish girl that you just happen to have a crush on was unbearable.

As the ship's hum numbed over them, Quentin's nose began to ache. Blanker really put it through the ringer. Scrunching up his nostrils pig-style, Quentin stretched the thing out to see if that would make it hurt less. It didn't. Even gently squeezing his snout provoked a sharp, piercing agony as though it were being stabbed from the inside.

"Ahhhhhhhhhhh!!!" he yelped.

Opening one eye, Trinta glanced over to Quentin gritting his teeth in pain.

"Yeah, that's one of my father's favorite moves," she remarked. "Said it always worked best controlling the grapuggles back on the Styxille feedpens. Especially as those beasts had eight nostrils and you could grab 'em with both hands."

"But should it still hurt like this?"

"I don't know. He never did it to me."

"Your loss. It feels like . . . like he left a sticker in there or something. Or a burr . . . It's like – " Moving his nose just right though (or "wrong" if you want to see it that way), the piercing pain shot through him again:

"YeaaaaaaaaaAAAAAAAOOOOOOOOWWWW!!!"

Strangely excited, Trinta grabbed him by the face and stared at his sniffer.

"Okay, the plan is . . . I'm never gonna move my nose again," Quentin said, trying hard to keep his face completely still. "I'll just never smile. Never cry. I will be Mr. Blankface. Well, until I sneeze and my whole freakin' face blows off."

"Sneeze . . ." Trinta muttered to herself. Stuffing the rest of the jerky in her pocket, she jumped up and sprinted out of the room.

"Trinta? Trinta? What are you – Where are you going? Trinta!" But with the last word being shouty, his nose-apocalypse went off and he howled again.

"Owwww-oooooowwwwwwww . . ."

Trinta raced back in, dragging Roddy with her right hand and holding something unseen in the left.

"What am I doing—" Roddy asked.

The question hung unfinished as Trinta opened her left hand to reveal a palm full of green powder that she blew right in Quentin's face. The Earther blinked several times as the powder fully infiltrated and tickled his nasal passages. A big sneeze was coming. He tried desperately to hold it back, terrified a sneeze might rip his whole damn nose apart. (And Quentin was partial to his nose, even if it was bigger than he'd have liked. He preferred to be nosed than noseless.) But the green powder (a spicy Darhuntian powder for meats) was too much for his schnozz to ignore and his head snapped back, readying an unholy torrent of sneeze.

"Ahhhhhhhhhhhh . . ." he sputtered, queuing up the requisite first syllable of the two-syllable sneeze dance.

Instantly afraid, Roddy's optical orbs went to the size of grapefruit as Quentin's head cocked back and then shot towards them. A fine spray of nose juice spread across the room with an outrageous wrath none of them had ever seen. Especially not from a nose. And never with such a disgusting torrent. Quentin tried to cover his nose as he'd been taught, but it was no good. It went everywhere. And it went loud.

"—CHOOOOOOOOOOOOOOOOOOOOEEEYYYYY!!!"

Each of them more than a little sickened (and the sneezer more than a little ashamed), they let the post-sneeze stillness drift over them. Quentin was about to search for a Kleenex to wipe up his mess, but Trinta held up her hand, stopping him:

"Nobody move!"

Roddy didn't move. He merely looked as revolted as any robot could after withstanding the sneeze tsunami that had drenched them all.

"Hey, my nose feels better," Quentin said blissfully, scrunching up his snout.

"Scan the room," Trinta said. "Again, nobody move. Stare up every single inch of the place. It's got to be here."

"Look for what?" Quentin asked. "What's got to be here?"

"I'm not sure . . . but something . . ."

Trinta's eyes darted about the room, from ceiling to floor, trying to catch a glimpse of whatever Blanker left her. She didn't know how, but somehow he did come through. She knew it. No matter what happened before, he was still her dad.

Quentin scanned the room as well. His own father often referred to him as a "snot-nosed kid" (even when he wasn't particularly filled with mucus), so he never thought there'd be anything great about his snot now. That changed when he noticed a small speck on Trinta's grey bed frame no bigger than an ant. Turning his head just right, it glimmered violet.

"Is that . . ." he nodded toward the oh-so-tiny purple circular dot.

Trinta squatted down, eye-to-eye with it. Carefully picking up the dot with her fingernail, she whispered a thanks to her father.

"What is it?" Quentin asked.

"Hair," she said proudly.

"Hair? That's hair? And it was up my nose? Gross."

She unspooled the dot slowly and carefully, revealing a long line of several of Blanker's hairs tied together. Holding the hair up to the light, she read the marks along it, marks her father must have made years ago.

"So, what? You going to go catch some flies with that?" Quentin joked.

"I'm going to catch something. My father left me this. It has everything we need to find your people. And for me to get a little something, too."

"A twofer then," Quentin said.

"Yes. A twofer."

Roddy cleared his non-existent throat. They turned to him.

"Can I clean this sickening spray off me now?" requested Roddy, exasperated.

"Sure," Trinta said.

Roddy walked out of the room and went down the hall muttering, "Just disgusting. 'C'mere, I need you.' You didn't say, 'I need you to get slathered in face goo.' Thanks, breathers. Glad to know I'm so utterly useful."

Trinta read the tiny hair note with the squintiest of squinty squints. Her father had to have carved this up with excruciating patience. It didn't matter that he had absolutely nothing else to do while contained. It was simply the kindest thing her dad had ever done for her. And she was touched. The message wasn't all for her though. His own unfinished business certainly played a part, too.

"What's it say?" Quentin inquired, wiping his nose on his shirt sleeve.

"It gives me a seventeen digit transponder code to

her beacon."

"That sounds . . . good?"

"Yes, very good. But right now, all we really have is the potential we were missing before. We should be able to get to her. Or to her city-ship at least."

"And then what?"

"That's a great question."

"Thanks."

"Now, all we have to do is come up with a great answer. One that doesn't include us most likely dying."

Trinta said that last bit with a wink. A confident wink that made Quentin smile. A confident wink that sent shivers down his back. A confident wink that let him know in no uncertain terms that things were about to kick off and that he'd better be ready. He had no idea if he was, but he didn't care. Because here on the cusp of what might be their own private annihilation, he finally realized he was more than just attracted to her. It wasn't just that she was the only one on board. (Hell, he'd probably have felt a little something for Roddy if the viadroid did himself up right.)

No, he was in love. And not the old puppy love he'd been fostering 'til now. This was full grown-up dog love. Nothing could change that now. Quentin McFury was full of all the nerves and courage and foolishness that love provoked, all for the tall girl he only just really met and it kinda scared him. Despite the fear, he was ready to follow Trinta anywhere she took him. He only hoped he'd get a chance to kiss her again before they died.

CHAPTER TWENTY-ONE
THE WORMHOLE CORRIDOR
OF QUEASINESS

Their plan was built purely on irrational hope and unbelievable stupidity. But at least all three of them knew it. No one entered this escapade without knowing exactly the ridiculousness of such a plan dependent on so many necessary coincidences, happenstances, and maybe some good old-fashioned lucky socks.

First, they had to hope that the beacon code Blanker gave them still worked to pinpoint the escape hole to the Mother's den. Then if that worked, they had to get past the defense systems with a code that surely had to be outdated. And if by chance it wasn't, Trinta would then have to try to whip up an override on the spot so they could get to their real destination.

Should they make it through to the Mother's floating

city of wormholes, debauchery, and antiquities, they'd then have to find a way to gain access to the Mother herself. That would require a spoonful of technological chicanery mixed with a ton of argy-bargy to get through the security that they'd surely be outnumbered, outmatched, and outpowered by.

However, the three of them did have nothing better to do.

For Quentin, this felt like the first round of soccer districts the season before . . . well, before everyone went bye-bye.

North Platte had the worst soccer team in the state. They weren't the worst team athletically. They just rarely worked together as a team. And because of that, each game was pretty much a guaranteed loss with the only thing in flux how much they'd lose by. But in their district game against Hastings, things changed when those North Platte Bulldogs accidentally scored in the opening minute. Unexpectedly, Andy Loya took a random shot from a mile away and, catching a fortuitous gust of wind, the ball crawled into the upper right corner of the goal. It surprised Hastings's unsuspecting goalkeeper. (It surprised Andy, too, as he admitted later he was just trying to pass the ball.)

After that, the game stayed close because that initial ray of hope made everything seem possible. The Hastings' team didn't even equal that initial goal until late in the second half, largely due to Quentin and the rest of his defense playing out of their collective heads. Quentin liked to think that if he, Trinta, and Roddy were able to fight with that same unyielding surge of pluck and luck, they might have a chance here.

(Of course, he conveniently ignored the fact that Hastings scored three goals in overtime and that their goalie Craig Jewell unintentionally kicked him in the face.)

They all sat silently in the cockpit, knowing they were at the point of no return. In the center of a revolving asteroid field, they studied a lush turquoise asteroid covered in wintry silicon trees and flowing lavender streams. Several miles wide, it spun around slowly, the stars dancing playfully in the background like an intergalactic kaleidoscope.

As the asteroid turned around, an enormous glacial palace revealed itself glimmering on the surface. Before the palace spun away from them again, Quentin thought it one of the most beautiful constructions he'd ever seen, elegant yet icily sinister.

"Wow," he whispered.

"And that's just the escape hatch," Trinta said.

"The 'escape hatch'? It's a freakin' palace!"

"Yeah, it's that also. But for us it's the honey to get to the Queen Bee. This is basically just her parachute-slash-vacation home."

"And we know she's not on vacation?" Roddy asked with concern.

"No," Trinta answered. "This is just one of her homes. Each one has a gateway to her city-ship. This is the one she'd go to if everything went bad. Now, the bad is coming to her. Going this way, we transport right aboard and avoid flying any suicidal missions through her fleet of a thousand Strikers."

"Yeah, but let's be honest, this is only slightly less suicidal, right?" Quentin said. "'Cause once we jump on her ship, we still need to get past her regular non-shippy security. Or is she just guarded by teddy bears and huggy unicorns?"

"We'll burn that bridge when we get to it, kid," she said.

As the young Earther blanched from being called "kid" yet again, they watched the palace spin away once more while the surrounding asteroids oscillated wildly. Each one – easily over a dozen – was a different color, but only one had a monstrously huge palace. To Quentin, the asteroids looked like giant Fruity Pebbles that mutated and drifted away from Earth, just waiting for a bowl big enough to hold them. He wondered how much milk he'd need to eat them. (Admittedly he was hungry while thinking this. Being scared shirtless always made him peckish.)

"So this is it?" asked Quentin.

"Yup," Trinta replied with a firm nod. "We all still in?"

"I guess so . . ."

"You 'guess so'?" she bristled. "You 'guess so'?! When are you going to know? If not now, when, Quentin? I have a lot at stake here – primarily my life – and I know I've made my decision. What about you?"

"Yeah . . . I said . . ."

"I haven't known you long, have I, Quentin? And in that time, you react to everything. Almost every choice I've seen you make is riding along someone else's choice. When are you going to grab the stick and go? When are you going to stop asking questions and start making statements? When are you going to stop being a guy stuff happens to and be the guy who makes things go boom?"

"Look . . . I said I'm in," he sputtered defensively. "I am. I gotta get my planet back. It's where I keep all my stuff."

Quentin wasn't all in though. Not with what Trinta shared about the Mother. Not with how the Mother sounded worse than any nightmare he'd ever had. Not after hearing her victims learned not to beg her to let you die because that just guaranteed she'd keep you alive longer. Alive longer in horrifying agony for her own malevolent pleasure.

In addition to that gooey, spine-tingling fear, saving his people felt too immense any more. So unfathomably real. What if he couldn't save them? What if he had to die so that they may all live? Could he do that? That seemed like an awful lot to ask for a planet of people who loved crappy music and reality TV stars and who generally seemed to not like him. It was a lot to ask of a sixteen-year-old kid who hadn't really lived much yet.

Basically, all he really wanted to do was go where the pretty girl went. They were having fun and she *was* very pretty. He didn't need much more than that. But there *was* more than that. There was also the fleeting chance he might be close to finding out that all his people were dead. And that . . . that was too much for him to consider without completely freaking out. So he focused on the pretty Trinta instead. It was easier that way.

Irritated at what she took for indifference, Trinta snapped, "Yeah . . . well, I've got a message to deliver for my father and I'm going with or without you."

Gravely, Trinta took out a knitted skullcap from her jacket pocket and pulled it over her hair, now grown back to the spiked pixie-do Quentin first encountered her with. She then pulled out a pair of fingerless gloves and slid her fingers in for a snug fit. She wiggled her fingers around and they melded to her like a second skin.

"Hey, are those my gloves?" Quentin said. "I wondered where those went."

"They look better on me," she said. "Everything looks better on me."

Quentin couldn't disagree and seeing those gloves, attained so long ago for his first road trip, he realized he never wore them much while flying the Havok. Mostly because they reminded him of what this all meant. It meant everyone and everything he ever knew.

"And you, Roddy?" asked Trinta to the viadroid sitting stoically on his own makeshift throne of orbs in the corner. "You in?"

"You obviously don't have any real connection to this, man," Quentin told him. "So if you don't want do it, I'd completely understand."

"I wouldn't," Trinta said. "But I won't kill you much or anything."

"Thanks," Roddy said dryly, picking up the remote Trinta made and looking at it intently. One of his orbs opened and closed over the remote a couple times. There was a long silence before he spoke again. And when he did, his words were said seriously and with much thought. "There are many reasons for me not to be a part of this. Self-preservation being number one.

Hanging around with you breathers can't be good for anyone's health. But knowing your planet familiarly as I now do, Quentin, that puts me in the 'let's do this thing' camp."

Quentin gave Roddy a playful punch to the shoulder. Speedily processing that this wasn't a violent attack, he gave him a playful punch back.

"Owwww," the boy yelped.

"Sorry . . ." Roddy apologized.

"Just kidding," Quentin laughed.

Trinta laughed, too, and Roddy started chuckling as well. It would be the last time they all laughed together like this. At least one of them would not make it.

The Havok gently touched down on the far side of the asteroid, at least a mile from the palace. Trinta estimated there'd be a security contingent of dozens of scanners, weaponized defenses, and thirty plus cyborg, humanoid, or mutated equivalents waiting for them.

The fact that the Havok was able to land without any problems gave them all a bit of encouragement. As they exited the ship and waded through one of the asteroid's many lavender streams, they passed a huge artillery cannon hidden behind an embankment that clearly could have ripped the Havok out of the artificial sky.

"Whoa . . ." Quentin muttered.

"Yeah, I'll second that," Trinta said, shaking her head at their luck.

The whole place seemed unnaturally still. Not that Quentin knew what a normal asteroid should be like, but it felt odd. Unsettling. He almost screamed when a flock of green four-winged birds shot out of a nearby brush. The binderbirds flapped wildly up into the air and over the palace with such speed he wasn't sure it actually occurred.

"Maybe that's all the security they have," hoped Quentin.

"You're a cute kid," said Trinta sweetly yet patronizingly.

As they hiked up to the palace, the red dwarf in the distance glimmered off the interwoven icy beams, making the palace look like the green crystal bowl Quentin's mom kept on a shelf in the basement. He considered the palace like that bowl – something pretty to look at, but nothing you should ever touch.

Walking up the frigid steps, the palace gave off a frosty chill that nipped through their bones as their breaths carried wispy exhalations of vapor. Columns lined up across the front with no visible doorway. That is until Trinta reached out and put her hand on one of the columns. Instantly, the column turned blue and viscous, like clay on a potter's wheel.

"Wasn't expecting that . . ." Quentin marveled.

"Now, if I can remember my father's directions just right . . . we should be on our way to the big show," Trinta said. "If not . . ."

"If not, then I'll never get to take you to prom," he joked.

"Yeah, so I definitely better not screw this up."

Trinta moved her hand through the gelatinous "keyhole", rotating her thumb and pinky in one direction while swirling through the center of it with her middle finger. Moving from one movement to the next and hoping not to stumble in the process, it felt like the old games she used to play as a child on the shadowed moon of Thrice. There, in the sticky mud puddles left by a storm between storms, she and her brothers would race outside to play Sluice the Gates, write their names in the mud, and draw rude imaginings of their pets doing horrible things to their parents.

One time, her father caught her older brother Hane in the midst of a particularly graphic mud drawing featuring the seven tails of their aquiditer lizard ripping through every hole in their dad's head. Blanker didn't blink. Just grinned and said, "Nice likeness, but my ears ain't that big." Then he sauntered off. It was one of the few times her father didn't overreact like a jerk.

Indulging such memories, she kept her mind off the task literally at hand. Precisely, she swirled and gestured her way so that seconds later she disappeared right through the crystal column.

"Trinta!" Quentin shouted. But she was gone. "Trinta!!! Trinta!!!" Frantic, he turned to Roddy, who happened to be rotating his head, scanning for the next sign of trouble. "Where'd she go?"

Roddy shrugged an "I don't know" that moved up and down his body of balls like a world-class (the "world" being Earth, of course) breakdancer.

"Time to follow the leader," Trinta said from somewhere beyond the column, her voice like a whisper miles away. Quentin looked around, hoping to see her, but all he saw was more crystal palace.

"Trinta?" he said.

"Follow . . . the . . . leader . . ." she replied and then her voice faded away.

The Earther turned to Roddy, "You first?"

Roddy shrugged and rolled towards the wall. He stopped for a second prior to touching it and then pushed through. The column poured over every ball and he, too, vanished behind it.

"Okay . . ." Quentin muttered.

Not liking that he left himself for last and now was quite alone, Quentin closed his eyes and walked through the column. He giggled as it globbed over him like Jell-O. Though he enjoyed the gelatinous feeling, he didn't like coming through the "door" and . . .

. . . Falling straight onto his face. Falling straight onto his face against a green crystalline floor with a slim layer of frost on it, sending up tiny little waves of dissipating wispy green clouds. He instantly jumped to his feet both for fear of his friends laughing at him but also because the floor was so chilly.

"Yeeaoowww, that's freeeezzziiinnnggg!" he yelled.

Quentin expected to face an amused Trinta and an unimpressed Roddy, all bathing in his humiliation. However, they didn't even see his fall. Their backs to him, they faced a long corridor, unmoving. For a second, the young Earther had the horrible dread that they were both dead, just waiting to keel over. Then he thought maybe they'd become zombies whose faces had been ripped off. Or maybe . . .

But before he could conjure up more horrendous outcomes for his two friends, he saw what captured their undivided attention. The hallway undulated from the walls and the ceiling outwards with charged waves coming out of them. He felt an intense motion sickness like the two times he went fishing with his dad on Lake McConaghy. But what really threw him off was the end of the elongated hallway where rested a wall of pure and utter blackness, the longest emptiness the young McFury had ever seen. It was like looking into a bottomless hole, except this hole went indefinitely sideways and not down. Staring at the undulating walls leading to this unmoving infinity made his brain hurt.

"Whattt'sss gooooiiing onnnnn?" said Quentin, sounding almost drunk. "Is anyone else feeling . . . not so good?"

"I'm fine," said Roddy, staring quizzically ahead.

"It's the waved hallway," said Trinta unsteadily. "That, coupled with the . . . with the wormhole at the end, won't let our eyes make sense of what's going on."

"I really don't feel good," the Earther groaned. "I feel urpy."

Roddy slid away from him, knowing Quentin's gag reflex was terribly low and wanting no part of the boy's heaving matter should it come up.

As Quentin went to lean against a wall, Trinta grabbed him violently: "Stop!"

"I'm . . . losing my . . . balance . . ." Quentin said, tilting towards the undulating walls. "I just . . . I just need to . . ."

"Don't touch them!" Trinta shouted, a little wobbly herself.

"But they look so soft . . ." he whined.

Trinta pulled out the jerky from her pocket that he'd given her so long ago and tossed it at the wavy wall next to him. The jerky exploded, the undulation ripping it to shreds with ferocious, tiny lightning strikes. Although still queasy and disoriented, Quentin snapped straight up and away from the wall.

"On someone like yourself," Trinta said, "that would have been more bloody and smelled more like a barbecue."

"Can't we just go back out?" he whimpered, closing his eyes and blocking out all movement. "Just for a minute . . ."

Trinta's head hurt from the room's dizzying dynamism. She doubted they could make it to the end of the hall without the walls zapping one, if not all, of them.

"No," she said, disappointed. "No, we can't. It's a one-way trip. There's a code to get in. A code to get out. We only have the one."

Staring down the hallway, she noticed the wormhole's emptiness receding into the distance. Their one-way trip appeared to be leaving.

"And we gotta go now!"

Quentin opened his eyes, squinting blearily, "But we'll never reach it. Let's just nap here and wait for somebody to . . ."

"No!" Trinta yelled. "I don't know how we're gonna . . . but we're not . . . giving . . ." Trinta couldn't even finish the sentence. The wormhole drifted further and further away as she felt more and more like giving up. They'd been through so much already and she couldn't think straight. It was all too much for her brain to handle.

For Roddy though, he didn't get it. When he stepped into the corridor, his ocular readings instantly put him off-kilter. But switching to a lower frequency visual range, he reassessed the corridor without any problems. He knew Quentin and Trinta couldn't do the same thing, but he still found their queasy mewling annoying. Grabbing their hands, he figured he'd lead them on, as much to silence them as to save their lives.

"Come with me, you animals," Roddy said.

Roddy tried to pull them down the hallway but, with their disoriented vision and discombobulated balance, Trinta and Quentin immediately bumped into each other and nearly tumbled against the undulating lightning wall. Thankfully, Roddy yanked them out of harm's way and held them together uncomfortably. If he hadn't, they'd surely have been lost in an eruption of smoke.

As the boy and girl wobbled woozily, Roddy considered leaving them or even just shoving them against the walls to put them out of their misery.

"I can't . . ." Trinta mumbled. Each word felt one word closer to vomiting or passing out or a horrible combination of the two.

Quentin, however, closed his eyes tight and just breathed, thus feeling slightly less nauseous. After a few moments, he nodded to himself. He had something . . . a plan.

"Trinta, close your eyes," Quentin said. "And take a few deep breaths."

She did as he said and instantly she only felt "*mostly queasy*" instead of "*puke-your-intestines-gall-bladder-and-spleen-out queasy*".

"I've got an idea," he said. "Roddy, is the wormhole thingy still there?"

"Yeah, but it's still receding," Roddy said. "It's at

least a hundred yards off."

"A hundred yards . . ." Quentin said. "Wow . . . well, guess we gotta do what we gotta do."

Holding out his hand to Roddy, Quentin said, "Grab our hands again and go fast. We'll close our eyes and run. I trust you, Roddy. You can get us there."

Roddy stood speechless. He didn't know what to say. He'd never experienced much guilt in his life, but he felt a ton right there. Now, he didn't know whether he hoped Quentin survived or not, his own betrayal festering through him. Festered and blistered, making it difficult to work out how best he'd be helping his new friend. If he left him here, he'd be fried toast. But if Quentin *did* make it . . .

"You want us to run blindly down a hallway with zappy deadly walls and jump into a wormhole that'll lead us into even greater danger?" Trinta asked incredulously.

"Yep," Quentin said proudly.

"Damn," she snickered. "Disappointed I didn't think of it my own self."

Trinta held out her hand. Roddy stared at the two of them in disbelief, both with their eyes shut and their hands out. He didn't know what to do. The fact that this Earther kid trusted him so much baffled him beyond reason. Trusting him without knowing him hardly at all only touched him all the more. (It also made him consider that the kid might not be too bright, but the gesture still hit Roddy hard.) So Roddy did what he had to do . . .

"When I say 'Go', go," Roddy said, grabbing their hands and lining Trinta and Quentin up for the long run, their eyes shut tight. This is the point when breathing things would take a breath and then go. Instead, Roddy just jumped into it: "Alright . . . let's go . . . NOW!!!"

Roddy rolled down the hallway slowly at first, getting a feel for the pace needed for both Quentin and Trinta to run. But at the end of the hall, the wormhole shrank further and further into the distance. And if they didn't hurry, Roddy knew it'd disappear for good or be so far away that they'd be crispy wall critters before they even got close. So Roddy ratcheted up the speed and dragged those breathers along, each galloping in a blind sprint. They huffed and puffed with every step, like Olympic sprinters in their final heat, bearing down on the wormhole, now less than fifty feet away.

Glancing back and noticing the Earther drifting towards a wall, Roddy gently squeezed his hand in such a way he smoothly moved over while keeping up the same frantic pace.

"We're doing it!" Quentin screamed ecstatically.

The undulating walls tightened the further they went. Trinta and Quentin didn't notice, but Roddy did and brought them closer together as they continued their mad dash. Only forty feet to go but the corridor kept narrowing perilously.

"Single file!" Roddy yelled, placing Quentin's hand in Trinta's.

There wasn't time enough to think as instantly they raced down the tight corridor single file, Roddy followed by Quentin followed by Trinta, all praying they'd reach the wormhole fast. And there it was, right in front of them, so tantalizingly close. (Not that Quentin or Trinta could see it.) Proud of their blind trust, Roddy rolled faster and faster knowing they only had seconds to make it through or lose their chance forever.

Roddy leapt first through the wormhole, holding tight to Quentin. An electric tingle charged through Roddy's whole body as he disappeared into the blackness. A second later Quentin followed behind. And then Trinta.

Silence . . . Total silence . . .

They all experienced one whole second of total silence in engulfing blackness. Something none of them had ever fully felt in their lives. And even though it was only one second, it felt like it lasted a day.

A coldness gripped Quentin's soul – quiet and all encompassing. There in his mind was a quick flash of Trinta's face, crying out. And then another woman's face that he couldn't quite see.

And as that second – that one tiny second – ended, another second began with a cacophony of noise and light so overwhelming it nearly knocked the Earth boy unconscious from the sheer unrelenting juxtaposition of it all. His eyes confirmed that they made it where they wanted to go. But his heart . . . his heart was cowering under its heart-bed in fear.

Outside the Mother's glacial palace on the asteroid our heroes just left, Baiwyk Stanz stood before seven of her elite retrievers. In the distance, more retrievers boarded the Havok and prepared it for takeoff.

"Let the Mother know they're on their way and we'll be right behind them," Baiwyk barked in her comm.

Surveying the flowing lavender streams, Baiwyk allowed herself a moment to savor the penultimate stage of this hunt. The kid had been much more of a challenge than she'd ever hoped. *Without the robot's assistance, who knows how much longer this would have gone on?* she wondered.

In the distance, the Havok's engines roared to life, snapping Baiwyk out of her wandering thoughts. The two retrievers at the ship's controls awaited her signal before taking-off. Baiwyk knew that and kept them waiting for the sake of her control.

They should always know that their leash is tethered right to me and me alone, she believed.

After minutes of nothing, Baiwyk gave the pilots a nod and the Havok tore up off the asteroid like a rabid pit-bull chasing after a succulent mail carrier. Baiwyk knew the importance of priming her retrievers' pumps. They needed to be ready to act, ready to attack, ready for anything at all times. And now more than ever. Because it's always at the end that things can go dodgy. For everyone.

"Let's cuff 'em and snuff 'em!" Baiwyk shouted as she and the retrievers headed into the palace, fraktors raised and eyes narrowed.

Tingling with the intoxicating mix of excitement and anxiety, Baiwyk kinda wished the kid would get to live. But she knew what she had to do and she was going to do it. She always completed her missions. And she always would. Which wasn't good for Quentin, Trinta, or Roddy. It wasn't good at all.

CHAPTER TWENTY-TWO
MEETING THE MOTHER

Quentin had only five minutes in this bizarre new world of blinding light and deafening sound before being knocked unconscious. But it was a lively five minutes where his eyes kept startling him with the madness they saw and his ears kept jarring him with the ruckus they heard.

A three-legged man with claws for hands rode a green elephant-like creature down the street, chased by a horde of snarling, cackling fero-dogs who tumbled over each other like kids chasing after an ice cream truck.

Bulging tubes ran across and along nearby buildings, all filled with people shooting through them in a vibrant red liquid, screaming their heads off – whether joyfully or excruciatingly Quentin had no idea.

Above, people flew around like amped-up superheroes, wielding long glowing red poles and trying to smack the hell out of each other. One glowing pole hammered a man in the chest and he crashed to the ground a block away. As the guy exploded in flames, a crowd cheered lustily.

Turning to Trinta, Quentin asked, "Where are we? Are we here? Is this it?"

"Yeah, this is it," she said soberly.

Quentin had only been to one real high school party in his life. He'd been accidentally invited and he spent most of the night in a corner watching his classmates get drunk and act like total asses. The Mother's ship felt a lot like that – except for the being on a spaceship with flying crazy people and strange day-glo creatures part of it. And even though the young Earther didn't see any alcohol, he felt secure in the belief that most (if not *all*) of the people were on something.

"So what now?" he asked. "Storm the Mother's throne room? Blow up a giant generator? Fight a thousand of her elite warriors with your honed berserker rage and my mad breakdancing skills?"

Trinta gave him an amused chuckle as he scooted out of the way of a frict-bike riding messenger zooming down a brick wall onto the street and then back up a building's green glassed windows.

"I don't know," Trinta finally said.

"You . . . don't know?"

"Nope. You got any ideas?"

"Uh . . . no, especially as, to be honest my breakdancing skills aren't that good," Quentin said. "I bet Roddy could do a pretty good Robot though." It was then he realized their party of three was only a party of two. "Hey! Where's Roddy?!"

They both searched the surrounding crowds of creatures, people, and chaos, unable to see anything ball-like anywhere. Worry furrowed across Trinta's brow, but as she went to verbalize her concern, a concentrated sonic blast rained down on her from above, instantly knocking her out.

"Trinta!" Quentin shouted.

Picking her up, he hoped she wasn't dead. He didn't know what happened but he suspected they were in danger again (and that they were probably never once out of danger. Once you're *in* danger, it's difficult to get out as a lifestyle choice). He tried to spot where the blast came from to avoid suffering her same fate. Thinking it had to have come from one of the shimmering onion domes of a cathedral above, he ran for the shadows with Trinta in his arms.

Suddenly though, his face brusquely met the front end of a fraktor, dropping him to the ground with the force of brass knuckles. Just before he blacked out, Quentin gazed up to the maliciously grinning face of Baiwyk Stanz.

"Good to see you, Earther," Baiwyk said. "Time to take you to your kennel."

That was the last thing he heard before everything went very, very dark.

The Mother's ship wasn't a ship in any traditional sense. It was a colossal space-traveling city that required more energy to power it on its travels than most entire solar systems put out. And wherever the Mother's ship went, it ruled the galaxy in its vicinity (and all the planets and peoples therein). Very rarely would the city-ship come across a system with enough firepower and/or insanity to rebuff it, so most just accepted that for the few days/months/years the Mother's ship was near they were part of her domain.

There was a dusty list of planets foolish enough to try to fight off the Mother. Each one was left either as a ghost planet where entire populaces simply disappeared without a trace . . . or suffered such a barrage of destruction that what few survivors remained lived the rest of their lives in a shell-shocked hellhole barely resembling the planet they knew before. With fleets of fighters all designed for maximum destruction along with on-ship weaponry that reduced entire continents to buckets of smoldering rubble, the Mother reigned wherever she went whenever she wanted. Occasionally, she'd let a planet slide by without facing her control or her wrath. But those were aberrations. Aberrations caused by her napping as they passed such places or her being distracted with abusing her very mighty power on other "amusements".

In her expensive and expansive sitting room, the Mother waited expectantly. The "room" was less a room than an arena with luminescent ceilings that stretched upwards over five stories high. Pulsating orange columns bent and spun wildly around the cavernous, poorly-lit chamber.

The Mother – big as a garbage truck and twice as smelly – lounged languidly on a massive settee that held her massive frame. The darkness hid a lot of what was wrong with her. Her immense oval face housed a mouth overflowing with cascading teeth. Her body seemed fused from a hodge-podge of many different creatures – three legs like a lion, four slimy long tentacles, and two bulky arms with talon-like fingers. But her two eyes – the universe's general average amount of eyes per being – were where the terror truly began and ended.

On their own, those two overwhelming yellow eyes would beam like moonlight, drawing in the most hard-hearted of people. But those big eyes were connected to such a dark and evil hunger, it turned them instead into beacons of horrific futures to come. (In fact, many brought before the Mother often took their own lives after only making eye contact with her, unwilling to face the torturous conclusion those eyes always guaranteed.) Currently, those evil peepers darted around the room, taking in her contingent of friends, suck-ups, and in-betweens. And boy, did they light up when Baiwyk led her team of golden-vested retrievers into the great hall carrying an unconscious Quentin and Trinta.

The murmurs grew from the entrance and built to a loud crescendo as the prisoners were dropped in front of the Mother like two heaping cuts of meat. The Mother smiled. (Or actually the Mother *tried* to smile. Having a gargantuan egg-shaped face with a mouth that looked like the victim of a tooth grenade, the Mother's smiles always resembled the frozen moment right before an animal tears into its prey.)

The crowd of acolytes and sick sycophants gathered around Baiwyk and her captured bounties, tut-tutting at how small and pathetic the prisoners were.

"So which is the Earther?" the Mother inquired.

Baiwyk kicked Quentin with her boot and he gave out an unconscious grunt.

"Careful, dear," the Mother said without much real concern. "I don't want him too damaged. Otherwise the set will be worthless."

Two of the Mother's gangling, scuttling tentacles reached out, feeling all along the sleeping boy to make sure he was more or less intact. As she did, Quentin rolled away drowsily and tried to push her appendages away, giggling.

"Stop it, Mom, that tickles," he said, eyes still closed. "I'll get up in a second . . ."

Titters spilled from the crowd as she continued to examine her specimen. Her tentacles squeezed the boy's arms. She shrugged, unimpressed. She smushed his face with her tentacles softly, not too hard. All that patting and prodding was just enough to bring the Earther back to the land of the living.

With his squished-up, smushed-up face only inches from the Mother's startling visage, he did the only thing any space adventurer could do. He screamed until his lungs hurt!

"Yyyiiiiiiiooooaaaaaaawwwoooo!" Quentin yelped, scrambling away from the Mother.

A mostly humanoid older man chuckled at that unflattering reaction. And even though well-hidden at the back of the crowd, the Mother knew who laughed and narrowed her eyes on him. Instantly, a heaving red securiton – a menacing robot built for terror – hovered over, placed a strip of metal over the man's mouth, and carried him out for slaughter.

"Welcome, boy," said the Mother, turning back to

the Earther.

"Who the . . . *What* the . . . *Who* the hell are you?!" he spat out, trying to regain the courage that seeped out with his childish screams.

However, the Mother didn't care about his "courage". She found it off-putting. Standing up from the settee, the monstrous Dowager Empress peered down over Quentin. *It's like having an angry house glare at you*, he thought. When the Mother scooped him up in her tentacles and brought him near again, he instantly regretted his boldness.

"I can't imagine you'd taste too good," the Mother said, drawing her long, creepy fingers along Quentin's neck delicately. "I expect more gristle on my meat." Those gnarled, strangely moist fingers sent a squirming shiver down his spine. There, up close with the largest, longest, most teeth-filled mouth he'd ever come across, Quentin really, really, *really* hoped she wouldn't eat him. (A secondary hope was she'd just move him back a couple feet as her breath smelled so gut-wrenchingly horrid he had to breathe through his mouth.)

"I guess you came to visit as I have something you're interested in," the Mother said, motioning to a thin green cylinder behind her. "Something you should actually be *in*. Which is why you're interesting to me. Very interesting."

"*Hoo 'r' ooh*?" Quentin asked, still refusing to breathe through his nose.

"She's the Mother," Trinta said.

Straining to turn his neck as the tentacles held him tight, the kid from Nebraska happily spotted his Thricer friend standing unflinchingly below.

Trinta snarled softly: "The big ol' Mother."

The Mother dropped Quentin harshly to the ground and glowered at the impudent girl before her. Two of Baiwyk's retrievers grabbed Trinta by the arms.

"So he's the last Earther," the Mother said, "and what are you?"

"Me? I'm no one," Trinta said calmly. "I'm just revenge. And before this little dance is done, you'll be dead."

The Mother tutted as though she'd never heard anything so preposterous. She then thought back through all of her long and gangrenous life and realized that she *had* never heard anything as ridiculously far-fetched as that. Then she laughed, her hideous cackles reverberating and echoing through the room like steel being shredded. Soon, the Mother's entourage followed suit and chortled uproariously as well.

Even Trinta chuckled and gave Quentin a confident wink.

Quentin didn't smile nor did he laugh. Nor did he wink.

"Over your dead body," the Mother said to Trinta.

"Eh, I'll take it any way I can," Trinta said.

And in a blink of an eye, Trinta dropped to the floor with all her weight, taking the two retrievers holding her arms down with her. Without missing a beat, she kicked each one in the face, snatching a fraktor from one before he even knew it was gone.

The Mother's partygoers weren't used to such a hubbub. They were used to watching the Mother destroy civilizations and torture people. They were used to being on the winning side of every battle and every skirmish in a total blowout. No one breeched the Mother's inner sanctum and started kicking people in the face and grabbing fraktors from guards. That just wasn't done. So the Mother's entourage did what the ridiculously affluent and powerful did best when their world was turned upside down . . . they ran around screaming like hysterical freaks.

Quentin, however, did nothing. He watched gobsmacked as Trinta fired the fraktor at the three hulking red security robots that dropped from the ceiling. Not in the mood to get captured again, Trinta ran for the waving electro-banner columns that crisscrossed the room like orange flowing arches.

Climbing one of the orange arches, sparks shot off Trinta's boots and hands. She knew getting up in the air would give her an advantage. For as the arches flowed around the room, she could jump from one to the other, better avoiding the blasts sent her way, all the while raining down her own.

"C'mon, you grunters!" she yelled. "Let's see if you have any fire!"

Her gloved hands black from directly taking the waving column's electrical charges, Trinta reached the top of the arch and stood up, scanning the room for immediate threats. There, she let loose a barrage of fire on the security robots, drilling one in the head. That robot, head holey and askew, plummeted, smashing into a wall before shorting out in a flurry of sparks.

Meanwhile, Baiwyk's team branched out into the shadows, a tactic that didn't escape Trinta's attention from up above. Ignoring the two retrievers Trinta left splayed in front of the Mother, Baiwyk motioned the other six to join the hunt.

Her green tongue flitting across her buckets of teeth ever-so-dangerously, the Mother commanded: "Bring her to me before I, or something less important, is damaged. Otherwise, for each of you, I will give you . . . torture, torture, TORTURE!"

Trinta fired a blast down below. The shot took out a retriever who'd been running in the open to draw her fire and distract her from noticing the two others climbing the crackling arches at the far back. Her head on a swivel, Trinta spotted them from the get-go but decided to let them get a little closer, just to have two less people firing on her at the moment. Instead, she focused on taking out the two remaining securitons unleashing rapid bursts out of their cannon arms at her.

The young Earther had never witnessed anything like Trinta's dexterous avoidance of all those attacking her. As she jumped across the arches, Trinta only barely missed being tagged from one second to the next. But what amazed Quentin most was the accuracy of her return fire. How she nailed a retriever in the leg followed by a dead center kill shot on a securiton in one single fluid motion showed him how scary-good she was.

Noting all the attention paid to Trinta and not him, he grabbed himself a fraktor from one of the downed retrievers and leapt into the action with a rabid fervor. As the last securiton aimed both his arm cannons at Trinta, Quentin fired his fraktor at it, scorching its shoulder.

"Take that, you red turdbot!" Quentin yelled.

Unfortunately, the blast did little damage and the securiton angrily turned around with both cannons aimed directly on him!

"Oh, shirt," he croaked.

But before the security robot could blow him to bits, the Mother bellowed imperiously: "NOT HIM!"

Seconds after the securiton drew down his cannons, Trinta let loose a volley directly at the back of the robot's head, causing the newly ex-securiton to litter the floor with jingle jangle jingling.

"Thanks for baiting him," Trinta hollered down.

"Yeah, 'baiting'," Quentin muttered sarcastically.

He then went right back to firing at the retrievers targeting Trinta. Darting in-between the conical columns floating around the room's periphery, he kept himself out of harm's way, sneaking up behind the retrievers firing on her. About to take an unsuspecting one out, he stepped on the metallic memory coil of an ex-securiton with a loud crunch. The retriever turned with weapon drawn and Quentin froze, dropping his fraktor. His one hope of Trinta saving him was lost as she currently struggled to stay alive herself, pinned down by fraktor fire from the rest of the retrievers.

Turning to his retriever, Quentin grimaced, "So what now? You gonna kill me? Or do something worse, like make me wear one of your stupid vests?"

The retriever's finger twitched, wanting to blow the kid away. He held back, knowing if he did, he'd probably suffer a fate worse than death. Maybe death with a heavy dose of torture. Or maybe just perpetual torture with no end in a Mother devised tor-box. With those unappealing choices, the retriever drew down his fraktor and raced into the shadows, still pursuing a decent angle to bring down the Thricer.

Up above, Trinta had eliminated two more pursuers, even with her steadiness on the moving arches deteriorating. Her nimble footwork kept her from falling, but being up there so long began to throw off her balance. Not to mention the fact that her boots were now melting. It was almost like she had been surfing and jumping from one cresting giant wave to another, all keeping her wobbling high above the fray.

While she only had a few more attackers left, her agile prowess had visibly dipped since she started this fun little skirmish. Catching the end of Quentin's interaction with his retriever though, she gleefully realized he must be off-limits. And him being off-limits for the Mother's marauding minions meant something good for her.

"Quentin!" she yelled down. "Get the cylindro and make a run for it!"

He shrugged, shouting back, "Get the what?!"

"The green thing by the Mother! They won't touch you! Get it and run!"

Her attention diverted, two retrievers unleashed a flurry of firepower on Trinta. A shot grazed her arm! She groaned angrily and then took out that annoyance on the retriever who tagged her, riddling him with pinpoint blasts from her weapon.

Meanwhile, Quentin glanced towards the front of the room to the Mother who watched the battle with both amusement and irritation. As he slipped into the shadows to make his way to her, he came face-to-face with another gun-toting retriever. Instead of shooting him, the retriever sneered and ran off behind a column.

"She's right," Quentin muttered. "I'm frick-frakkin' untouchable."

With that realization, he made a mad dash towards the Mother on her chaise on the dais, noting the long green cylinder behind her was a good twenty yards away. Running to the edges of the room and sneaking through huddled partygoers, the young Earther snuck towards the Mother with great stealth. (Far more stealth than he'd honestly ever used before.)

While the Mother watched entranced as Trinta continued her dance on the arches firing down on all comers, Quentin carefully crawled up onto the dais. Nearing the two-foot long "cylindro", he marveled that even though it was mostly opaque, tiny, tiny little bursts moved through it as it hummed ever-so-slightly. With no idea why Trinta wanted it, he silently crept up behind the Mother, ready to snatch . . . and . . . run . . . .

And that he did! Grabbing the cylindro, Quentin dashed straight down the great hall with it tucked under his arm like a football.

"Sprint your butt off, Bulldog!" Trinta hollered with a big, throaty laugh.

Trinta didn't think they'd get this far and was amazed that it looked like they might actually make it. Or at least make it to the next obstacle. And that made her happy. Made her even smile, tasting a little dollop of victory on her tongue. She didn't savor it long as she still had people firing on her, so she quickly returned the favor, throwing blasts back their way.

Quentin, too, grinned as he ran for the doors, scrambling like an ace Husker quarterback of days long gone. (What with his former disdain for his state's football team, it would have been ironic had he thought of it.) Thrilled to see Trinta jumping from one arch to the next, both of them frantically heading towards the entrance, he assumed once they reached the doors, she'd slide down and they'd race out while firing back on their assailants with relish and gusto. He was wrong though. They both were.

Back at the dais, the Mother narrowed her eyes and soon the arches Trinta had been using to protect her became her literal downfall. Swiftly, the arches proceeded to disappear, starting with the one Trinta was standing on, fifty feet above the ground. At the last moment, Trinta noticed it dissipating under her and frantically leapt to another. Which then began to dissipate as well, leading her to scramble to another one . . . and another one . . . and another one . . . like she was in some bizarre videogame. The problem wasn't solely that the arches were going out one by one. It was that each went out drawing her back to the Mother.

Waiting at the doors for the imperiled Trinta, Quentin felt helpless and hapless as he watched on with the taste of their imminent escape still on his tongue. And in the few seconds it took for the last of the arches to disappear and Trinta began her plummet to the ground from several stories high, the boy from Earth winced as the Mother grinned horribly. It was the widest grin anyone had ever seen and Quentin knew he'd never seen anything so terrifying.

That is until he noticed the Mother extending a

tentacle to catch Trinta. He had the briefest of hopes that this was a good thing. One surprising noble act by a reprehensible tyrant. But he was wrong. Up from the tentacle's end snapped a sharp-pronged spike like a mace. This was the Mother's wrentacle. And before anyone could say anything/do anything/pray anything, the wrentacle's spike gouged straight through Trinta's chest with a sickening glush.

"Trinta . . ." gasped Quentin.

All those in that room gasped. It was a brutal way to die. A far too wretched end to anyone. And as the Mother tossed the girl's limp body to the floor, everyone turned away, unable to watch any further. The thud of her body on the cold hard ground rang in all their ears far longer than any of them could stand.

Quentin rushed to Trinta and scooped her brokenness up in his arms.

"You're a good kid . . . for a bulldog," she sputtered, coughing up blood and holding back tears.

Clutching her tight, Quentin knew she was hurt and hurt bad. This wasn't like the Cheeve fight. This was savage and unforgivable. This was mortal and forever. His eyes watered as she trembled against him with staggered breaths.

"It's gonna be okay, Trinta," he said, voice cracking. "I promise. It's gonna . . ."

"You can't lie for shirt . . ." she muttered, trying with her last reserves to smile up at him. "C'mere . . ."

The Earther bent his head down close. Trinta tried to make words but couldn't. She motioned for him to come closer still. She motioned for him to kiss her. Choking back tears, he kissed her softly on the lips. It was the most powerful moment of his young life. Before his lips had left hers, she was gone.

As she died there in his arms, Quentin's heart broke. This wasn't how things were supposed to go. He should never have been here. It should never have been her. As he embraced her lifeless body, he wanted to yell angrily in anguish. To scream. To howl so loud and so long that he wouldn't be able to speak for years. But no noise came. Only tears did. And they flowed with a tender fury.

CHAPTER TWENTY-THREE
THE REMOTEST REACHES OF SPACE

Quentin didn't wail. He wanted to. He wanted to weep like an abandoned infant dropped in the middle of a busy street. But the boy didn't sob. Didn't moan. Didn't really even move. That didn't stop the tears though. And those tears silently drifted down his cheeks, off his chin, and onto the unmoving, lifeless girl in his arms.

"Is he done?" the Mother aloofly inquired.

Snapping his head up, Quentin glowered at her. Glowered at her superabundance of limbs and her enormous oblique head filled with so much evil that it pushed its way out in mutated malevolence. Eyes narrowed and full of rage, he set Trinta down gently then stood with fists clenched in front of the heinous monstrosity that killed his first real love.

"Am I *done*?" he snarled. "Am I *DONE*?!! No! No, I'm not DONE! You'll know I'm done when your ugly egghead is cracked and scrambled, humpty frakkin' dumpty!"

The Mother rolled her yellow gravy-like eyes. How another tiny being dared to threaten her today was rather amusing. Made only more so by the fact that . . .

"I wasn't talking about *you*, boy," the Mother snooted. "I was talking about *him*."

Holding her wrentacle out for a servant to clean, the Mother pointed another tentacle towards the entrance. Quentin turned slowly, shocked to see Roddy standing there.

"Roddy . . ." a confused Quentin spluttered.

"Come forward, viadroid," the Mother said. "Mother wants to thank you."

Roddy rolled forward, adjusting his height so that he towered over Quentin. But that wasn't why the Earth kid gawked at him strangely.

"Does this wretched egg-turd . . . know you?" the boy asked him.

Chagrined, the viadroid responded, "I was instructed to—"

"Oh, didn't you know, Earther?" the Mother interrupted, malicious joy seeping out of her mouth. "He set this whole thing up. Using my 'wormhole escape' and getting the retrievers to welcome you once you boarded the ship. He even warned us that we might be in for a scuffle based on his assessment of the Thricer. And she did *not* disappoint. My hearts hadn't beat with such excitement in four decades. That is until she went – " the Mother used her tentacle to mime Trinta's gory demise with a playful popping sound effect.

This was all too much for Quentin, who grinded his teeth in anger. Anger at the Mother's flippant regard for Trinta's death. Anger at his own inability to do anything about it. Anger at Roddy's unbelievable betrayal.

"He is just a robot," the Mother said. "And on top of it all, he's given me everything I need to know about you. Downloaded, uploaded, fused right up for us. Which is lovely because I want to find out all about you. Because you aren't right, boy."

"What . . . what are you talking about?" Quentin mumbled, numb from the emotional juggernaut of the past few minutes.

"When I had my people scoop up your planet," the Mother explained. "You remember? The Edbu brothers almost had you at the . . ." The Mother glanced up, scanning her own cortex for the downloaded memories she'd just received from Roddy. ". . . At the fun park . . . prior to you running off with their ship. (I'm glad to have that back now. Not as glad as the Edbus will be.) Well, those fellows scooped up every single Earther for me easily, unmessily, and instantaneously. Put them all right in here."

The Mother shot out a tentacle and grabbed the cylindro Quentin had dropped at his feet when he witnessed his first love die. The Mother held it up to her eyes and spun the cylindro around, observing all the little bursts floating and popping throughout it.

"And all of your insignificant and obtuse little people went quietly into the cylindro like good little pets," she continued. "Except one. And do you know who that one was? You should. Because he looks almost identical to you. No, wait, maybe it's because all you Earthers look alike, but I think it *is* you! Oh, it is! IT *IS*!!!"

As the malicious Dowager Empress mocked him, her entourage chuckled. Quentin didn't care though. He didn't care about anyone laughing at him ever again. Blankly, he stared at the cylindro, thinking: *Everyone I ever knew is in <u>there</u>? Mom . . . Dad . . . everyone . . . All right there?*

"But you were a unique Earther," the Mother gestured with all of her tentacles around him as though presenting him like a princess to high society. "Not scooped up when every single other one was, you intrigued me. Because never before had this ever happened. Ever. Not once. And do you know how many civilizations I've collected? I'm sure I've eaten more than you could ever guess. So why it didn't grab you is a mystery. And I like mysteries."

"Well, good for you," Quentin sniped. "Maybe you could get Sherlock Holmes to come solve the mystery of why your mouth reeks. Seriously, did all your misshapen freak teeth take a dump in it?"

The entire room gasped. Some say words can hit as hard as a fist and these words definitely did, connecting with the force of an unsuspecting uppercut. For someone never told no, never insulted, never told harsh truths to, the Mother recoiled back.

"I mean maybe instead of having all those killer robots and super duper retrievers, you could come up with a giant toothbrush robot," Quentin added. "With giant bristles for hands and an awesome mouthwash cannon. Because that face-hole is something atrocious. C'mon, there's some rope over here. I'll give you a floss.

I'm sure that guy will help." He pointed at a guy who quickly shook his head no to his offer.

"How dare . . ." the Mother sputtered out.

"'Cause really what do I care? You killed the girl I loved. You turned my new viadroid pal against me. (Not to mention he's not 'just a robot' like you say.) And you've got my entire people captive for whatever sick plan you have in mind. So with all that goin' on, for the sake of the galaxy, I'm willing to do a little dental work – provided you have the coverage. I mean, c'mon, you all have gotta be able to smell that! And you've said nothing?! That's just mean."

"*'Mean'?!* You don't know the meaning of 'mean'!" she shrieked, grabbing him with her tentacles and lifting him high into the air. "Now, I've had enough of your unguided jabbering. I want you to jabber where I want. And if you don't –"

"What?" Quentin scoffed. "You gonna kill me?"

"No. I can't kill you. But . . ."

The Mother unfurled her gruesome grin, so long and wide that the Earther's newfound bravado scampered away and hid in a mousehole. Her arms held up the cylindro, caressing it until her fingers stopped on one tiny bubble in it.

"Oh, there's one . . ." she chortled.

Instantaneously, a holographic image magnified itself out from the cylindro overhead. It was Jane – Jane from school, Jane his first unrequited love, Jane from so very, very long ago. Frightened and confused, she peered out at Quentin.

"Jane . . ." he whispered.

"Yes, your emotional memory definitely has your

tags all over this one," the Mother said. "Thanks again, Roddy."

"Q-Q-Quentin McFury? Is that you?" Jane shuddered. "What's going . . . on? Where are . . ."

Without warning, the Mother tapped on the cylindro and Jane disappeared.

"So borrrrrrrrrrrring that one," the Mother sighed. "She knows you're you. Why would she ask, 'Is that you?' Such a stupid question. And asking 'What's going on?' and 'Where are we?' What does it matter, silly girl? If she knew all that's transpired and that her life and the life of all of your 'people' depended on me, would that make her feel better? Worse? Like eating a gooey pudding? What? How ridiculous!"

Quentin scowled at the Mother. He tried to slip from her tentacles but she easily held tight, prodding him in the gut with one of her arms to show him who's boss.

"Let's see if we can find someone with a little more juice," she said.

The Mother's fingers slid along the cylindro as faces of people from Earth materialized before them all, holographically hovering high in the air. The Mother stopped and suddenly Steve Z appeared. Quentin couldn't believe it was him at first.

"Ooh, you don't like *thissss* one," she hissed with delight. "Not at all."

Steve Z gawked at Quentin, puzzled and hurt. He tried to find words . . . but stopped. He didn't know what to say.

"Well, that's dull," the Mother said. "How you loathe someone who can't even talk is beyond me!"

The Mother then flicked her nails across the

cylindro, vanishing Steve Z and tickling across the green cylinder until finally Quentin's mom coalesced above. She gazed out, calm, gathering her bearings. When she realized she was looking at Quentin, there was a sparkle in her eye. The sparkle soon grew watery, so overjoyed to see her son again.

"Quentin . . ." his mom said softly.

"Now, we're getting somewhere," the Mother said. "Let's put a pin in that one."

The Mother jabbed a nail into the green cylinder and Quentin's mother disappeared back into the cylindro writhing and screaming.

"Let her go, you piece of—" Quentin spat out.

But the Mother had already brought up someone else. The only someone else that could stop his anger in his tracks. The only someone else who before all this could enrage him in an instant. His dad. His own infuriating father. And of all the expressions on the faces from the cylindro – fear, confusion, sadness – the boy saw on his father an expression strange and unseen so far . . . *guilt*. And he couldn't figure out why.

"Quent . . ." his father stammered. But then he stopped. He didn't know where to go from there. "I'm sorry . . . That's it, kiddo . . . I'm sorry. That's why I gave you the phone instead of me keeping it. That's why I hope he—"

Quentin heard the words his dad said but they didn't make any sense.

"Oh, yes, this one's a hoot," the Mother said. "He's hilarious."

Turning back, Quentin's father shouted, horrified to see the Mother: "You?!! No! No! NOOOOO!!! That wasn't part of the deal! He promised me that—"

The Mother ran her finger along the cylindro and he disappeared into the ether.

"*Who* promised him *what*?" Quentin demanded. "How the hell does my dad know you?!! What the hell is going on?!!"

"You are now back to being totally and unequivocally unexciting," the Mother said blithely, setting Quentin down next to Roddy. One of her tentacles even patted the boy's head with genuine pity. "I expected more from you. Something interesting. Something special. But you're obviously not. What a waste. And I thought it was maybe you weren't entirely human or something. Or that you had special powers. But if you're just a child . . . just an Earther child . . . I've wasted my time. And I hate wasting my time. Now I wish I wouldn't have killed the girl. *She* was significantly more fascinating than you."

The Mother turned to Baiwyk: "You can take care of the robot. He should have picked this up beforehand. No excuse really."

As Baiwyk turned her fraktor on Roddy, Quentin yelled, "Noooo!!!"

But it was too late. The oval set of orbs that was Roddy's head exploded and all that was Roddy sank to the ground. A puddle of lifeless balls.

"Roddy!!!" the Earth boy screamed.

"What do you care?" the Mother said, completely baffled. "He betrayed you. I think you merely like being noisy!"

"He was still my friend!" he bellowed. "What is wrong with you?! You can't just do that!"

"I just did. And I will continue to do so, despite what an Earther says," she stated with a wave of her wrentacle. "That's why having power is so important. No one can tell you what to do."

This was by far the worst hour of Quentin's life. And, astonishingly enough, it looked like it'd still get worse. Because "death" kinda trumps everything. He at least hoped that his would be instantaneous and the night's misery would finally end.

"It's a shame," the Mother said. "The Council thought you might be something worth keeping around. Something worth mining for some further use. Too bad they were wrong. They so often are. (I say so all the time.) And if the rest of your people are as useless as you, I might go and eat the whole thing, even though they wanted to peruse the populace first. You'd probably all give me indigestion anyway. Of course, I must wait for the Edbu brothers to finally show up to really have some fun. Surely, they'll want to exact some pain from you for marooning them on your shabby planet."

As she spoke, Quentin drifted off, reflecting on all that happened:

. . . everyone on Earth vanishing . . .

. . . dogs chasing him . . .

. . . aliens chasing him . . .

. . . stealing a spaceship . . .

. . . wrecking Los Angeles . . .

. . . flying through space . . .

. . . fighting spaceships . . .

. . . meeting Trinta . . .

. . . taking out Cheeve . . .

. . . meeting Roddy . . .

. . . Blanker's screams . . .

. . . the wormhole corridor of queasiness . . .

. . . Trinta's death . . .

. . . his parents . . .

. . .(and what the hell was the deal with his dad?). . .

. . . Roddy blown up . . .

All of these moments, all of these epic monumental life-changers made him decide he wasn't gonna accept his death. Not now! Not ever! He refused! His life overflowed this past year and he wanted more, even with every loss he suffered. And thus, he vowed to fight the Mother with whatever he could. If all he could do was punch the ugly old thing with his fists, then that's what he'd do. If he had to bite a tentacle, he'd bite a tentacle. He'd prefer it if he had something bigger, something better, but he'd make cake with whatever he had.

Scanning the floor for a stray fraktor, he frowned, disappointed to find nothing. Just a short time ago when the whole scuffle was going down, there were freakin' fraktors everywhere.

"Council?" asked Quentin, hoping to buy some more time. "What council?"

"The Prudent Council, child," the Mother said, all of her guests guffawing at his ignorance. "Do you know nothing?"

"Nope," he said. "It's what I'm known for. Knowing nothing."

"I am not surprised," she said. "Now, back to our most pressing issue. We must decide on how you should expire. I could repeat my wrentacle thrust from earlier."

The crowd murmured unenthusiastically with that suggestion, especially as they'd seen it so recently and it still kinda disturbed most of them.

"Or perhaps I grab a limb with each of my tentacles and pull. Might see if there's something interesting inside him yet."

The crowd oohed enthusiastically with that thought.

"Or I could order in some torture-bots to flay his skin off first followed by . . ."

As the Mother spoke, Quentin noticed the pile of balls formerly known as Roddy move slightly. When shot, the viadroid collapsed, reduced to a random clump of orbs resembling an enormous splattered ice cream cone with sprinkles. Now, the balls had spread out in a circle like some sort of tapestry. And . . . in the middle of that circle . . . rested a small silver disc . . . the Havok's remote!

Quentin's eyes went wide as the balls bounced ever-so-slightly again, beckoning him to the silver disc. Maybe Roddy wasn't dead. Maybe Roddy wasn't dead *and* they could somehow escape. Maybe Quentin McFury would not die painfully this day. His mind raced:

Now, just need to grab the remote, hit the button to bring the ship in, then get the two of us on it (along with the cylindro thingy and Trinta's body), and race as far, far away from this Mother-freak as fast we can . . . I can do that . . . no problem . . . at . . . all . . .

Of course, that was an awful lot to ask. Especially with Baiwyk and her retrievers standing guard. Especially with the Mother being so psychopathically murderous herself, hungry for his Earther blood to spill. Especially with Quentin himself so doubting the feasibility of such a ridiculous plan that he almost gave up right there and then. But that's when he smiled instead. If the Mother hadn't killed Trinta, he wouldn't be so reckless, so unconcerned about his own well-being. Now with nothing to lose and a grudge to guide him, he grinned as the center circle of balls leapt ever-so-slightly once more, inviting him to jump on in.

"So Earther," the Mother continued, "I do believe you've provided enough entertainment for this evening. The decision has been made and—"

Quentin interrupted: "Yeah, the decision's been made! And you're done, Miss Mother Inferior! You should never have pissed off this Earther!"

Before the Mother could respond, Quentin jumped into the middle of Roddy's fallen "body" and grabbed the remote. He pushed the button, certain that the Havok would come crashing in, only awaiting his guidance for where to land. If not that, he'd at least hear the comforting rattling hum of the ship making its thunderous approach.

Unfortunately, there was no sound. There was nothing. A fat man in a green robe chuckled snidely.

"Uh . . ." Quentin stammered.

The Mother turned to Baiwyk: "Kill him and get it out of here. I want to nap."

But as Baiwyk and her retrievers trained their weapons on the Earther, Roddy brought all of his orbs together around Quentin like armor. With the boy wrapped up, Roddy then sped the two of them off on a set of three wheelie balls, tearing off through the room like a cat with its tail on fire. The retrievers fired on them, Roddy zigging and zagging to narrowly avoid their blasts. Roddy made himself a new orb head and put it up next to Quentin's.

"I thought you were dead!" Quentin said.

"Why would you think that?"

"They shot you in the head, man! Brains all over the place!"

"Why would I keep my 'brains' in my most exposed area? That'd be stupid. Might as well not even have 'brains' then."

"Uh . . . that's where I keep my brains . . ."

Hearing that, Roddy hastily doubled the amount of balls around Quentin's head. Blasts ricocheted around them as guests screamed and Roddy weaved in out of the columns and right through the partygoers. Anything to keep them safe for another second. A fraktor's salvo shattered one of Roddy's orbs and he screamed in pain.

"What are we going to do?!" the Earth boy squealed as the wall right next to them exploded, chunks crumbling off and bouncing off Roddy's body.

"We wait for the Havok to show. And then you get us out of here!"

"And if it doesn't show?"

"Then we die. But let's not be negative."

"Hey, that's my bloodtype," joked Quentin.

"That's the worst joke ever," Roddy replied as they laughed despite themselves and rolled faster around the room.

While they were talking, their attackers had fanned out, surrounding them. Roddy scanned the room, noticing they were only seconds away from being checkmated by the retrievers. Realizing there was only one way to go that would keep them safe for a few seconds longer, Roddy spun around and headed right back towards the Mother.

"What the hell are you doing?!!" yelled Quentin.

"They won't fire on us if there's a chance they'll hit her."

"But then she'll hit *us*!!!"

"One thing at a time, Quentin. One thing at a time."

As Roddy went faster than he'd ever gone before, the Mother salivated, watching them with eager anticipation. She envisaged grabbing them with her tentacles and ripping them to shreds while smashing them against the walls and floors. Then she'd eat the Earther's fleshy pieces prior to settling down for a big long nap. But just when they got in range, Roddy spat Quentin out sideways from his protective shell of orbs. The kid rolled over and over and over before slamming into the far wall with a crunchy oomph.

In that instant, the Mother threw out her tentacles to grab the two of them, but only came back with Roddy. Rapidly, he reformed, wrapping long strands of balls around those tentacles like handcuffs (or tentacle-cuffs in this case). She tried to pull Roddy apart, but he held tight, making sure her tentacles weren't going anywhere. And every time she tried to smash Roddy with her wrentacle through his "body", he swiftly reformed, making gaping holes wherever her wrentacle whiffed away in vain.

"You useless, asinine robot!" the Mother shrieked.

The Mother pulled her tentacle-cuffed tentacles

towards her head with all of her strength. Trying to bring him close, she'd peel every ball off her tentacles with her teeth, swallowing the shredded remains of Roddy as she did. She'd use every limb, tentacle, and tooth she had to crush Roddy and then do the same to Quentin.

Trying to fend her off, Roddy growled angrily: "I'm NOT a . . . robot! I'm a viadroid!"

Shaking off his pain from being tossed aside, Quentin grimly watched as Roddy made his last stand. But the boy's grim grimace soon turned into a grave grin as he heard the Havok's familiar approach, knowing they were too far in to make an escape now. He had to do something more.

"Hey, you Mother!" Quentin yelled across the room. She turned to him, halting her imminent destruction of Roddy for only the few seconds Quentin needed to say, "Eat HAVOKKKKKKKKK!!!"

The Havok came screeching through the roof above, debris raining down on all. Holding the remote and motioning his first two fingers toward the Mother, the ship hurtled towards her with unforgiving force. Catching site of the ship, Roddy let go of her and fell to the ground, a long string of balls speedily slithering away.

The Mother said nothing. She had 1.79 seconds to say something and she chose not to. That's when the Havok crashed into her, smashing her into the ground as a meaty pulp of flesh and malice. She died unlike the way she lived her life . . . quietly. And that silence gripped the room . . . until the Mother's entire entourage ran out crying and holding their heads in shock, their tiny world of privilege, sycophantism, and callousness destroyed.

Moving past panicked feet, Roddy slithered over to Quentin as a serpentine line of balls. He reformed himself into a humanoid shape just as Baiwyk approached them with her fraktor drawn. Quentin considered trying to squash her with the ship, too, but didn't think he had the time or precision not to kill himself in the process.

"Nice work," Baiwyk said, impressed.

Quentin winced, waiting for her to take him out.

"You better go," she said. "The Council will be sending teams after you."

"Aren't *you* supposed to . . . get me?"

"Not until they order me to. Since she's dead," Baiwyk said, nodding to the ex-Mother mass, "my last orders are both null and void."

"But won't the Council send you?" he asked.

"Probably. That's why I want you to have a head start. You're a fun chase, man."

Giving him a wink, Baiwyk motioned to her team and they followed her out.

"Shall we get out of here then?" Roddy asked.

"Yeah," Quentin said solemnly. "Let's grab Trinta and go."

"Grab . . . Trinta? But why?"

"She deserves a proper burial. Away from here. She deserves that much."

Roddy stood with arms crossed in a manner many angry teens adopt to show hearty disapproval, hoping that would carry more weight than words. It did not.

Quentin reverently picked the Thricer girl up and

marched sadly toward the ship. With each step, he couldn't help but look at her and feel that any chance he had to live a life with any glimmer of happiness was lost forever. He'd effectively "won" today. But he'd have rather lost everything so as not to lose her.

As the ramp descended from the ship (with gross strips and bits of the Mother hanging off), Quentin nearly stepped on the green cylindro. Amazingly, it appeared unharmed from all the crazy chaos. As Roddy followed, Quentin turned back and said:

"Could you grab my people for me? It's late and I gotta get 'em home."

CHAPTER TWENTY-FOUR
HOME AND AWAY

As the Havok lifted off, ripping out the rest of the Mother's ceiling, two very annoyed figures meandered in amongst the catastrophic mess. Like unkempt, smelly travelers who've sat through a hundred delays before their plane finally departs, they approached the Mother's gooey remains and exhaled, irritated beyond belief.

It was their time on Earth that made them so miserable. Their only source of communication destroyed by Quentin's wreaking havoc on them with the Havok, they spent the better part of a year trying to get off that rock. Now returned to their benefactor to rejoin their paused lives, their depression only increased as they trudged over to their former employer's corpse.

The taller figure turned to the rounder one: "Weedoss, what do we do now?"

The potato-like figure said: "Dasimon, I don't know.

I really don't know."

"Wait for the Council," Dasimon said forlornly.

"Yes . . . wait for the Council," Weedoss said forlornly.

They sat down and stared up into the sky as their starship flew off again without them.

"I miss our ship," Dasimon said.

"Me, too. Me, too."

As the Havok entered space proper, no one was at the wheel. Quentin had to use the bathroom and when he came out, Roddy stood peeking in on Trinta's body in the sleeping quarters. Quentin placed her body on her bunk when they boarded. It seemed like the only place she could go, as anywhere else just seemed rude.

"Where else should I put her?" asked Quentin defensively. "It's not creepy."

"What are you planning to do with her?" the viadroid asked.

"Get her stuffed and mounted. What do you think?!" Quentin snapped. "Just take her back to her home. I guess. So they can bury her or . . . whatever they do . . ."

"We could wrap her up and eject her from the cargo hold," Roddy suggested. "It's a noble funeral. Like your sailors do. It would be respectful. And more hygienic."

"I don't think my sailors do that. I think you're misremembering my memories or something. She needs a real funeral. *I* need a real funeral for her. She deserves that."

Roddy nodded sullenly as the Earther chewed the inside of his cheek, stewing on where his life could go now and how he could go on. A melancholy playlist of songs he picked played through the Havok. Earlier, it was LCD Soundsystem's "Someone Great" and then the Pogues' "Rainy Night in Soho" that hurt him in the heart, but now Maximum Fisher's song "All Done and All Gone" echoed through the corridors. The verses ricocheted through him.

"All I got is the chip on my shoulder . . .
Just above the heart on my sleeve . . .
I wanted you for me forever . . .
I thought you'd never leave . . .
Now, I'm all alone on this highway . . .
And nothing is what it seems . . .
Everyone tells me they see you around . . .
But you're only in my dreams . . ."

While Quentin wondered how he could live his life with any joy without Trinta – the measure of *his* dreams – he was taken out of his melancholic reverie by a question.

"Do you know where we're going?" Roddy asked.

"Either to bury Trinta or to Earth. Probably bury Trinta first. That'd be more respectful, I guess."

"And she might smell soon," the viadroid said.

"Not cool, man."

Quentin glanced back at Trinta, so at peace. Turning and skulking back down the corridor, he felt she should be alone. Plus, he had to figure out where she needed to be.

In the cockpit, the sorrowful McFury had fallen asleep in the pilot's seat again. He didn't plan to, but he'd been through a lot. When you accidentally fall asleep, any noise can startle you awake. Which was just the case when Roddy rolled in and sat down in the corner.

"Holy shirt!" Quentin shouted, bolting up.

"It's only me," Roddy said. "You can keep sleeping. Not like we're going anywhere in particular at the moment."

Rubbing his eyes, the exhausted Earther slowly typed "Thrice" into the nav. Nothing came up. "She's called a Thricer, right?"

Roddy nodded.

"Then what's her planet called?"

"I don't know," Roddy said. "The Thricers were known to occupy several small planets in the Daviker system. But they spread through the universe after the fall of—"

Suddenly, a female voice interrupted with disgust, "First off, it's a moon. And secondly, why the hell would we want to go there?"

Quentin swiveled quickly, ludicrously hoping to see good old Trinta in the doorway. But it wasn't good old Trinta. It was a slightly violet woman several inches shorter than her. This woman looked to be another Thricer. About the same age as Trinta. Or maybe not. He didn't know. She was definitely not as tall as Trinta. Maybe an inch shorter than Quentin now. She was less lean, too. Whereas Trinta was all sinewy tautness, this woman was more playful and curvy, almost bursting out of the longer, more lithesome Trinta's clothes.

This girl stole Trinta's clothes?! Quentin fumed. *That is sick.*

One way she was similar to Trinta . . . was that she was absolutely lovely. A different lovely but still . . . Absolutely lovely.

"Uh . . . wha . . ." responded Quentin, struggling to figure out what was going on.

"I wouldn't go to the Daviker system if you paid me," the woman said. "And to be honest, Quentin, I know you can't pay me, so we are *not* going there. Not over my dead body."

The shaggy-haired boy glanced over to Roddy who merely shrugged. Turning back to her, Quentin asked, "Uh, who are you? And how do you know my name? And does this ship just pick up cute purple women all over the universe? I mean, seriously."

The woman lowered her head and stared at him. He felt uncomfortable with the unyielding intensity of it. And when he spotted a glimmer of recognition, she spoke:

"It's me, Quentin."

Sauntering over, a familiar scent wafting up his nose, she kissed him softly on the lips.

"Trinta . . ." he whispered.

"Yeah, it's me. And that's how I know your name. And no, I hope this ship doesn't pick up cute purple women all over the universe – I'd get a little jealous. Nice to know you think I'm cute though. I was concerned how I'd look this time 'round."

"But how . . . I thought you were . . ."

"Funny thing about us Thricers. We get three lives. Sorta in the name."

"You . . . You what? Three . . . How was I supposed to . . ." he stammered. Then he grinned a giant goofy grin and she kissed him again. She seemed so different, in personality as well as appearance. She was *definitely* more affectionate. (Which he was totally cool with.)

"What happened, by the way?" she asked. "How the hell did you two survive and *I* didn't?"

"Because we got mad skills, Purple Rain," Quentin bragged. "That's why."

"Oh, and I 'died', too," Roddy said.

"And he betrayed us," Quentin said.

"But then I saved us!" Roddy interrupted.

"Yeah," Quentin said. "He sorta did. Hooked me up with the remote and I rammed the Havok right down the Mother's throat."

Trinta nodded impressed: "That's sort of your go-to, isn't it?"

"Hey, if it ain't broke . . ." he joked.

"Were you brave?" she asked.

"No. Just angry."

There was an awkward silence where none of them knew what to say next. In that vacuum, Quentin stepped forth with every question that came to mind: "So how does that work with Thricers? Aren't you shorter now? Is this your first life gone? How do you Thricers do that? Do Thricer dudes do that, too? Can you choose what you look like or how big or small your parts get? You wouldn't want to have stumpy little wiener dog legs and really long spaghetti arms, would you? Do you just – "

"Hey, why don't you go get me some of that jerky?" Trinta interjected, playfully nudging him out into the corridor. "Because I am starving! Then let's get goin'! We've got places to be, right?"

"Uh . . . sure, no problem," he said. "This is the . . . I can't believe it! This is the absolute best thing to happen . . . just . . . ever!"

Quentin almost skipped down the hall, so happy was he that Trinta was alive. He thought this the single greatest moment of his young life and that it'd never be topped. (Not getting her some jerky, but knowing the dead girl he liked wasn't dead and that she now really appeared to like him, too. All in all, it was pretty damn near perfect.)

After Quentin left, Trinta put a hand on her hip and narrowed her eyes on Roddy.

"So what does he know?" she asked.

"Nothing," Roddy said. "Assuming you mean about Thricers and the such."

"Good. We'll keep it that way, right?"

Roddy didn't say a word. She continued:

"Because if we don't keep it that way, we'll have a little game to see who can live the longest. You or me. And even though you might think you have the advantage, you don't, Roddy. Trust me . . . you don't. Especially as I always keep some fun tricks with me at all times. You never know when a damper patch might come in handy."

Roddy didn't move and didn't say a word. Quentin returned with jerky for Trinta and a Swiss Roll for himself. Surprisingly, her eyes went wide for the Swiss Roll.

"I want *THAT*!" she said.

"I thought you'd rather eat Cheeve's butt than one of these."

"I . . . want . . . *that* . . ." she said again, licking her lips.

He shrugged and tossed her the Swiss Roll. Without

a second thought, she stuffed the whole thing in her mouth and furiously ate it, cream spilling out of her mouth like a rabid dog.

"Thersh irsshh fantashhtic!" she garbled, smiling a huge gooey grin.

Quentin giggled, so ecstatic that she was alive. *And* that she enjoyed Swiss Rolls now! *And* that she seemed even more perfect! *Everything* seemed perfect.

But Trinta and Roddy knew it wasn't. They both knew things would at some point get very uncomfortable between the two of them. And that Quentin would probably suffer because of it. Since that wasn't now though, they continued on in silence, letting that Earth boy mistake their peace for perfection.

Days later as the Havok orbited Earth, the three of them peered down as they passed over hills and mountains, rivers and streams, former cities and towns.

Dressed in better fitting yet still more revealing clothes than her previous incarnation wore, Trinta leaned forward, surveying everything about the planet below. She soaked up Earth the way you do when visiting a friend's house for the first time, trying to put together how it made up the person who lives there.

"So you came from here?" asked Trinta, face scrunched up.

"Yup," Quentin said.

"No wonder you're so soft."

Roddy chortled despite himself and Quentin gave him a dirty glare. This made Roddy laugh harder.

Embarrassed, Quentin changed the subject: "So,

Roddy, you sure you can put 'em all back?"

"Yup. Should be no problem," he said, still chuckling.

"And they just pop up like nothing happened?"

"Yup. Although some might feel a little woozy, but no more so than coming out of a long, drowsy sleep. Except . . ."

"Except what?" Quentin asked, not liking that "except".

"Except those that the Mother accessed and showed you. They'll remember some of it. They may not know what exactly happened and it might just feel like part of a bizarre dream, but they will remember."

"Okay . . ." Quentin said, running his hands through his hair, unsure what was about to happen and what it would all mean for him. "So when can we start?"

"We can do it now if you want."

"Yeah, let's do it. Let's repopulate the planet, mwah-ha-ha-HAAA!!!"

Ignoring his friend's goofiness, Roddy picked up the cylindro and placed it against the far panel. Suddenly, a sheath slid around the cylindro and a holo-pad appeared. Roddy typed some swirls into the pad and moments later the green cylindro glowed intensely. The holo-pad stated: *Population Download Commenced.*

"Wait!" Quentin exclaimed. "What about the people who were on planes and stuff?! They're going to fall from the sky!"

"Oh, no!" Roddy screamed hysterically. "You're right, they'll just . . ."

Quentin's eyes almost sprinted out of his head. He was about to leap and grab the cylindro when Roddy sat him back down in his chair.

"I'm just kidding," Roddy said. "They'll all be put back to their last default safe position. They'll all be fine."

Slouching back into his chair, Quentin breathed a huge sigh of relief. He didn't care that his shipmates were snickering at him. He just rested his head on his hands and watched as his Earth re-populated itself. Home was home again.

The McFury backyard was known throughout the neighborhood for wiffleball tournaments when Quentin was younger and had actual friends. It was a huge backyard, perfect for playing. His parents made sure it'd be spacious when the house was built back when they planned to have more kids than just Quentin. They also planned to host fabulous parties for the entire neighborhood in that big backyard – which, like having more kids, never really happened. Instead, the backyard only served to be a big butt-pain their son had to mow every summer when it was a million degrees out.

Of course, that same backyard also could serve as a tremendous place to temporarily park a spaceship, which it now did. Trinta and Roddy gazed out at the surrounding houses from the cockpit. A little past eight in the evening, every home had lights on in their living rooms with families interacting more peculiarly than they used to. They may not have known what went down, but they knew something did. And it appeared that these people would find comfort in the strange days ahead with the people they found most familiar –

their own families.

Almost all of the houses had lights on. One did not. The McFury house. The Havok had landed stealthily in the backyard and sat in relative silence. (Well, except for the sound of crying from Steve Z's house. Quentin figured that was due to Steve Z's smashed up truck or the loss of their precious, precious chimney the Havok knocked off when leaving Earth so long ago. Steve Z's family always seemed to care more about things than people.)

After staring at these homes wordlessly for almost an hour, the kid that saved Earth built up enough courage to go in and talk to his parents. He didn't know what he'd say to them . . . what he *could* say to them. Especially after such a strange and extraordinary year. But he needed to see them. To hug them. He had to know what his dad was sorry for. Before anything else, he had to know that.

So when he slid open the back patio door, he knew he had a lot of questions. He just hoped to find some answers.

As Trinta and Roddy watched from the cockpit, lights in the McFury home flicked on one room at a time. First the kitchen, then the living room, then the downstairs basement, then the bedrooms upstairs. And then one by one, each of the lights went out.

Moments later, Quentin skulked back out of the house and into the Havok. He entered the cockpit shaking and shocked to silence.

"They . . . weren't . . . they weren't there," he finally said. "Could they have been dropped off somewhere else?"

Trinta bit her lip and shook her head. She didn't know. They turned to Roddy, who ran a scan on the cylindro. The cylindro, now a pale green, had been emptied of all its contents. As the scan raced through the cylindro and the billions of individuals it dropped down on the planet, it listed Quentin's parents with question marks next to them.

"What does that mean?" asked Quentin.

"I don't know," Roddy said.

"Are they alive? Are they dead?"

"I don't know. They should have been with the rest. Maybe the Prudent Council would know . . ."

Quentin plopped down and held his head in his hands. Prior to this, he had no idea what he was going to do after this adventure. He assumed he'd talk to his parents and probably go back to school and return to his life as a semi-normal teenager. But his missing parents definitely changed the playing field.

"Okay . . ." he said. "I thought that now that I rescued Earth – "

Trinta interrupted: "Now that *we* rescued Earth . . ."

He looked up and gave her a "Really?" glance.

She apologized, "Sorry."

He continued: "Yes, now that *we* rescued Earth, I thought things would all fall right into place."

"You should never think that," Trinta said. "It never does."

"So now . . . I've got no parents . . . I hate school . . . and no one here really likes me anyway."

Quentin turned to his two new friends and raised an eyebrow.

"But I suppose I do have a spaceship to travel the universe to get as far away from this place as I'd want. Plus, I'd be learning a hell of a lot more than I could ever learn in high school." He nodded to his two friends and smirked. "Guess my decision's sorta made for me, ain't it?"

"Only if it means we're not done with you," Trinta grinned.

"No, not yet," he said.

"Good. Because I wasn't gonna let you stay anyways."

"We gotta find my mom and dad. If only so I can know how they got me into this mess."

Offended, Trinta asked, "Are you calling us a mess?"

"Yeah, a little bit," he said, all of them still pretty battered and bruised.

Trinta kissed him on the cheek and said: "Well, I appreciate your honesty, kid."

Sitting up straight in the pilot's seat, Quentin McFury fired up the engines.

As Trinta and Roddy got back in their positions, the young Earther grabbed the stick and they lifted into the air. The Havok slowly ascending into the sky, Quentin looked down on his town of North Platte, wondering if he'd ever come back. Then he wondered whether he even wanted to. He was young and didn't know how much home weighs on you when you're older. But for now, he was excited.

Quentin McFury grinned from ear-to-ear at the promise of more adventures to come and an entire universe for his playground. (He also grinned at the thought of more kisses with Trinta across the stars.)

ACKNOWLEDGEMENTS

My Wookiee life debt goes out to Maggie Bandur, Maia Peters, Jeffrey Schuetze, and Sarah Watson, each of them absolute heroes who helped me make sense of the book early on and improve the book immensely. I couldn't be more grateful to have their input and more importantly their friendship.

I also want to thank my parents, John Blankenchip, Steve Sansweet, Mary Franklin, Jeffrey Bell, Evan Cavic, Nick Simon, and April Johnston.

Also, a billion thanks to my wife and kids for putting up with this writing nonsense.

ABOUT THE AUTHOR

Patrick T. Gorman has been writing since he had hair. He started off as a playwright with plays performed to acclaim around the world. His plays – such as *Star Wars Trilogy in 30 Minutes*, the stage adaptation of Quentin Tarantino's *Reservoir Dogs*, and his own play *Four Guys Eating Out* – yielded glowing reviews such as "unfailingly imaginative" by *Variety*, "quick-witted and pithy" by the *London Stage*, and "extremely funny" by *Star Wars* creator George Lucas. After years of being a playwright, Patrick became a screenwriter, selling scripts to Universal Pictures and 20th Century Fox. After working as a playwright and then a screenwriter, he's now become a proper book author with the new *Quentin McFury* series and the upcoming *Normal Regular Human*. After the whole bookwriting thing fizzles out, he plans to write misfortune cookies.

He also was born in Nebraska, now lives in California, and hopes to one day have his own TARDIS where he can take long naps.

To find out more about Patrick, please go to:
www.patricktgorman.com
To follow Patrick on Twitter, please go to:
www.twitter.com/patricktgorman